Poison Magic

Josh D Sanders

ISBN: 9781717870469

I want to thank the people who helped me finally make this a reality. I'm sure I've been hard to deal with, but you have all supported me. You've given me the strength to make it to the end. I hope I can repay you all in the future.

Special thanks to:

CW who introduced me to my salvation and publication method, you will never want for a drink when I'm around.

And

Kareem Miskel who has always listened to my ideas and helped me flesh out even the worst ideas, thank you, and I hope I can be half as much help to you as you have been to me.

CHAPTER ONE

Wednesday night was a bit chilly. The last couple days had seen the first real rain of Spring and it was the cold biting rain of a world not yet ready to give up on Winter. It felt far more like a liquid snow than the warm rains children like to run outside to play and romp in. I was not truly prepared for this since, like most, I had been reveling in the warmer weather that had graced the area recently.

An old friend of mine had contacted me about a client who wanted to meet me. The client was his since he ran a private detective agency. I didn't have clients and I rarely wanted to meet anyone who was looking for me. For some reason I had an odd feeling about this one and decided to take Alan up on his request. I could listen and still reject any offer I didn't like. Which was most offers I heard.

I walked to his office, deciding that the best way to handle this cold snap was to staunchly deny that it existed. If I refused to admit that it was cold outside, the world would realize this and bring back warm weather like a pouting child. Every year I had this fight with the elements. I don't like to talk about the success rate of my plan since bragging is considered gauche.

The building in which his office resided wasn't large.

Just a three-story facade downtown. For anyone who has been to Chicago or New York, this building is hard to even notice, but here it made up a significant portion of the downtown skyline. Marksboro wasn't a large town, of course. Many citizens claimed thirty-five thousand out of sheer optimism. Maybe that worked much like my hypothesis about the weather. Who can truly say how the world works?

There is a charm to small towns that I have found. For many who have only lived in a city there is a strong belief that everyone in a small town knows everyone else. It's a common misconception held by so many people. Really, it is not very hard to get lost in many of America's small towns.

Americans like to have their privacy and in towns this size there truly was the space for it. There were still enough stores and restaurants to rarely ever cross paths in the course of a normal day. Even people in these towns got the idea sometimes that they knew everything going on. Then the shock of having an abuser next door occurs and they find out just how isolated they truly had been.

I stood outside of his office for a moment in the rain. I looked up from across the street at the lone light that burned in Alan's tiny office. As I stood under a street light, I had a moment of seeing this through the perspective of an outside observer. In a spotlight stood a man about six and a half feet tall with a long black duster made of oil cloth and a black wide brim hat. I must have looked like an exorcist or traveling preacher here to kill a widow. I half expected to hear sirens as I stood there.

I crossed the street and entered his building. Alan had made sure to leave the door open so I could get in since it was after regular hours. His office was tiny. Very tiny really. He had a wooden desk he got from a resale shop years ago. It looked like it had spent the better part of a teacher's career holding apples and homework. Behind it sat an old ratty chair that no longer sat upright when no one sat in it.

On the other side of the desk sat two chairs for clients. They were the almost comfortable type used in churches for meetings held outside of the sanctuary. He had the obligatory grey metal filing cabinet with an old coffee maker on top and a couch that had probably seen a lot of teen sex in the seventies. The door to his office had a frosted glass window with Alan Dores etched on it. The true sign of success.

Alan and I passed no words when I entered. He was not a very talkative man and I was focused on the upcoming meeting. I did not like to have any preconceived notions when I spoke to a potential client. Well, not a client really. I did not run any kind of business, but people seemed to find me occasionally with requests to perform services. They always seemed to think I had the skills they needed to fix some issue they had. Many times, most really, I wanted nothing to do with their requests, but occasionally, I would take on the job of fixing someone's problem. That night had an odd feeling about it. I didn't know why, but I had a feeling this one might be interesting.

The two of us were sitting quietly in the office when the potential client entered. Alan sat behind his desk while I sat on the couch, unseen behind the door. She was tall and lean. Surprisingly tall for a woman. I would say she was at least six feet two inches tall and looked taller considering how she was built. She was dressed very well.

Somehow, however, she seemed very uncomfortable in the well-tailored black suit. She had a silk blouse opened at the throat making her neck look longer. Her skirt showed a lot of leg. It was not an overly short skirt, the length looked quite formal, she simply had a lot of leg to show. Her hair was cut short with the longest in the back reaching about to her collar with the rest slightly spiky on the top and in the front. Her hair reminded me of Meg Ryan's hair in *French Kiss*. They shared about the same color of blond as well.

She walked to the desk and sat in one of Alan's client chairs. For but a moment she seemed out of place, but took command of herself very quickly. She sat still for a long moment looking directly at Alan silently. She did not seem scared as much as she seemed to size him up. Finally, after many quiet moments she spoke firmly.

"I would like to hire someone for a job. It's quite straight forward, but not easy."

Alan met her gaze evenly for another moment before speaking, "Well, that's a good place to start. What is it, exactly, that you want done? You were very vague in your initial message."

"Well," she stopped for a moment seeming to collect her thoughts as if she had not expected to get this far. "I want someone to attend a party with me. For protection. I was told that you are strong and capable."

"I see. Is there a reason you will be needing protection at this party? Correct me if I am wrong, but I was under the impression that parties are supposed to be fun affairs."

"You see, my son is getting married and his wife-to-be is a wizard. The party is being held by her family."

"Ah, okay. That explains your message better. And while a mad wizard is dangerous indeed, this still seems to be a joyous occasion. Again, why the need for protection? And why did you describe it as 'particularly powerful?'"

I noticed that her back was very tense. She kept herself still, but there were signs she couldn't hide. Something was definitely wrong that she wasn't saying and didn't seem to want to. I have a general policy about taking jobs from people who held back information: don't.

Now, most people held information back at first. They don't understand that the more I know, the better I can work. Usually, it's a bit of personal or embarrassing information. That kind of information made sense and I could usually get them to speak with a little coaxing. This, however, felt like something much bigger than cheating on a spouse. Something inside of me said there was a big issue at hand and there was no way I was going to take this on without knowing what that might be.

Again, there was a long silent moment as she seemed to wrestle with something in her head. All three of us waited. Silence can be persuasion's best ally. Often getting information from someone has more to do with saying nothing than what, specifically, is said. Nature deplores a vacuum and so do most people. If nothing is being said they will rush to fill the air with words. Finally, she came to some decision and spoke up.

"I am a member if the Humans First Coalition."

There it was. She left it hanging out there all pink and naked. No wonder she was concerned about this party. Imagine going to an interracial marriage as a member of the Ku Klux Klan. Now I could see why she thought she might need some kind of protection.

"I assume they already know that."

"Yes. My son has told them so. I'm quite a prominent member. Some of them probably knew that before he said anything. I assume they know my name."

"Okay, so am I also to assume that you are opposed to this wedding as a whole? Have you tried to stop it?"

"I want my son to be happy, but yes, I'd rather he not marry a wizard. Of course, I've talked to him about it and he knows my feelings about the whole thing, but I haven't taken any actions to stop it. He's very strong willed and, in the end, he'll do as he pleases. Boys love to defy their mothers."

Alan leaned back in his chair as he said, "Well, this seems fairly straight forward, wouldn't you say?"

I finally spoke up, "I have a question or two before this is decided."

She snapped around as if she were slapped. She was noticing me for the first time.

"And who might you be?" There was venom in her voice. She was not accustomed to being caught off guard.

"I'm Trevor Harrison, the man you wish to hire."

CHAPTER TWO

It took her a moment. I had done this to her on purpose. I found it helpful to see how people acted from the angle of an observer. Most of the time when people put on a show or lie they aim their actions toward a targeted observer. All the facial expressions, emotions, and body movements are targeted specifically at the person watching. A third party can usually see all the actions for their true intentions. Lying in a group is another beast all together. That has a lot to do with why few people are truly good actors. This case was one where I had noticed something I expected she did not want me to observe.

She turned to Alan.

"I thought you were Mr. Harrison."

"In your message you asked for him specifically, but that account comes to me. I'm Alan Dores. I often act as his gatekeeper. I contacted him on this one because of the tenor of your note. This is entirely his show now."

Alan leaned back in his chair and made a big motion of putting his hands behind his head. Clara turned back to me.

"One question: do you intend to initiate the situation?" I fired the big gun right off.

She never faltered for a moment.

"How dare you? Why would I do that? And where do you get off accusing me of lying when you orchestrated this whole farce? I don't like to be played for a fool."

"And yet you joined the club and surrounded yourself with them."

"And what, exactly, is that supposed to mean?"

I smiled at her and leaned forward just a bit. "I find it funny that no matter what is happening in the world, bigotry always finds a target. In other times I am sure that you would have hated niggers, or injuns, or spics, or camel jockeys. You see problems in the world and must find a safe target. Right now, you and your little friends have found hexers. God forbid you try to take responsibility and solve your own problems"

I leaned back, crossed my arms, and let a smug look cross my face. This was fun.

Her face turned red. It turned bright red when I considered how tan she was to begin with. The shade of red did still match her blond hair strikingly well. I dare say that this might have been a more natural tone for her.

"You son of a bitch! I never use that term. Where do you get off?"

"Here," I spat back leaning forward again. "If I feel you're not being honest with me I get off here and now. I don't care about your politics. Whatever rhetoric you want to use to justify the actions you had intended to take are bullshit. I do, however, care about someone lying to get me to a wizard party to set off a bomb or start shooting. I will not see to it that you're safe during your act of terrorism just because you hate your son's girlfriend."

She sat for a moment. She almost seemed to be shaking in her skin. She spent a few moments trying to collect herself with visible effort. The red tone drained away as she gained control of her emotions. I had to give her credit for her self-control. I had hit close to the bone and she was handling it well. Most people only saw what this woman wanted them to see. I had an extraordinary gift for making people angry.

She sighed as if releasing something big into the world. "I do not like being fooled, Mr. Harrison. I also do not like being accused of bigotry. You have your way of looking at the world and I have mine. Yes, you are correct. I would love nothing more than to start something at that party. I don't want my son getting involved with these people. They're dangerous by their very nature. Anyone should be able to see that. However, I'm well respected in this community and it would not behoove me to cause strife on my own doorstep.

"I have no intentions of starting anything, but I fear that they will. With my background in the Coalition I would make a great target for some young rogue who wanted to make a name for himself. The police won't offer me protection and I doubt they're well suited for a situation like this anyway. If everything goes well you'll come to a party, have a few drinks, eat your fill, and be bored for a few hours. But I would feel more comfortable with you there in case that is not the scenario. I've heard that you can handle a crowd. Even a crowd of their kind. I'm losing my son, Mr. Harrison, please afford me this one request."

Her speech seemed to calm her more still. She had control again as if it had never been lost in the first place. Impressive emotional control.

"Yes, I can handle a crowd. And yes, I can offer you some protection from this particular crowd. I'll go with you to this party. Maybe it'll at least be interesting. Understand, however, that if you or your people do start anything I won't get involved… on your side. I will not be brought in as a weapon for your agenda. I have no sides in this business. No harm will come to you. That is what I offer with reasonable assurance. Do you accept that?"

She sighed and stood up, "Yes, that'll be fine. It's the best I'm going to get either way." We discussed payment and reached an agreement easily. She had enough money that arguing my price was not worth her time. She wrote me a check and handed it over.

I looked down at the check and held my hand out.

"So," I looked down again for effect. "Clara, when do you want me to show up?"

"Sorry, my name is Clara Edwards. I forgot entirely to introduce myself. I thought my message had done that, but you didn't receive that. The party is Saturday at eleven in the morning. Thank you."

She wasn't going to forgive me for this rouse anytime soon. She walked to the door and opened it. Her forward momentum halted and she turned back toward me.

"You don't like me very much, do you?"

"I don't know you," I paused. "But the forecast is cloudy now with a chance of rain."

We sat quietly for a time after Clara left. Alan made a new pot of coffee with a jug of water he kept nearby for that reason. He had told me before that he thought running water to his office was a ridiculous notion when I had suggested it. We kept the silence marathon going as the coffee maker chugged along making the dark brown fluid that seemed to sustain Alan's life. I had come to believe, with time, that there is such a thing as a coffee vampire. This supernatural beast must suck the life essence from coffee plants. They have discovered, over time, that the best way to do this is by running water through their victim's seeds. They are very efficient predators in that way.

As we sat refusing to break the calm we had created, I took the time to study my friend again. It had been a year and a half since we had seen each other last and things can change in that time-frame. We had known each other for eight years at this point. We had worked on a few cases together in that time. Alan was the best investigator I had ever met. He had built a very respectable practice on his reputation alone. People knew him as a tenacious man with an agile mind for mystery. He could not suffer a mystery to live so, by nature, he had to solve them once involved. On that same note he maintained his reputation by carefully picking his cases.

Alan was a wiry man who seemed jumpy and jittery. His path to detective work was a truly unique one. Unknown to the local legal structure, Alan had spent years as a mafia shooter. Well, the legal structure knew well of who he used to be and the man he is now. They just had no idea he was the same man. Of course, as it goes, things went awry for him and he chose to turn state's evidence. The Witness Protection Program had set him up in a new area with a new identity: Alan Dores.

His choice of work was as much an act of negative reinforcement as it was a job. Bust criminals in one manor to keep himself from becoming one. He kept all his skills sharp as an obsession and he was still the best shooter I had ever seen. He stood five feet ten inches tall and fluctuated around a hundred-fifty pounds. He had a very cool, almost icy edge to his demeanor, but always felt like a spring wound too tight. There was an energy that seemed to be stored deep inside of him. I had seen him move before. No, scratch that. I had seen the results of his having moved before. I am still not entirely sure I have seen every frame of his action.

His mind was tailored much like his body. Though it seemed to relax and just allow information to seep in as it flowed through the world around it, it could rapidly snatch that information and process it. He could find connection between facts much like The Flash does housework. Detective work mostly involves trying every possibility you could think of until one worked out. Alan could create and try them rapidly in his head, but had the patience to wait out trials when he needed to. Watching him work was a pleasure akin to watching a beautiful stage performance live. Two of my previous encounters had found me through Alan. I imagine there were others who wanted my services, but he had turned them away. His judgment was something I trusted intrinsically, so I had never asked for confirmation.

After more time passed I walked to his filing cabinet and poured coffee into my mug. I turned and refilled his as well, put the pot back, and took up residence in one of his client chairs. I looked across the desk for a moment and took a drink.

"So, what are your thoughts on Miss Edwards?" He had won the contest of wills; I broke the silence.

"She wants you to be there to witness something." He turned in his chair and looked out his window. He lifted his mug and took a drink. His mind was racing through possibilities. This was truly his element.

"She wasn't at all concerned that you refused to help her if something went down of her own volition. I doubt she intends to directly start anything. I also doubt that anyone would plan a straight hit on her at a party for her son's wedding. That would look terrible on the host. That having been said, something is going to happen and she wants a witness who isn't connected to law enforcement involved. I would guess that it will probably be violent and that someone will get hurt. I think she wants someone around who can stay calm when the shit hits."

He took another drink and turned back to me from his window gazing.

"My advice to anyone else would be to leave this whole thing be. It's going to be bad and there will be collateral damage."

"And your advice to someone who is me?"

"Keep your eyes open. Don't get into fights with wizards. And no matter what, you should keep the World's Greatest Detective nearby for assistance."

"No dice, I checked and Inspector Gadget is busy."

"I guess you'll have to take me instead."

"My loss, you don't have a niece or a dog."

CHAPTER THREE

So, after that we split ways and, seeing as I could conceive of no other way to prepare, I went home. To be entirely accurate this wasn't my home. I was only in town because Alan had contacted me. I prefer to stay roaming as I am harder to find that way. So far, I do not maintain a regular home in any one place. There is no city I consider home. There have been numerous places I have enjoyed, but none enough to stay. It might be a nice thing to find a home city one day. For now, though, I visit and when I do visit a town I do not like to stay in hotels. They are always so sterile and impersonal. Hotel rooms never quite feel like home. Also, a hotel always reserves the right to enter your room and muck about, and I can't have that. So, instead, I find a house or an apartment for rent.

When I bed down anywhere I tend to keep many tools of my trade with me. While some of these tools are simple, many are different weapons or items that could be mistaken for weapons. These are what most managers object to my keeping when a house keeper enters the room. I never know exactly what I might face on a specific case so I must remain prepared. On that note, when I have used a hotel I was way too easy to find. Policy or not hotel employees are too easy to convince to give up room numbers and keys. For that reason, I tend now to leave many traps for any unwanted visitors wherever I might be staying. Hotel managers really object to those.

Over the years, I have played with numerous different traps. I have tried shotgun rigs, bombs, pits, and the whole lot. Kevin McCallister didn't have shit on me. I have tried various iterations of each, but always there was too much chance for collateral damage. I do not want things to get messy. There was a very unfortunate shotgun rig that ended up decorating the door across the hall with very red brains that did not well match the Christmas wreath already there. Now on this place, like all my more recent places, I use psychic traps. Cerebral mines if you will. The reason Clara, and so many before her, seek me out is that I have a great knowledge of the supernatural. I myself am a psionics user.

That's an attention getter.

I tend to fare better than most with or against more magical beings. As far as I have found there are no others like me. I don't use magic. Let me be clear on that. I do not cast spells, use talismans, enchant items, or call spirits. There are many people that do those things and I have employed them over the years in different ways. However, I use my mind to affect the world around me. There are drawbacks for sure. I pull from a finite source within me so I can exhaust my supply. I have a large supply, but my mind will eventually fight back if I tax it too far for too long.

Wizards are more open in how their power works. A wizard, given enough time, can construct a spell to do most anything. It all has to do with channeling energy around the world in the manner that they want. I can learn to expand my power and new applications for it, but that takes time and effort. Anyone can make use of magic, but most require far too much effort to move any significant power to actually learn. The ability to channel energy freely is referred to as talent. I have never had any real talent with magic. I know about it in the way that anyone can know something without working with it. I have read about it and talked to many magic users about the finer points, but I have no real understanding. Try as I might I have just never felt the magical field in any tangible way. I can feel when a wizard is drawing energy together. I am very good at that, but I can't seem to access it myself.

Of course, there are rules with magic. There are groups of wizards who take it upon themselves to maintain some semblance of order in the use of magic. This is on top of the basic physical laws around magic. The problem with the different groups is that they are only as powerful as the members allow them to be. There is no governing agency or overall law that all must obey. There is no one mage prison or any major magical court system. The different groups can't even agree on what laws should be formed. Thus, there is no code or even ethics aside from basic human law to govern them all. Being a wizard is a highly political position since everyone is trying to be the one on top to control it all.

I can do without all that. I hate politics. No one governs me aside from the usual law, IRS, physics, and possibly the gods of old. As anyone can see, I live a free and relaxed lifestyle of my own making. No outside force controls my dice rolls.

So, I generally have a series of psionic traps laid on any place I stay. Psionics, for me, seem to work well by using my thoughts and reading the thoughts of a target within range of the trap. So, for example, I can lay a mine that scans a doorway for any being with malicious intent. I can adjust the sensitivity of any so that it requires a certain strength of conviction to trigger. I can also adjust for the particular target of thought. This does well to protect postal carriers and Jehovah's Witnesses. The strong stuff I keep for those who actually breach a doorway or window.

I walked to my fridge to see what I happened to have inside. I have a bad tendency to keep a bachelor's fridge. I grabbed a Red Stripe beer having seen nothing else that looked desirable. I tried to find new things whenever I could. Life gets dull when you only drink the same beer all the time. I popped the cap off this one and took a long pull. As I tasted the ale, I turned toward the kitchen window and peered outside. The sky was a solid iron grey almost featureless above the low local skyline. It seemed quite apparent that the rain was not far from falling again. I decided against taking a walk.

Eventually, I ambled into the living room in search of a more comfortable perch. This job seemed incredibly simple. That was a problem. All that was being asked of me was attending a party of, most likely, stuffy and dull people and assuring the safety of a woman whose greatest threat in the world was probably a stock market decline. When I added the variables of wizards and the fact that my client was probably planning something, I still figured that this was well within my skill set. I had just one question then: why did I agree to take on a case that seemed so simple?

The first beer was dead and no answers were forthcoming so I decided to interrogate another golden brew for the answers I sought. I took this witness onto the porch for a change of venue and to watch the sky and maybe a storm. As I drank my second beer I realized that something had kept drawing me outside. I stood for a moment before settling in a rocking chair that had been provided in this fully furnished rental. Once again, I found myself contemplating a long walk when the phone rang. This struck me as an odd situation. My cell phone did not ring so it was not Alan. Instead, it was the land-line phone that rang. I had never given out this number, which would also have been a problem in itself since I had never started service in the first place.

I moved toward the sound eventually finding an old style rotary phone attached to the wall in the second bedroom. It had rang now for a solid minute and showed no signs of stopping soon. I gazed around the room to find one window. I crouched down low and scooted over to the phone. I grabbed the receiver and threw myself to the ground far from the phone. Land-line phones are a great way to set up assassinations and I had not stayed alive this long by taking loads of chances. Okay, yes, I take chances, but not one like that. Okay, I had done so before, but I had learned from my error. I paused for a moment to see if anything happened, but no hail of bullets came through the window or wall. Finally, I remembered what phones were for and spoke into the receiver.

"Hello."

"Trevor Harrison?"

"Look, don't play dumb with me. You obviously had this phone service started here so that you could pull this little trick. You know who I am and where I am staying. What do you want?"

The voice was had a soothing tone. My guess was that the speaker was a singer or orator as a cover. He sounded like a large southern, black man who should narrate documentaries for a living. For a moment I had quick flashes from the Electric Company.

"Look," he said, sounding friendly. "You have no stake here. This isn't your town or your people. We can pay you so much more to give the bitch back her money and just walk away. Hell, keep her money and walk away. We don't care. We have no problem with you."

"Oh, that's too bad because now I have a big problem with you. I do not like being threatened, even by the penguin guy. Now you've also corroborated my client's story. This was one of the dumbest moves you could have made. I hope this call is being recorded for quality assurance. I want your boss to know you fucked up."

"Look, man, I get it. You're a tough guy and don't want to be pushed around. Don't look at it like that. We are offering you an alternative to the client you took. There are two sides to every story and you cannot be sure that yours is the correct one."

"True," I paused a moment. "But you had to know that this is a terrible way to go forward with your plan. You create sympathy for my client and cast a shadow over yourself and those connected to you."

"Look, you don't wanna do this, man. You don't know who yo messin with." The voice lost its smooth quality.

"No? Did you go off script? I know this: if your plans keep degenerating like your grammar I need wait only a few more minutes before you fall on your own gun."

"Fuck you, asshole! Stay away from that bitch and stay away from that party. Hear me?"

"Well, whatever your goals let me RSVP now. See you Saturday."

I hung up the phone before he could answer. I figured I wouldn't be able to understand it anyway. I got up and walked back into my bedroom. I slipped on my shoulder rig and unpacked my .357 Chiappa Rhino. I checked the load and slid it into my holster. Assured in my assessment of rain, I put on my hat and duster. I guessed the weather was going to get a shot at me after all. Only an idiot would stay stationary after a call like that.

I turned out all the lights in my place from back to front and then went out the back. The light was fading, but seeing in low light was one of the first tricks I had learned. I scanned for any trace of movement. It was extremely quiet, which played to my favor at that moment. I moved out and took the alley to the main street. I walked calmly through the street not hurrying or lagging. I have often found that moving with self-assuredness is the best way to go unnoticed by most people. After about ten minutes of a casual walk the sky decided to drop the rain. Fortunately, my hat and duster kept me completely dry. I just continued to meander around with no real destination in mind.

Finally, it became obvious that I was being followed. They must have picked me a up along the way because they had not been at the house. That is baring the use of magic. I am dealing with magic users so a cloaking spell would have concealed someone nicely. However, if he were using a concealment spell, why drop that now? Having a shadow, now I needed a plan. I wanted to know who was following me and I wanted to know before Saturday. Maybe I could wrap most of this up quickly. I walked into a corner pharmacy that was closing in about ten minutes.

I had asked the woman at the register to use the phone. In a world of cell phones, she looked at me like I had asked to see her underwear. I just smiled big and she finally acquiesced to my demands and pointed to a phone on a different counter that I could use.

"You have to dial nine to get an outside line. We close in ten minutes."

I nodded and called Alan at his office. I knew he would be working late. This whole thing was greatly bothering him too.

"Dores Detective Division, how can I help you?"

"Hi Stan, it's Trevor."

"Excelsior." His voice was flat and disinterested.

"I'm down here at William's Pharmacy and you won't believe who I ran into: Lamont Cranston. You really should say hello."

"Ah, well, I'm a bit busy right now. Say hi for me and tell Mr. Cranston I will see him another time."

"He will be very sorry to hear that. Can't blame a guy for trying, though. I'll be here for a couple more minutes in case you change your mind."

Alan disconnected the call. I knew he would be here in about five minutes. I shopped around for the last couple minutes they were open under the hawk's gaze of the girl at the register. Having not found the fictional product that I didn't want I decided to leave. Alan would be in place by now. Let's see where this goes.

We were walking through an industrial district. We had been walking now for almost twenty minutes. I was giving him time to make his move, but he was quite patient. The rain was steady and cold making the night very foreboding. I turned to head toward a more commercial district. I maintained a pace like I was just out for a casual walk to clear my head. That illusion was a bit strained with the rain, but maybe I am just a fucking moron. The weather made it hard enough to see that he would have to keep quite close to me. I was hoping that moving to a busier area might spook him and make him move.

I turned into the downtown district and merged into a

light crowd. With the university in session students were out rain or shine; it was a night and there was drinking to be done. I spotted a record store and stopped at the window to look inside. Well, a music store I corrected to myself. I took a few moments to look and kept my eye on my shadow. He took up a spot nearby so I could not disappear in the crowd.

I took a breath and then turned back on my previous route heading right for the shadow. He had gotten a spot quite close and Alan was close as well. As I walked by where he stood I reached out and took his collar in both hands. He started to pull away but Alan materialized at his side and as quickly his gun appeared in the man's ribs.

"Nice evening," I said. I walked with both into the alley leading behind the store. We all walked back down the alley to get out of casual view or the sidewalk. I pushed him back and let go of his collar. I looked him up and down to see just what I had caught.

He stood a few inches taller than I did and was quite a thick fellow indeed. I was quite surprised at how well he could move through a crowd at his size. Any NFL team would be happy to have him as a linebacker. His skin was an odd bronze that he probably bought in a bed. His hair was unnaturally uniform in its tone. It was all the exact same black with almost no shine whatsoever. He kept it in a standard military crew cut that fit his strong jaw line and large nose well.

He seemed relatively normal all told but for a few traits that most people wouldn't notice and his eye. That's right. He had only one eye and a simple black patch covering his left eye. His right eye was steely and trained directly on my eyes. He seemed to ignore Alan entirely and remained preternaturally focused on me. His body, however, seemed very aware of Alan's gun pushing strongly into his ribs. That was just the way I liked it.

"So," I looked hard into that gaze trying to decipher what seemed so odd in his eye. Something familiar, yet wrong. "As you can plainly see you have been caught. It is cold and wet. You might as well make this easy and tell me why you are following me."

His look never faltered for even a moment. Were I less intrepid I would have collapsed under the weight of it. Finally, he broke his silence with a voice that seemed to shake the very earth we stood upon.

"You dare to question me, Failure? You have no standing so to do. You have caught me because I have allowed you to. As to whom I serve, it will take more than you have to wrench that information from me."

I took a moment. His presence was great, but I know a trick or two. Few beings can truly hide much of their mind. Though *reading* someone's mind is a bit of a misnomer, I can glimpse surface thoughts easily and delve deeper if need be. The process is messy and more than a little painful. I rarely employ a deeper method, but I could tell that his resolve would not crack any time soon.

I gazed up into his eye as I wormed my way into his mind. I worked first to simply gain control. Much like taking a beach I have to form a base and fortify that. Surprisingly, people's minds do not like to be invaded. Everyone forms barriers and weapons to fight back against any invading intelligence. Even verbally most people have experienced the feeling of barricading against an invading thought. That is only natural. Of course, skill and training effects the level of resistance any mind can produce. Willingness to change also comes in to play. Sheer willpower can form an amazingly strong front, but few people can muster that kind of tenacity.

I worked my way in slowly, trying to get a foothold on

his most surface thoughts. From there it should become progressively easier to decipher his mind the more I learn. The more knowledge I can gain, the less I must fight because it's like getting bits of the code. People's thoughts carry in them the method in which their mind works and thus the pathway to understanding it. Or controlling it. That is the reason people instinctively rally against having their true thoughts guessed and known. Even therapists use methods similar to that, but they're required to work far more circuitously, as they must get people to talk about their thoughts and feeling.

As I worked to pierce the veil of his mind a thick steel wall dropped down and completely barred my passage. It had the feel of an unconscious mechanism more than a conscious action. So hard did this wall fall that I was forcibly and completely ejected from his mind. Painfully. I had never encountered defenses that worked like this. That felt more like hitting an incompatible zone than just a defense. Many people had tried to set something like that up in their mind, but this one gave me the impression that it was rejecting my very power at a very fundamental level. I could think of no way to bypass that.

As the wall came down I got a quick vision. An image blared into my mind crystal clear and bright. Some minds can transmit thoughts well while others can only receive. This goes for everyone. Everyone has some ability to connect minds, but it's an ethereal feeling and most people don't trust what they get from the connection. Some call it sixth sense while others talk of instincts or their gut. The problem with trusting these flashes is that mental communication between people is so broken that no one ever gets the whole picture or even a complete thought. This time, however, I got the picture.

I saw one giant eye with a trident standing upright in

the pupil.

When I snapped out of my reverie he was laughing. Alan almost seemed concerned, but his gun never faltered from its position. I steadied myself and met his eye again with both of mine.

"So, you have found your limit. Good. I find no evidence as to why you are so favored. Know this, Failure: if you continue on this path I will end you. If you stop now I am bound by law to leave you be… for now. I truly hope that you continue, however, I want to finish you now."

His mouth smiled, but it never traveled past that. No light touched his eyes. He stepped back and turned to leave. I shook my head at Alan and he lowered his gun and let the man pass. We stood for a time watching him walk back out to the street and then stood for a bit longer.

"What happened," Alan finally asked.

I shook my head, "I don't know, but I intend to find out."

"Not going to give this up?"

"That would be the smart thing to do…"

"Yeah, I didn't think you would."

CHAPTER FOUR

Having met the man who had been following me, I decided that I could go home. It was late and there was not much left to keep me away. A good meal and a night's sleep would get me ready for the next day. I needed to find out more about the woman I was supposed to protect. Very quickly this simple project was becoming complicated. Why on Earth would they send an enforcer of that caliber for this job? I could understand why they wanted me to leave. That was fairly common-place. Why risk a fight and why send someone so heavily armored toward my specific abilities if this was simply a family dispute?

My questions were not getting answered as I walked home, so I turned into a small pub on the edge of the college student district. There were a few people here, but not many. This was obviously the place for people who were not popular enough for the clubs, but refused to admit it. I got the distinct feeling that most here were too cool for that crowd. This was also the place where town outliers, who want to meet and maybe pick up students, came to feel like they were still young. Oh yeah, this was a great place for me to get a drink and a burger.

I stood just inside the door for a moment and surveyed

the room both visually and mentally. Visually I saw people drinking, talking, and dancing in a small area provided. Mentally, I found what was always to be found in these places. It was easy, for most, to deride this crowd for being outcasts. In turn, it was easy for this crowd to deride anyone not here for being vacuous.

In both cases the people making the judgments were lonely. Students in a town that isn't really home searching for friends who probably won't last; town inhabitants who have trouble meeting friends their age venturing back to the last time they felt part of something. All of them were searching to make connections with other people.

No one approached me as I stood there. It was not hard to know why. This was the reaction I usually cultivated in any populated area. From their point of view, there stood a tall thick man wearing a long black coat with a large, wide brim, black hat. Very little of him shown to viewers outside of that. His jeans were worn and faded blue and ended in black leather engineer boots that were scuffed and old. What skin he was showing was olive toned and no one could see his eyes. This was not a welcoming visage for a middle class, mostly white bar.

After a moment I walked over and took a seat in a corner booth. I wanted to eat and drink near people, but I wasn't really looking to interact much. I figured most of these people would be enough into their own lives that they would have no interest in the odd man in the back. It was a certainty that I would be included in stories told of this night. I stood out so much that I would add to a normally dull set piece. By tomorrow I will have hit on many of these girls and fought many of these guys. My ass will have been kicked at least ten times tonight. I will have gotten into arguments with the intellectuals in the crowd where I was both a conservative and a liberal. All of them will have gotten the best of me. One couple who broke up here tonight will have done so because of my involvement. Of course, it is certain that I will have had thirty different names. At least in the stories where I had a name that is. I have always wanted to hear some of those stories of the man in black.

A waitress came over to my table after she had served everyone else. I don't mind being last. She was young and pretty or would be if she would just trust that fact. Hard to look pretty when she was so frazzled. I would guess this place was perpetually short-handed and she needed the money.

"What can I get for you?" She was trying to be friendly, but she was near her limit.

"Do you have any draft beers that are good?"

"The usual and a craft from a brewery in Southern Illinois. We are trying them out for a few weeks. We try out a lot of places."

"Hmm, I'll have one of those and a burger with ketchup and pickle. Some fries if you have them and they are any good. That sound all right to you?" I tried to smile and make her feel a bit better.

"Sure, the fries are the best thing here. Sorry about the burger though."

I caught her smile and laughed. Had to do something to make her night a bit better

"That'll be fine then. Thank you."

She walked off into the fray once more. I continued to glance around the room to see what I could. While I could scan minds here for some thoughts, there really wasn't much reason to. There was not much to learn from the surface thoughts of most people. Most people tended to think about the same things: sex, food, work, and play. No one's true self can be gleaned by these basic opinions and any deeper scan will hurt them to a degree and be noticed. Despite what some people want to think, most people are not in the business of spending their time deep in thought about the deep matters of the day. Even when they do, "I'm hungry" is a much louder thought.

Sure, someone here might have been thinking about Clara's son and his wedding. Someone here was probably a wizard with some level of magical ability. Someone might have even known more about the man who was following me but, and here's the thing, they wouldn't be thinking that out loud. Unlike in the movies no one learns much from eavesdropping aside from a bit about some issue not concerning the listener. Serendipity was not going to crack my problem, so instead I was going to enjoy myself by people watching and having a drink.

The waitress returned with my beer. She had no name tag on so I had no clue what her name was. Names are another thing most assume would be in surface thoughts, but people rarely think of their own name. There are a lot of names floating around so how would I discern hers from all the others? She put down a napkin and put a glass of a light red beer in front of me.

"It's called Saluki Dunkledog. I have not tried it but a few people have said it is really good."

"Well, thank you," I took a drink and was surprised by how good it was. "Wow! Thank you. This is really good."

"I'm glad. Your burger should be a bit longer." She walked off smiling again. Another story might be in the works currently and this one might be closer to true.

I sat and drank what was becoming one of my favorite beers and felt good about my choice to stop here. As I sat, a girl slid into the booth across from me. Let me be more specific about that. A small young girl slid into the booth across from me. Her hair was long and dyed jet black. She had taken care to get the color correct all the way through. Her clothes were chosen with the same care. She had a tight crop top that was black and had most of the logo for a Japanese band on it. I could see the kitsune fox head covering her chest. The shirt cut off right below her boobs and her ripped denim jeans dipped low to her crotch leaving most of her torso exposed. Her boots were black and had heels so high she appeared to be a ballerina. Her face looked very young and the way she dressed along with her size accentuated that. I doubted she was old enough to drink.

I looked at her stoically and remained quiet. She seemed to be quite accustomed to drawing a lot of attention from any room she was in. Most certainly, she drew lots of attention from boys and old perverts. I figured she expected me to be awed by the very cute girl that had slid into my life. I wanted to deny her a reaction and see what she would do with that. We sat for a moment or two quietly. I was beginning to think she would just get up and leave. This may have been a bet situation.

"Hello there. What brings you into my bar on this dark and stormy night?"

Good god, she actually said that to me.

"Oh, aren't you a little young to own this place? What killed your parents? Or husband?"

"What? Oh-" she laughed like a stage actor who had long trained for a scene that required a laugh. It sounded great, but the emotion never truly touched her eyes. She was already off put by my reaction. How could this thirty-some year-old guy not be ecstatic to have her here?

"You're a funny guy. No, I am just a regular here and everyone knows me. I've never seen you around here.

You look different from the guys I see around here."

"Well, I'm new but just visiting. I came for the beer but will stay for the show."

She tilted her head to the side like a cat might and smiled at me. Again, I could see how many guys and girls would find this adorable. Her act was spot on and she was going for the Oscar tonight.

"You look like a character out of an anime with that coat and hat. Are you cosplaying someone?"

For just a moment I realized that this must look like I was trying pretty hard myself. The difference was that my stuff was all very worn but maybe that, too, was part of the look I was working toward. Maybe she thought I had come here to pick someone like her up. I guess I do not spend much time around this type because it never dawned on me that this might be attractive.

"Interesting. Am I doing a good job of it?"

"Depends. Who are you supposed to look like? I don't really recognize it. Maybe D from *Vampire Hunter D* or some detective?"

"No, this is just how I dress. Especially when it rains. All of this is waterproof. Are you cosplaying someone?"

"No silly, I'm just the kind of crazy girl who dresses how she wants not how people think she should."

Jesus Christ.

Now we were onto a subject she liked. This was very comfortable territory for her. She wanted me to know how much of a rebel she was and how she didn't care what I or anyone else thought. She had to be very certain that I understood that fact well. I was beginning to think that I might remind her of her father as we sat there. How much more cliched could this get?

"I see. So, this particular getup expresses who you are as well? This tells me all that I am supposed to know about you?"

"Well, this and my actions and attitude."

"Stop!" I interrupted her. "I am really good at this. Let me see if I can tell you about yourself. If I'm right you buy me a beer. A Dunkledog. Deal?"

"Sure," she smiled wryly at me then asked me the next obvious question. "What do I get if you are wrong?"

"Anything you want. You name it and as long as it isn't illegal it is yours. I can make your dreams come true."

Playing this part was getting to be a little fun. Too bad I was about to ruin her night and make for another story about me.

"Well, I bet you're good in bed. If you get this wrong I get you for the night. So, really, you win either way. But no cheating, you have to try your best. No guessing wrong just to have sex with me. I can tell."

"Don't worry, I take this skill very seriously. Now, let me look at you for a moment."

She stood up at the side of the table so I could see her better. She started to pose like in a magazine or Madonna video. She turned to show me her back and ass. She bent and turned and thrusted out all her features so I saw it all. As I sat I had my hand on my chin with a very contemplative look on my face. I nodded at moments to seem like I was figuring her out. As time went on she tried to distract me more. She pulled her shirt up a bit to show me she had no bra on and tugged at her pants to let me see her complete lack of underwear. I continued to react a bit.

What she could never know was that I was carefully looking into her head. She wanted so much to impress that she had left herself far more open than most people. It was a part of what people all naturally find repulsive about desperation for attention. The human mind can instinctively tell that they have their mind open and out and that feels very repulsive to people who do not want to manipulate. Of course, it was an open calling card to those who want to control. After a few minutes of her show I had the link I wanted. At that point I could coax information out of her fairly easily. Time to assure that I go home alone tonight.

I sat back, tented my fingers, and began, "Okay. Obviously, to start, you are quite attractive and you know that. You were always cute as a child and people have tended gravitated toward you. Your parents were quite happy with you when you were young because all parents like a cute kid.

"As you got older you stayed small and cute as you got into school. Teachers liked you because you were friendly and played up your cute nature. You stayed very agreeable. Not much changed for you all the way through middle school. School liked you and you liked school. Your grades were always good, but never too good. You never made people feel uncomfortable in any way."

So far so good. She stood there and smiled. She liked the story I was feeding out. This part was very positive. Two of the girls who had come with her had joined her and figured out what I was doing. They had motioned over a young man, probably her current boyfriend. This is where her plan really came into play. In her mind I had seen that she didn't really like him. She either wanted him to leave or do favors for her to regain her interest. She wanted me to lose so she could leave with me and make him angry. She would then hope to get a call soon and use the guilt to leave me and go back to him. Or, if they broke up, she would have someone to make her feel wanted for the night. She had not even considered the other options.

"In high school the world started to blossom for you. For the first couple years you were so popular. The guys wanted you. The girls wanted you. You kept your grades at the right point. Smart enough to be liked by all but hated by none. You joined the right groups and carefully watched your image. Your parents were so happy with you. Doing well?"

"Fairly. It wasn't an image. I was just being me as always. Please, go on."

"Okay. In your junior year girls were filling out more and giving you more competition. More and more the boys wanted you to put out for their attention. This was the first time you had a lesbian relationship. You flipped to that side because you were less afraid of sex on that side and you were, by far, the most attractive girl in their court. This went on the rest of that year until summer. You had your first serious relationship that summer."

"Hey! I never changed sides. I just realized that I wasn't straight."

"Sure, that's what you tell yourself. That's what you let him believe too. He first approached you at the end of the year and you really liked him. However, you were afraid that he was only interested in you because he wanted to turn you. So, you played it up and let him. You found out that you liked it on both sides and that you liked him. Now you had to carefully play that you had turned, but only for him. The stress got bad as you watched how you spoke and what stories you told. Your past got edited and you started to fold under the stress of keeping it up.

"It didn't last long as that fall you caught him with another girl. He had gone after another lesbian. A girl you had been with the year before. You were hurt, furious, and terrified. He told you he didn't care and that you were just a dyke. Hearing him say that cut straight to the bone. You ran out and cried for a month."

"No! I don't know where you are getting all of this but you are full of shit. Come on, Jeremy, let's leave?"

"Wait. Don't you want the rest? The colleges you applied for but found out that years of keeping lower grades kept you from affording or getting accepted? Your parents informing you that this was the only place they could afford without scholarships? The first time your father looked at you with disappointment?"

"Bullshit! My parents were cold. They never cared about me. My dad was a dick once he realized that getting me out would cost him precious money. The rich kids got what they wanted. No one ever really cared for me."

"Oh, is that your story? Well, I got it pretty wrong. Let me finish my beer and we can go back to my place. It's pretty close."

"What are you talking about?"

"You said that if I got it wrong I had to sleep with you. You said that I would win either way. To tell you the truth I would have rather had the beer, but I never welch on a bet."

I drained my beer and stood up, "Let's get going."

"What?! I would never say that. I'm with Jeremy. You are some kind of pervert."

"Wait," Jeremy said. "You made a very similar bet at that party a month ago. I lost at guessing a list of questions so we went back to my place. Your boyfriend called and you left him. You cried all night and we got together."

"Karen played you, Jeremy. It's easier if you just accept it and move forward with the truth."

"Shut up, fucker! Karen, I'm leaving. Fuck all of you."

Jeremy stormed away. One of the other girls ran after him. I think she was intending to pick up the pieces. Karen and her friend looked at each other. The look on her friend's face told me something similar had happened with her and she shook her head and walked off alone. Karen looked at me and hung her head low.

"You're an asshole," she stormed off into the night and I just leaned back in my seat. I needed another beer.

The waitress came over right about then and she was laughing. She set my plate down and continued to laugh for a bit. I waited because it seemed like she wanted to talk after she got herself under control. Finally, her laugher wound down until she could hold it back. She paused, took a few breathes, and then spoke to me.

"Oh, that was great. She deserved every bit of that."

"Why?" I asked very frankly.

"Oh, she comes in here and acts like she owns the place. She works to take every man that she sees whether she wants them or not. Most of the girls too. She has hurt a lot of people and it was great to see you give her what she deserved."

"Oh, she didn't deserve that. I wasn't trying to teach her a lesson. There was no comeuppance or karma there."

"Then... why did you do it?"

"Look, there is no point in trying to teach someone a lesson. You don't know what her story is. That girl has plenty of problems of her own. Nothing I could do would modify her behavior. At least not in any way that I could predict or control. That is without physical force. No, treating someone terribly to teach them a lesson is a giant waste of time.

"Doing something harmful with a point is a horrible thing. Doing something good to set an example is terrible as well. If you have to rationalize an action or require a reward to do something, you should not have done it in the first place. There is no karma, no balancing force. The universe will not reward your deed or punish your transgressions. You will not succeed in modifying anyone's behavior. If you must rationalize an action then you know you shouldn't do it. If you hope to gain favor or set an example then you might as well not do that either. Do something because you want to. Just be sure you can live with what you have done. There's nothing more to it."

"So, then why did you hurt that girl?" She was perplexed now and no longer enjoying this.

"For the same reason that I told you all of that, because I wanted to at the time. I do not like people who try to manipulate me so I made her go away. I told you the truth because I want to be honest. There is nothing more to it."

She dropped the check on my table and walked away. She did not return for the rest of my stay. I came in here with the desire to watch people and eat. All seemed to have worked out. Only time would tell what else might come of this. I finished my food and went home for the night. I was done spending time with people. I wanted sleep.

CHAPTER FIVE

I woke up in the morning feeling refreshed and ready for a new day of pissing people off. Thursdays always felt good for pissing people off. Get a jump on the weekend. Which was a very good thing as I had decided that I needed to get more information from Clara. There was information there that I didn't know that was making someone aggressive enough to come after me. I got the impression that she did not want to talk about it almost as much as she did not want to see me. It was time that I went to anger my employer for the first time. This surely would not be the last.

I put in a call to Alan first to see where Clara lived since she was not forthcoming with the personal information. While he checked into that I sat in my kitchen and had some breakfast. I preheated my oven and put in a frozen pizza. I added crushed some red pepper to a sausage pizza so, clearly, you can see that I am quite the gourmet. While I was waiting for that to reach well done, my phone rang. Alan had found her address. I took that information and my pizza to the living room and started to plan my day.

It probably would not help to get to her place in the day without an appointment. I did not want to announce my coming; I wanted to see how she would respond to my showing up out of the blue. My best guess was anger. I might have to get her angry to start getting some information. I knew that bigotry can run hot and with all the money her address suggested it could explain her side, but I didn't think she tried to scare me off a case she hired me to take. That would be a swerve, though.

So, at this point I had to assume that it was someone on another side that wanted me out. It could be the family of the girl who wanted me gone. I guessed that this could be a cliched romantic tragedy. If that turned out to be the case, I would be extremely disappointed. There was nothing interesting about feuding families when the basis was money, position, or bigotry. People needed to come up with new reasons to fight. The old ones have all become boring now.

So, I finished my zero star meal and put the rest in the fridge to throw away in a few days and started to get ready. The day was cool and the sun was out so this was obviously the day to wear my duster and hat. I decided that after last night I needed to be sure I stayed armed at all times. Psionic powers were very useful and can turn the tide of a fight, but sometimes it was just easier to use a gun. People have a natural fear of staring into the open maw of a gun barrel. Sometimes using my mind could be slow or too subtle.

I showered and dressed normally. I saw no reason for formality on a day like today. I wore a black T-shirt with the original Gojira on it and blue jeans. My engineer boots and coat were layered over that with my Rhino concealed under my coat. I put my hat on and headed out into the sunlight. I took some of my time this morning to load a few items into my trunk. In case of a need for a costume change, I dropped in a bag with a couple shirts, a pair of jeans, and some underwear. I also laid in a couple weapons that might be useful. It was always good to keep a few items in a rolling base of operations.

I spent some time driving around town. It had been long enough that I wanted to get my bearings again. Though towns didn't seem to change much to those who live there, it could be shocking to an occasional visitor. Landmarks change, making navigation almost impossible. New things get built while old ones are torn down. I figured it might help me in the future if I had a better idea of the town as it stood. Also, I had a little bit of time to kill.

I figured that I could check on Clara at about three or four. I wanted to catch her off guard and before dinner. I needed to do this meeting on my terms and not hers. I had a feeling that I could get more information from her if she were not prepared to meet with me. So, I took in the sights, ate lunch downtown, and generally acted like a teenager who had nothing to do but avoid responsibility. This was far more fun when you skip class to do it.

Around three-thirty I pointed my car toward Clara's and headed that way. I didn't know what all she did during the day, but by that time she should be wrapping up the official stuff. Even if she wasn't I wanted to break her concentration. At that point I had a fairly good idea of who sent my shadow, but I needed a better idea about why. This had a feeling of being bigger than I had originally expected.

The address Alan found was out in a ritzy subdivision. Clara lived on Honey Lane. Most people in town referred to this area as the Sweet Spot. Streets like Sugar Creek, Molasses Avenue, and Honey Lane made the name almost inevitable. Marksboro was a fairly small town but it had a fairly large population of well-off white people.

The bulk of the town was working class. It was built of mining, the railroad, and a few big factories. Of course, there were a couple areas with a poorer populace, but those areas were quite small. That, however, was not the real surprise. This town had an alarmingly large population of rich people. There were multiple subdivisions of the upper middle class and minorly rich. Then there was The Sweet Spot. No house in this area was worth less than a million dollars and most were larger than that. People there had serious cash available to them and many were power players around the country.

I turned into the development and immediately felt out of place. I had to drive back to the older area to find the Edwards' residence. Honey Lane was the first part to be built out here. At that time rich folk just bought land outside of town to get away and this happened to be the road that connected them all. The rest of the area built up around it to leech off the aura of this spot. So, I drove my black 1987 Buick Grand National back through to richer and richer areas. I realized that an American car may not have touched some of these roads since they were built. I was expecting to see people standing in their yards and staring at me like I came from a movie starring a white rapper.

I pulled into her drive, which was obscured by a few trees. The drive wound back into a much larger copse of trees through which I could see the house. The house was very large and the front had that southern plantation look with columns that were large and white. On top of them was a large balcony and on the ground in front was a large porch. The landscaping was lush but not overdone. There were two paths that wound off to the left and right going behind the house. There was probably a small army of landscapers who maintained all of this. I drove up to the house like I did this every day. Nothing odd about the lady of the house having her hired thug show up for an afternoon visit. Nothing to see here.

I sat in my car for a moment and took the time to scan the area for minds. At this point I was really trying to identify sentient beings who are within a certain range more than any threat. Here I found only ten people which seemed fairly reasonable for staff and occupants. I stepped out of my car to have a look. I could get a sense of their location as compared to mine as I looked around to match scenery to what I felt. Glancing around casually I saw two gardeners within view. The rest seemed to come from inside the house. Since I doubted that either in the front was the world famous and ever deadly gardener assassin, I decided to walk up and see who was in the house.

I strode to the door taking long steps with my long legs. My long coat made each step look longer still. There was a breeze blowing around me. I thought of this once again as it dawned on me how odd and cinematic this scene must have looked. I had to remember that rich people were very sensitive to appearance and protected themselves with police. I had to steel myself to the idea that I might have to speak with a few authorities over this impromptu visit. Continuing to the door, I rang the bell. I figured the best thing I could do was act like I was supposed to be here and hope that it created a shield around me.

I stood for a few moments at the door and waited for any response at all. Finally, the door opened and a boy stood on the other side. He stood five inches shorter than I and was at least a hundred pounds lighter. His hair was long and messy. Well, I say messy, but I imagine that it was a very cultivated look that took him an hour to create.

The more I looked at it the more I could see the hard work and effort involved. His dress was more obvious. He wore a button-down shirt unbuttoned to the third button and tucked in. The lines of the shirt added to his thin look. His hair and collar also made his neck look long and thin. His whole appearance had a birdlike quality to it. He seemed a bit nervous when he saw me.

"Yes?" he sounded uncertain, but he was trying to hide it.

"Hello," I put my hand out. "My name is Trevor Harrison. I would like to speak to the lady of the house."

He never took my hand.

"I see," he turned his head and called over his shoulder. "Mom! Some guy's here to see you."

He then closed the door leaving me outside. Who said manners were dead?

Another full minute passed as I waited. I spent some of that time wondering if a phone call might have been placed. I stood half waiting for the door to open and half waiting to hear sirens. Finally, the door opened again and this time Clara stood on the other side.

"Why are you here?"

"Hello to you too," I smiled.

"Well?" Her stone facade was unperturbed by my wit and charm. Her willpower was truly breathtaking.

"I was hoping to talk to you for a moment about the party and a few other events in recent memory."

"I told you where and when. Just meet me there at that time."

She moved to close the door. I caught the door in my hand and held it open.

"Look, there have been developments. I'd like to talk to you about them before the party. We can do it out here, but your neighbors already find my existence odd. How about we do this inside like civilized people. You could even find it in you to offer me a drink along with this basic hospitality. What do you say?"

She sighed dramatically, "Fine. Come in, then."

I stepped inside, past Clara, and she closed the door. Behind her stood a man who, I assumed, was there to greet guests. He seemed uncomfortable with this situation. I stepped into a large foyer, or entryway, or whatever you call it. It was large and vaulted with dual staircases leading to a second story. The floor was a dark rich hardwood with all the accents done with a gold flourish. Most of the cloth I could see was a rich crimson that look velvety. This room dripped age and money. There was no doubt the impact that was made on any first-time visitor.

Clara lead me into a small den off to the left side of the room. This room was set up as a sort of office for more official meetings. There was a mahogany desk and two wooden chairs on one side and a high back chair with wings on the other. The walls were lined with bookshelves stuffed with books. The high back chair faced the window at the front of the house. Again I could feel the impact this was all intended to make on anyone who found them self here. This whole house was created to give the family a serious home field advantage in any dealing they might have.

As we walked into the room, she motioned to the bar on the wall. I took her meaning and asked for a bourbon. She walked over and made a couple drinks and returned to hand me one. I took a drink and relished the money it took to purchase liquor like this. I stood next to the chairs and waited to see just how she wanted to proceed with this meeting.

She took a drink and got right into it.

"So, tell me about this development. I didn't hire you to play detective."

"No banter just business, huh?"

"Look, Mr. Harrison, I don't have time to waste while you amuse yourself. Please get to your point and leave."

"Okay, sure," I finished my drink and sat the cup down on the desk with no coaster. Take that fine wood finish. "Why was someone hired to scare me off this job?"

"I'm sure I don't know. I suggest you ask your detective friend to check. Is that all?"

"It seems odd that anyone even knows about this yet. Next, why would anyone object to you hiring protection for an event? You have to see how strange this looks."

"Who knows why any dirty mage does anything. I assume that they sent whomever you're talking about."

"Who knows indeed? You wouldn't happen to have more of a plan for the party than you have informed me of, would you? I'd think they would object to your presence far more than mine."

"Tell him, mother. Tell him why they don't like you."

I turned to see the same young man from the front door standing behind me leaning against the door frame. He seemed far more confident now dealing with his mother in their home. He stepped into the room and slide over between both of us.

"This is none of your business." She turned toward me, "This is my son, Victor. He's the one getting married."

"Why not? How is my wedding none of my business? Your involving some hired goon is definitely my business."

"Thug."

"What?" he turned toward my voice.

"I'm a thug, not a goon. There is a distinct professional

difference."

"Sorry, I guess you take pride in your work and all of that. Tell your *thug* why you feel the need to involve him in our lives."

She sighed that big sigh again, "I'm sorry for my son. He's under a lot of stress and tends to handle that with a rude attitude."

"Fuck you, mother. I'm no longer a child. I'll tell him if you won't."

He turned toward me with a cruel self-satisfied smile on his face.

"My mother dearest here tried to have my future father-in-law killed."

"That's a damn lie!" she spat.

"What else would you call that nasty business perpetrated by your little club last year?"

"Wait. Do you mean the attempt on Alexander DesChanes?"

"You heard about that, then?" Victor seemed to be taking almost perverse pleasure in this.

"You're marrying Jessica DesChanes? That is quite the ordeal. You're punching above your weight class, kid."

Alexander DesChanes was the head of the Neolithic Consortium. It was a huge international import/export turned banking corporation and the single largest cadre of wizards in the world. The name DesChanes carried a lot of weight in most any circle it was used. This group was well organized and well-funded. So, they were very powerful. I was beginning to see why this wedding was such a big deal.

"Yes, I am," he glared at me as he spoke. "She's been wonderful by accepting me despite my mother, but she," he pointed at Clara. "Is not willing to let Jessica's parentage go."

"Victor, you don't see these people for who they are. Wizards have no use for someone like you, like us, aside from using us to their ends. It isn't her father that is the problem. The girl is a wizard as well. Why can't you see that for what it is?"

"Mother thinks that Jessica is using me to get to her."

"Well," I said. "Is that a possibility?"

"You too? Why can't anyone accept this for what it is? She loves me and I love her!"

Victor got up abruptly and stormed out of the room to remind me of his youth. I took a moment to revel in the glory of youth. The whole act looked like a perfect scene from a daytime soap opera.

"Well, there you have it. All our dirty laundry is bared now. Are you happy?" Clara seemed, for the first time, to be showing her real feelings. This had been wearing on her for quite some time now and she simply could not take any more of the show.

"I didn't mean to stir the pot or make life harder on you, but I cannot do the job you hired me to do properly if I don't know the facts. This is the only way I can effectively protect you. I'm sorry, but I have to ask. Did the Coalition order the hit?"

"I can't tell you either way. I wasn't in any discussions to that effect. That is not my goal in the Coalition. Terrorism isn't going to get us where the world needs us to be. Suffice it to say, however, that Alexander believes it, along with my son. Now you know why I'm scared enough to need you there with me."

"Why not just stay away from the whole thing? Sounds like the safest decision."

"I can't miss my son's wedding. She may be a wizard, but he is still my son. I just can't do that."

"I think I can understand. I'll still help you as best I

can, but the same caveat goes as before: if this is a plot of any kind you'll not find me a friendly party."

"You as well? Can no one see my concern?"

She stood there looking me in the eyes. I could think of no reasonable response so I chose not to give one. After a moment she seemed to agree with me and we decided together that it was time for me to leave. She led me to the front door and opened it. I walked out and got into my car. I pulled out of the long driveway and as I hit the street I caught a glimpse of a mind that was new to me. I would have to stay on my toes. These were real power players involved.

CHAPTER SIX

As I drove back onto the county road that would take me back to Marksboro proper I noticed that a red truck was following me. He was quite open about the whole business so I figured that he had to be official to some degree. Either that or he was the worst tail in history. Just to be sure, I took a couple odd turns and headed into town in a roundabout manner. He stayed with me so I knew I had spotted him. I figure he knew that by now too. There was no reason at this point to play any longer so I found a good country road and pulled over. He did the same right behind me.

He sat in his pick-up for a moment so I took a second to check his mind as to his motive. The whole feeling that came back told me he was a cop. He was very self-assured and confident about the situation like he had done this many times before. He had been on the force for a while and knew what he was doing. I got out of my car and walked back toward his stopping between our cars to wait. Being rousted does happen in small towns, but I really wasn't expecting it here because of Alan. He was well respected around here and for the most part worked well with the police. I'd have to check with him later to see if there had been an incident.

The cop got out of his unmarked vehicle. He was dressed in more casual civilian clothes so I figure this might be an extracurricular activity. He sauntered up to me and crossed his arms. He was staring out from dark wraparound sunglasses. He was a fairly tall and thick man. I'm sure most people would find this treatment very intimidating. He knew how to stay silent while he stood almost unmoving. He was waiting for me to get nervous and move this along. I stared him down and waited myself. I also took the time to keep a check on his mental state not wanting him to become too frustrated. That could cause me more problems than it was worth.

Finally, he reached up and pulled the glasses down a bit to reveal his icy blue eyes. This guy was well built for his job. His slightly long but unruly hair and his unshaven face worked well with his heroic jaw line and square face. His nose had been broken and he had a couple light scars that proved he was not a pretty boy. He made a point of looking me up and down before he spoke.

"Well, you're a big one, aren't you?"

"I wouldn't throw me back."

"We'll see. So, you're the guy Ms. Edwards brought in, huh? You a professional security guy?"

"Something like that."

"She found you through Alan Dores, right?"

"Yup."

"Good man. I've known Alan a while now. Not too sure about you, though."

"Oh! Shit! You're hot for Clara," I sometimes get too excited when something hits me. This was one of the bad times.

"What makes you say that?" his eyes narrowed. His mind betrayed him, but his face never did. This guy was good. In for a penny in for a pound. Might as well continue.

"That's why you are following me on your own time. This is your truck. Didn't think the department had any official red trucks, but you never know in a small town like this."

"You think you've got it all figured out, don't you?"

Shit! I had fucked this up something fierce. Now he was getting pissed and increasingly suspicious of me and how I knew all of that. He didn't want to admit his feelings so I was guessing that she didn't reciprocate. Hell, she might not have even known. I couldn't tell him any of that. Damnit!

"Sorry, it was just one of those feelings that came to me. Yeah, she hired me to come in and watch out for her on Saturday."

"Well, you better be sure to watch it. If I find out you're just taking her money I can make life very difficult for you. You're a big guy, but I've dealt with big guys before. I have my ways. I'm not going to check you for a license for that cannon under your coat either. Just don't fuck this up, asshole."

He turned and walked away. I could tell he was more concerned about what else I might find out than anything I might do physically. His eyes were great. Most people could not tell what I had under my coat. This guy would be a great guy on your team, but I would not want to cross him.

I waited while he got back in his truck and drove off. I stood there for a moment and thought about what I had found out. Clara had a good cop who was either dating her or wanted to. Why not ask him to go to the party? He'd probably go for free and though he may not be a wizard, most people had no choice but to respect the law. In a small town like this the whole force would make life miserable if anything happened to him. I may have gotten more information, but I had even more questions now. Great.

I got back into my car and decided to go get some town gossip. The good old grapevine would probably know quite a lot about the cop and the rich lady. I thought I would head in to a couple diners or bars. Chat with a few waitresses and bartenders. They tended to have pretty good information. It may not be completely true, but there would be truth in there. Maybe I'd get lucky and this might even be a minor scandal. If so, they'd know a lot of good info. I'd also have to ask Alan later. He'd know some things, but he tended to stay away from gossip that was pertinent to a case at hand.

Ten-thirty that night. I had eaten two sandwiches (a good turkey, and a dry ham), an order of fries, mashed potatoes with watery gravy, a cup of chili, a cup of chicken noodle soup, two pieces of pie (best food all day), and more drinks than I want to count. All this food down and what did I have to show for it? Nothing. No one seemed to know anything about this situation. Here I would have figured that he was a loved cop and she the focus of town gossip, but I was wrong. I had one last bar to check before I was done with this whole thing. Maybe I was entirely wrong about the whole situation.

I trekked into a small dive bar on an old route through town. This one had the feeling of a local bar that town's folk used to get some personal service. I chose this one because earlier I had seen two police cars sitting outside for a bit. I was grasping at straws but maybe this was a local cop bar. Not many people were inside at this time on a Thursday night. More than I had really expected but still not many. The woman behind the bar looked like this was a career for her. She had that hard look in her eyes that you see in women who dealt with drunks, perverts, and assholes for a living and liked it. This was her bar no matter who owned it.

I sat at one end of the bar away from the regular patrons. Not many looked at me. I guessed they got a few odd people float through here, but eventually drove them off through aggressive unfriendliness. Fortunately, I was not here to make friends. At least not with any of them. I still had to try and connect with the bartender and see if she would talk to me.

I sat there for longer than a good customer should. She had looked my way twice while moving on to other customers. The woman at the bar was making sure I knew who was in charge and that I did not rate. I figured the best thing I could do here was patiently wait and see if I could get on her good side. In this situation I needed to play against the image I was creating and my natural tendencies. She probably thought I was either some hard ass or a poser trying to put off that image. Either way I needed to get past that and find her heart of gold, so to speak.

After her third look my way she finally sauntered my way. Stepping up she gave me the once over before talking to me. Apparently, she found me deserving of contact, as she did speak.

"So, what can I get for you?"

"You wouldn't happen to have Saluki Dunkledog, would you? I just discovered it and really like it."

"Is that some kind of a joke?"

"Probably," I spread my hands and gave her my best "can't blame a guy for trying" look. "How about something on tap that isn't light?"

"That I can do," she walked toward the tap and pulled

me a beer. There were only two handles so I had a pretty good idea what I was getting. If she wanted to screw up my beer her skill would not allow it. So effortless was her perfect pour that I don't know if she realized she had done it. The glass she brought was perfect. It could have been on a commercial.

"That's three bucks, no tab."

I pulled out my wallet and handed her a ten.

"Keep it. It's so rare that I get to meet a true master of her craft. That is a picture-perfect pint."

"Thanks," a slight smile escaped her. She was proud of her work and glad to have someone acknowledge it. "Would you like some peanuts?"

"Certainly. Thanks."

She walked off and returned with a wooden bowl full of unshelled peanuts. This bar would be perfect if only they could improve the beer choices. I sat while I munched nuts and drank my beer. The bartender went about her night. She moved between her customers and their conversations. All told I think she was in the middle of four or five different discussions around the bar. Occasionally, something would get yelled to her from across the room and she would answer as if it had not been ten minutes since they had last talked to her. I sat there for over an hour watching this dance going on simply fascinated by the spectacle.

After the third time she came by to get me another been and receive her third ten-dollar bill I stopped her to take a shot at getting some information. I figured it was now or never. Chances were she didn't know anything anyway, but I was here to try.

"So, is this your usual crowd?"

"Sure. Mostly local people to the neighborhood. We'll get a bunch of cops in an hour or so when second shift ends."

"You like catering to the police crowd?"

"Sure," she smiled big. "I get to act like a hard ass to anyone and they know not to mess with me. It also saves me the money of having a bouncer. Cops meet out in my lot throughout the day and people know not to fuck with me."

"So, you do own the place?"

"Yeah, what's it to ya?" he expression shifted down fast. I had hit on something.

"Oh, no reason. I had just thought so when I saw you work. You have the air of such pride and I wondered if you owned it. Had problems lately? You went all scary on me there for a second."

Her smile returned, "there have been a couple guys trying to buy my place. They've been threatening different things. So far, they have never tried muscle, but I wondered for a second..."

I looked down at myself, "Oh! You thought I might be muscle brought in to do something. Well, you're a good judge of character. I am hired muscle but I wasn't hired to cause you problems. No, I was brought in to guard a rich lady in town at a function coming up."

"Oh, you must mean that bitch involved in all that wizardy shit going on."

"Well, I think so, though with that description I'm not sure. I take it you have a problem with wizards?"

"No, I'm not even sure they're real. Mostly it all seems like tricks and bullshit. No, I have a problem with Clara Edwards."

"That sounds like a woman scorned. Not that it's any of my business, but I'd like to know more about the woman I work for."

"Just a moment," she slid off down the bar and served a

few people. While she did I sat and basked in the fortune that brought me here. If she didn't know anything about this than I was entirely turned around. She even seemed angry enough to talk to me. Good.

I waited while she did her work patiently and well. This place was her life and not even her anger was going to hurt the service she gave her customers. I had to applaud her for her work ethic. Finally, she walked back down toward me with another beer. I pulled out my wallet but she stopped me.

"This one's on me. If you have to be close to that cunt then you need this more than I need your money. So, yeah, there's a very specific hell for that bitch. See, her husband died twelve years ago and she takes over all his dealings. She blames the magic folks and so she joins that HFC a bit later and starts to bring their kind here. I may not believe in magic, but that sure ain't a reason to hate them. Can't stand hate groups. Only bring trouble with them wherever they go.

"So, she goes about all that just fine for a while. I hear a lot about it from all the police I get through here. I've had this place now seventeen years. Most of 'em don't like anyone who lives out toward the Sweet Spot. She takes over that group and small things start to happen. Nothing major, but suddenly students start to get more harassment and a few incidents of violence happen, but not so much that anyone can pin down who did it. I know, though. I can see it, and so can many guys through here, but they can't prove it.

"Finally, one good cop decides to really look into it. He and a handful of good cops decide to take some of their free time and see what they can piece together. They work for about six months and find a lot of good info. After a while, though, the guy in charge pulls further and further away. He starts to switch his view toward the magic folks. He starts to make things a lot harder on the other guys checking. Then their evidence starts to disappear before he finally just shuts it down."

"Did someone pay him off?"

"No, worse, he fell in love. He had spent so much time checking into Clara that he fell for her. Now he chases her like a puppy. Not that she shows it. He just chases like men do and she lets him."

"Big guy? Tall with messy hair and blue eye?"

"Yeah, that's Johnny, my brother."

"Oh," I now knew why she hated Clara so much. "Did he tell her how he felt?"

"He said she knew but he never said he exactly told her. He's chasing her and I'm waiting for him to come to his senses. I don't know what it is that men get in their heads about pretty bitches."

I finished my beer, "you said it. Well, it's been a good night. I hope it all works out for you along the way."

"That all you got to say about him?"

"Sure, but I do have one last question for you."

"Shoot."

"Where did you hear all these details? I didn't think cops would rat out one of their own that way."

"Oh, most of my information came from another of my regulars. Name's Chuck. He's a big supporter of the locals."

"Thanks. You've been a big help and a really nice conversation."

"Taking off?"

"Yeah, cops make me nervous."

She picked up my glass, smiled, and turned back to her patrons. I walked out of the bar and back to my car. So, now I know why he was so upset when I seemed to know what was going on. I hoped he didn't think his sister hired me for some reason. These family situations seemed, all too often, to get in the way of everything. I didn't want collateral damage, but in many cases, it was inevitable. If he did cause trouble I probably wouldn't even find out. If everything went to plan, I would have no reason to even speak to the police.

It had been a long day and I was tired, so I decided to go home. I figured sleep was the best course of action at this point. The way I saw it the world had had enough of me. No sense in pushing my luck. I had found out a lot more information about both my client and her son. I also knew a lot more about his bride and the other family. I had a lot of information to check and to think over.

With what I had already found out, Clara's reasoning was looking sounder. She did actually have some fear of reprisal from people who had the means to do it. Her biggest motive now, aside from possible protection, I guessed to be having someone account for her actions. I knew a few people in the Neolithic Consortium and my reputation was fair. I figured she wanted me to be able to say that she had no malicious intent and did nothing wrong. I could not get out of my mind, however, the idea that something really was going to happen.

I drove to the address that I called home at that time thinking of the shockingly easy fee I was earning on this one so far. Maybe I was working too hard for it. This could have been really straight forward. As I pulled up I realized the error in my thinking. Stopping in front of my rental I found my front door open and my house in disarray. Well, to be completely accurate, the front door was lying in the yard and the house was on fire. Flames were licking out of the front door and windows. I could already see that the fire had overtaken the house. I heard sirens growing louder while people from the neighborhood were standing on the lawn watching it burn. I decided to go to a hotel for the night

I recognized the damage immediately. A couple of my cerebro-mines, calibrated for malicious intent, had gone off. The problem with traps using explosive force and heat with a wooden building was that they tended to cause a fire. I was surprised to find no bodies on the lawn when I drove up. It was possible that someone had carried away the intruder to leave no evidence.

My mind raced. Though it was possible that this was a new attack, or an old one unconnected to this situation, those thoughts did me no good. For the time being I would have to assume that this was connected to the call and my tail from earlier. If it was the same guy, was it possible that he could withstand the attack that came from my mines? It seemed possible that he was some kind of super being. Shit. I would have to watch out.

Of course, I'm some kind of super being, so I should have been able to handle another. Of course, I was not sure that I was ready for my next move. Maybe it would surprise him if I got a hotel room and a good night's sleep. Tonight, I would sleep, for tomorrow I'd ride.

CHAPTER SEVEN

I woke up around eight the next day feeling great. I had slept well and my mind had a clear focus on what to do next. This was really a very rare situation for me. My professional opinion was that having my house burn down with a lot of my stuff inside focused me on a single track. I had called Alan last night and apprised him of the situation and we had agreed to meet today in his office at ten.

Having two hours to prepare myself, I grabbed a quick shower and got dressed for the day. Looking at what few clothes I had left, I decided to go shopping later for a few things. I got myself together and, considering last night's attack, decided that I could not go unarmed for the duration of this situation. It seemed that this whole situation was conspiring to keep me armed. Having it all together, I decided that it was time for breakfast.

The hotel provided a continental breakfast at no charge, but those were usually reheated and thawed patties that barely resemble food. I had a little time and a food-like substance did not appeal to me, so I decided to go get a couple sandwiches. Sonic seemed like the decision for sandwiches along with the largest orange juice they were willing to sell me. I congratulated myself on my superior taste in food and drove to meet Alan.

I arrived at his office a few minutes after ten thanks to the line at Sonic. He was already sitting at his desk with a cup of coffee and a couple donuts. I sat down in front of him and pulled out my first sandwich. We sat in silence as we ate and drank our incredibly nourishing breakfasts like the responsible adults we were. When I had finished my second sandwich and was crumpling the bag I decided to break the looming silence.

"So, I need to find out who torched my place."

"That, my friend, is a unique idea. As a trained detective I never would have thought to follow that line of investigation. I am obligated to remind you that it really wasn't your place, though."

"Oh good, you're in rare form already, today." Alan took a mock bow. "So, do you want to follow up on that line? And I know it wasn't mine, you jackass."

Alan sat stoned faced for a moment looking right at me.

"Is that all? Don't want me to stop a speeding train and rescue a damsel for you to kiss in the end?"

"Something getting to you on this one? You seem pissy."

"Look," he sighed. "There seems to be a lot going on here and some really bad dudes are probably behind it. With you involved they are probably wizards, or wolf men, or fucking Sith Lords for all I know. You know I'll help you out with this, but I have a really bad feeling that you are being taken for a ride here. I've already started investigation and things just aren't adding up right.

"A friend of mine with some specific magical talents looked over your house early this morning. She said some things had dissipated but that the fire was definitely magical. The magic was, and I'm quoting here, "smooth and sexy." She told me that the fire shot up rapidly to over forty-five hundred degrees, held for a short period of time, and quickly dropped to normal. That would explain some of what my contact with the fire department and PD had to say. That is some serious power. She also said there was a big explosion involved that may have spread it further."

"Well, the explosion was probably the mine I had set, but my trap wouldn't cause that much heat and I don't use magic."

"True, but she may not be able to tell the difference between the two. And if someone went to your door to set off your trap, where is the body? No sightings in the hospital."

"Burned up? Forty-five hundred is really hot. Maybe the body is gone."

"No, if the explosion was first then the body would have been thrown. There might be a charred corpse left, but a corpse should have been there. The police should have found evidence of a person involved."

"Maybe there were a few involved and they carried the dead away."

"Possible, but no one reported anything like that so I doubt it. This doesn't smell right at all."

"Look, if you want out that's fine. I understand that you don't like this stuff."

"I want you out, Trev. I wish I had just told her to take a hike. You may think you're an immortal, but you aren't. This is some serious shit and someone with this kind of power could have your number. That guy following you the other day did not seem too fucking concerned about you being a threat."

"Maybe, but I'm not ready to back away from this one. Something here is very wrong and I want to know what it is. The more I learn about the players, the more this doesn't make sense. This kind of money and power tends to fight in courtrooms and boardrooms. This is spilling over and I don't know why."

"That guy following you has really gotten in your head."

"Something about that was personal. I have to know why. Someone seems to be aiming for me specifically and I can't tolerate that."

"Fine, but let me start preparing. I have a few ideas that might help."

"Great! Like what?"

Alan shook his head, "No. The less you know about what I'm doing, the better. I need to work solo for a bit."

I sighed. Alan was not easily spooked. I could have forced his mind to open and tell me the plan, but that would serve no purpose. He would change his plans assuming he didn't quit entirely. That route runs the risk of seriously hurting him as well and it would most certainly end our friendship. There were only two choices here and I wanted him involved.

"Okay, Alan, what do you need from me?"

I left Alan a little after noon and thought, maybe, it was time to talk to the in-laws. Alexander DesChanes is one of the major players who were involved in this affair. To begin with, he was rich. No, richer. Richer still. There are many rich people in the world depending on how the word is defined. Those who sit at the bottom of the well have a very broad definition of wealth. In most of the world just living in a first world nation would make a person rich. As anyone's personal wealth increases the definition narrows. Now, even if that definition were to be narrowed to an almost non-existent line Alexander DesChanes would still qualify as rich. The DesChanes family had been wealthy for so long that it had passed into being classified as a scientific law.

Along with his copious amounts of wealth, came serious magical ability. Alexander's line had managed the business and core of the Neolithic Consortium since the last time wizards were trendy. The front name and business had changed down through the years as both societies and economies had evolved, but it always remained large, powerful, and shady. Finally, when Alexander took over, everything came forward and he publicly combined the business and the magic. Of course, he came forward as the leader.

Alexander had conquered that front the same way he had won every other battle he fought: sheer force of will. He was a powerful and ruthless man who took all he saw that was worth taking. For centuries there had been many organizations competing for control over mortal magic. The groups have always battled for membership and influence in the world. Many had held sway at different points along the way until another took it away. Alexander slowly moved through and around them all until he controlled the mass majority of them. With that control he combined them all into his Neolithic Consortium. There were still rogue groups out there operating independently, but they all feared Alexander and his Consortium. He was also said to wield tremendous amounts of magical power personally. I had only spoken to him a few times, but I believed much of what I had heard said about him.

When in his presence I could feel the easy way that he handled power. It was a manner managed only by those who control true power. There was no game playing or show to his power. This was a man who knew, in all situations, that he was the master of his own fate. With that in mind I knew that this meeting would have to be by the books. I could not show up and scare him into a reaction. That route was likely to leave me injured at best and dead at worst. I called his office and set an appointment for two o'clock, which gave me time to go get some lunch and prepare to meet with a man few ever shared a room with.

I drove downtown and had lunch at a small diner with very basic food. This unassuming place had tremendous chicken and noodle and it was on special that day. I made sure to get a seat near the back as I did not want to stir up any trouble. After I placed my order I sat back and let my mind wander. Over the years I had found great value in allowing my mind to meander the halls of thought. Allowing my mind to float freely around a problem often brought new perspective on the problem at hand. Most of our problems in dealing with others stem from getting stuck on one perspective and making assumptions. In this case I seemed to keep floating around the wedding itself.

I found that my mind kept coming back to the idea of why these two were getting married in the first place. How did they get together? What brought about their first meeting? I knew it was in college, but I assumed that they did not travel in the same circles. See? Assumptions. Of course, they both had money, but there were huge gaps in the levels of these two. Compared to Jessica, Victor was average. They could always have had classes together, but a chance meeting did not satisfy my mind at all.

I could see the possibility that Victor wanted to anger his mother. Many kids with powerful parents rebel by going after what their parents hate. For Victor magic could be a giant red button with "Do Not Press" written all over it. Anyone would have trouble not pressing the

History Eraser Button. However, that same scenario did not work for Jessica. Her father worked constantly with people on all sides and he rarely seemed to take notice of the Humans First Coalition. That, of course, was until the attempt on his life. That attempt was only last year and I doubt that these two got together after that. Also, if Alexander DesChanes truly wanted that organization destroyed it would probably be crumbling to dust as I sat at that table.

It could have always been true love between those two. Somehow that just did not feel right with at this juncture. She was a young, wealth, and extremely talented wizard from what I have heard. He was a snarky, less rich, nonmagical young man with mother problems that probably stemmed from dependence. There seemed to be little in the middle for them to have in common. All told, it seemed that I was missing a large amount of information so maybe it really was time to get a few questions answered.

I finished my simple meal and decided to go for a bit of a drive before my meeting with one of the world's true powers. I still had an hour until my meeting time; a little less when I consider that I should show up a bit early. I figured that I should show respect, but not bow down entirely. A five-minute gap or less should manage that attitude well enough. I was fortunate that Alexander kept a home here in town. He traveled all over the world and kept many different homes for his convenience. This residence was supposed to be a small house by a lake toward the west side of Marksboro. There was now a fairly low rent district built up around the lake, but one side was an area of old money.

I drove out to and around the lake for a time before I went to his place. Again, I decided to get the lay of the land should there be any problems. Many problems could be avoided if the time was taken to research escape routes. I once read that luck is the residue of preparation. That had a distinct ring of truth in my experience. I had no real reason to think that anything would go wrong at this meeting. Alexander was a very professional man and would guarantee my safety for this meeting. I took in the sights as well as I drove and let my mind wander a bit more on the issue. I found it surprising that the wedding was taking place here as opposed to some exotic locale. Maybe the plan was to fly everyone out somewhere for the actual ceremony. That seemed a bit more realistic for someone like Jessica DesChanes.

As time drew closer I drove to his estate. His small house resided on at least five acres of land with a private pond aside from the lake itself. The place looked like a castle of sorts but slightly less ostentatious. I would have hated to see his definition of large. I drove onto the land and began to follow the winding drive to the house. As I drove I checked the area for minds and found too many to catalog specifically. I did not sense any malicious intent so I decided to leave it at that.

When there was a lot of mental activity in range the effect was much like being in a very loud room. People's surface feelings and thoughts were projected outward from themselves at all times. The same way people emote with their face and body was what they do with their mind as well. For most people they receive only a slight feeling from this that they feel unsure about, but for myself it all came in loud and clear. For a moment it was oppressive so I took time to soak it in before closing off again into my own mind. I prefer to stay more closed with just a feeler out since most surface thoughts were useless.

Really, surface thoughts were just noise in anyone's head that sounded like words to them. These thoughts flowed out of all people as they had them, but were only interpretable by those who had a talent. These thoughts, like speech, go through all the usual filters of ego, pride, uncertainty, doubt, and any other walls put up because people, deep down, know that these were broadcast. With all that bullshit, thoughts were about as pointless as most words. It was possible to dig down deeper, but it was difficult and could be very damaging even when done by a talented person.

I walked from my beast of a car to the front door. As I was about to knock, the door burst open and I was hit by a thin, but fairly tall girl. She could best be described as haunting. She was quite attractive, but in such an ephemeral way as to set any potential admirer off. She seemed to glide as she moved quite rapidly into my chest. I was only certain that she wasn't a ghost when she hit me with a solid force. She bounced back a step thus ending her career as an NFL defensive lineman.

"Who the fuck are you?" she stretched her neck up to look me right in the eyes.

"I'm Trevor Harrison," I stuck my hand out. She did not take it. "And who might you be?"

She glanced at my hand and then looked over the rest of me. She seemed to scan me like a star ship and came to a decision that did not seem positive.

"I'm Sica DesChanes. Now, if you'll excuse me." I moved slightly and she walked past me out the door. I watched as she walked down the drive and was met by a car.

"They grow up so quickly," said a voice that was familiar to me.

"Hello, Alexander," I turned to greet him with a smile.

He took my hand firmly.

"Come, Trevor. You are early as usual. Let us retire to my study and talk."

I followed him into his house and closed the heavy door behind me.

CHAPTER EIGHT

Inside he led me through the entryway to a study that could be someone's apartment. The room was adorned with rich woods and deep color dyed fabrics. The walls were lined with leather books older than myself and far more exotic. As I looked around the room, I dared not try to calculate the value of the contents let alone the house itself. We sat in a pair of leather high backed chairs off to one end of the room. This area was built for visitors. There was a circular rug under the chairs creating an intimate space somewhat separated from the rest of the room. A dark wooded table sat between the chairs, which were angled toward each other. A man almost seemed to appear from the ether rolling a silent cart of drink components. I chose a scotch and water while Alexander had a sherry. We sat and drank for a moment in silence.

"So, Mr. Harrison, what can I do for you today? I wish you had waited until Saturday. I have long desired to ask that on this, the day of my daughter's wedding." He laughed. It was a rich and full laugh with no self-recrimination. I laughed along with him.

"Well, I have been retained to go to the party on Saturday. I did not realize that the wedding was that day as well."

"I am aware that you have been so engaged, I was unaware that you did not know you had been invited to the wedding. That explains why you did not request an invitation yourself."

"Just so you know, I was told nothing about going to the wedding. I was told I would be attending a party. I would never think to invite myself to anyone's wedding. I don't even really know the bride or groom. I'm sorry if this has at all been insulting to you."

"Not at all. Clara is allowed a plus one and I am much happier that it is you over one of her other friends."

"Thank you, but I assume you will have your own security and I was concerned that you would find my inclusion a personal affront."

"It is my turn to be surprised. I had assumed she had gained great taste in men. You are not coming as her date?"

"No, I have been retained in a professional capacity to assure the safety of Clara Edwards."

He took a drink and nodded to himself quietly, "I see. You need have no worries, you have done nothing to insult me. In fact, now that I think of it, your skills are very welcome in this particular situation. Emotions run high between the families and many things can happen. You have always been a good bridge between people."

"I thought very much the same thing when this began and assumed my work was almost theft for being so easy. Since then I have been warned off numerous times and the house in which I was staying was burned down. This seems to have become more complicated."

"That incident last night was your house? How dreadful. Can I help? I could provide you with a place to stay and protection. At least let me speak with the police to end any discomfort that it might cause you."

"Thank you but no. Considering the situation and my employer it would look poor for both you and me. She is covering my expenses and the attack is a job hazard."

"Of course. I will still speak with the police if only to avoid their presence at the wedding Saturday. I would not have been pleased with myself had I not offered more. On the rest of the matter, have you any lead on the perpetrators?"

"Not yet, but I have trouble believing that it's not connected with my current employment. If you wouldn't mind I would like to ask you a few questions to understand my situation better. There're obviously things I still do not know."

He continued to look at me with the same relaxed eyes, but I could feel that he had heightened his awareness. That was one reason I chose not to be a detective, I have never been good at keeping people at ease. I tended to be too direct and people didn't react well to that.

"Certainly," he responded. "Proceed as you must."

"Thanks, first off, how did Jessica and Victor meet?"

"Straight to it, then? Well, it was a bit of an odd incident. You may not know, but Jessica has shown great magical talent from a very young age. We have known for sure since she was four years old and I had hints before that. I have taken great time and effort to train her carefully to gain a solid grounding of knowledge and skill.

"I have also been careful to challenge her so that she has to work for her goals. I do not want her to feel entitled or sanctimonious. Alas, she came along so quickly that the training was still easy enough for her to breed a serious feeling of superiority. Try as I might there is no way to stop the talented from knowing how talented they are.

"I tell you all of this so that you know that I understand

the question. I have also seen that Victor has a great fascination with wizards and magic. They met at college as he sought out more and more knowledge on the subject. She found his interest endearing and he is a quick study."

"That does makes sense," I thought cautiously how to ask him the next question. "So, what do you think she sees in him? Do you think he has much aptitude for magic use?"

"Do you not think that being a quick study is enough? Neither do I. No, he has no real talent for magic. He has learned history and mechanics, but he simply cannot channel energy well enough to perform. Of course, she says that she loves him and all that rot, but, as her father, I think he feeds her superiority since he seeks knowledge and she has it all. With no magical talent he can never truly challenge her in any meaningful way."

"That's a very jaded perspective."

"Yes, but it is also honest. I do not think my daughter could find love in any true sense outside of an equal equation. However, I do not think she will ever seek out such a situation. This seems to be exactly what she wants in life so I will work to see her happy."

"So, you're satisfied with their relationship?"

"Of course not. What father is ever truly satisfied with the man his daughter chooses? But they are adults, if just, and so I will let this run its course. She does not need my blessing, but I want her in my life so I choose to step back. There is very little that can be done here to change her mind, so why fight it? There is a reality, when it comes to children, and I choose to understand reality and work within it rather than tilt at windmills."

I thought about this for a moment. Something still felt off though I did not doubt his sincerity. I didn't think he was lying, but more that he might have missed an angle. He had obviously thought the question over before and was quite satisfied with the answer, but I had to check. Even a man as great as Alexander DesChanes could try to convince himself of a lie.

"Still, why not one of the many wizards she must have had contact with? She's an attractive girl and would be considered quite a catch by most any man who had the mind to understand the situation. Forgive me if I keep harping on this, but it seems to me that she could have all of that with a wizard and, possibly, even more as he would want to learn her power."

"I have heard that you have a very powerful mind and that you are capable of much that many, even wizards, consider impossible. I have also grown to respect and like you on a personal level. I assume that you mean no disrespect; however, I think that you lack the understanding of a young girl. She is willful and does what she wants. There is nothing else to say about the subject."

"You're correct. I lack that knowledge entirely having never been a young girl. On another note, what do you know about Clara Edwards?" Time to change the subject. There was something there, but now was not the time to pursue it.

"Victor's mother? I have met her only twice through all of this and she has gone to great lengths to erect walls between us. I would like to better know this woman who will soon be a member of my family, but she has no interest in knowing me. Her allies are a small-minded lot. As with so many of these types of groups they fear change from what they view as the correct established structure. They see us as monsters not unlike African Americans were seen after the Civil War.

"I sincerely hope that I can bridge the gap and foster a better understanding between us all. She seems to be a kind and caring woman. Both she and her son seem intelligent and capable. As a singular person I hold no animosity toward Clara, but in her position, I have to remain wary of her motivations."

I could not miss just how political his answer sounded. There was a stump speech hidden in there somewhere screaming to get out. I was beginning to think he was better prepared for this meeting than I had originally thought. There may not be any more good information to be gained.

"So," I continued with my line of thought carefully. "You have no plans to retaliate against the HFC?"

"Ah, the attempt on my life. I am not yet positive that they were behind the planning of that. From what I have found I think the entire plan was too well orchestrated to have come from their lot. They lack organization and any real cohesion."

"Huh," I turned that over in my head. I hadn't expected that to be his answer at all. From everything I had heard it was all but certain that the HFC was behind it all. This could be well placed doubt by Alexander or this could change everything.

"Is there another group that you are looking at?"

"I have people investigating the whole event, but there is no need to get into that now."

"So," I finished my drink and set the glass down. "It seems there's still a lot to consider. I may just have to wait and see how the wedding goes."

"Oh, it will be fine as far as security is concerned. You should earn an easy fee my friend."

"Thank you for your assurance. I'll leave you to the planning as I'm sure you're quite busy. Thank you for sparing some time to assist me."

"Certainly."

"I look forward to Saturday and the party."

"It will be one for the ages. Good afternoon, Trevor Harrison."

With that he shook my hand and I left the way I had come. Passing through the entry, I realized that, like a castle, this room could be fortified and turned into a choke point during an invasion. Not sure why that thought dawned on me, but there it was. I walked the short distance to my car and stopped about ten feet from it. Someone had placed a spell on my car in the time I was inside. The work was quite subtle, but my mind could detect magic right away. It only took a moment after that to realize that it was a tracking spell. Someone was still very interested in knowing where I go. I considered breaking the spell and speeding off, but it might do more for me to draw them out and find out who was behind it all.

Time to lead someone on a bit of a chase.

CHAPTER NINE

So, I've never been very good with magic. I have felt it and I understood the different ways it flows and, for the most part, how it affects the world around us. I simply didn't have any real talent for actually channeling magic, so I had no way to track the spell or counter it with magic. However, any conscious magic was always connected to the mind that controlled it and I knew minds very well. At some point the caster would have to tap into the field to get the information being sent from the spell. Often that is done with a device. Wizards will connect the magic with an item for easy interpretation. In the case of a tracking spell, tradition called for a compass while young wizards were beginning to use a GPS unit. No matter what, the actual translation of the spell is done by the wizard's mind. It acts like a CPU for a spell.

Now, changing a mind has never been an easy thing to do. In that way it was not like a computer at all. There was no basic code that could be changed to achieve the desired result. That was the case for myself outside and for the person whose mind it was. While the mind had a kind of coding, it was too fluid. Minds were constantly being reworked and changed by mere existence. Things were never as static as computer code. This made it all sound much easier to change, but that is not the case. Most all conscious thought, perception, and living was done in and through people's memories. The mind filtered ideas and emotions through what anyone already had programmed to help determine how to view the new information.

So, if I wanted to change a single small memory in someone's mind I had a real problem. A new memory or a change to an old one often showed up as a discordant thought that the mind would, fairly quickly, smooth out to something very similar to what it had been to begin with. That is why true changes were so hard to affect. To make a real change the whole line of memories must be changed. Of course, those are also connected to other memories in other lines. It soon become a titanic undertaking. Add to it the sheer effort required, and the problem of the change in personality that all this change always caused. The person on the other side might end up nothing like before.

Changes could prove useful in the short term, but very rarely as a long-term solution. Instead, once I connected with that mind, I could flip this situation and begin to track it as well. Most wizards knew nothing about my specific abilities, so they never knew to check for anything other than a standard counter-tracking spell. It was possible, and there were rumors of some wizards who are quite good at mental magic, but not probable. The real question: what, exactly, was the spell cast on?

I seriously doubted that the spell had been cast on the car as a whole. If so, simply changing an aspect of the car at all would diminish or destroy the spell. I could have simply removed a few bolts to break it up entirely. Magic spread out over the object holding it like a web. While a large object meant that great amounts of magic could be poured into that web, it could be picked apart piece by piece. This will make the whole web unravel. Like a tapestry, specific threads could be removed to change or destroy the product as a whole. No, the spell would be anchored to one small component of the car that would be hard to remove. A tracking spell did not require a lot of power so a small component was ideal. That is if the caster wanted the car tracked. Essentially the spell would track whatever object it was cast upon so it all depended on what he wanted to track.

I decided to drive down to a local coffee shop for one of those caramel coffee milkshakes that were so good. There I could try to figure this all out. It took a few moments at the shop to get the barista to understand what I wanted. He swore to me that they did not sell milkshakes, but persistence won the day and I sat to think with my shake in hand.

I was seated at a table in the corner with a view of the street. I took my sunglasses off and set them on the table in front of me. The table was covered with newspaper clippings from the area under a thick varnish. I was told once that this was called decoupage. I had no clue why I remembered that. Even my vast knowledge of the human mind did not remove some truly odd moments. The cut clippings sent my mind on a trip thinking of all the tiny items that could possibly hold the spell. I drank my shake as my mind slipped into neutral. To have the upper hand I needed to know the item, but it could truly be anything. Was this caster tracking my car or me? This thought process was making me highly paranoid wondering who was watching me and when. And, to add insult to injury, that damn song got stuck in my head. Remind me to find Kenny Gordie and hurt him… badly.

I sat and spun the gears in my head. The possibilities

were so large I could not seem to get a line on logic. I kept running through possibilities and shooting them down to resurrect many of them again. The whole time I had the constant dread feeling of somebody watching me lingering in my head like a bug bite. There had to be a way to figure this out. Then I could set into motion a plan to find out whom was behind it.

I finished my drink and began to fiddle with my sunglasses. When I was frustrated I tended to play with things in my hands. It just felt better to be doing something physical while my mind worked. I was just settling into the idea that I might have to check every part of my car. I could sit and focus on each area and try to triangulate where the connection was so that I could pin it down. The process could take hours. I stood up and put on my sunglasses and froze. What item was either always with me or always in my car? It was easy to get and a simple item to work with. Sunglasses.

I took them off again and looked at them. No wonder I could not shake the feeling of being watched. The wizard in question could be watching my actions now. I closed my eyes and reached out with my mind. It did not take long to find the tie between my sunglasses and a mind outside. It was probably a basic tracking spell, but it was possible he was seeing the world from my perspective. I stopped and shook my head.

"That's crazy, I could lose them somewhere."

I put them back on and strode out to my car with a new-found purpose. Opening the door, I leaned in and began to rifle through my car. I took a few minutes before I opened the glove compartment. With conviction I reached in and pulled out my registration card. I stared at it for a moment and smiled nodding my head.

"Perfect," I said out loud. "That never leaves the car

and no one would tear it up."

I placed it back in my glove box and smiled inwardly. I hoped that my ruse had worked. I didn't know if he had me wired for sound or video, but if I had convinced him that I thought it was my card, then he would continue to feel safe. Either way, I now had the upper hand. I could lead this trip where I wanted to go and be seen only when I wanted to be.

CHAPTER TEN

I drove around Marksboro looking for a good spot for my plans. I needed a place to have a showdown and a place to appear to watch. I had to carefully maintain the look of continuing my job so my watcher would not become suspicious. This whole confrontation needed to happen before the wedding. I did not want to have him able to act when I would have many innocent bystanders to protect.

After an hour I found a great spot that served all my purposes. I stopped by a convenience store for a sandwich and drink so I would look like I was settling in for surveillance. I parked my car at a lot with a view of the Neolithic Consortium building so I could watch it. I set my sunglasses down on the back of my chair so that the angle would appear close to normal and I walked down the block to an old empty department store. This would serve as my trap.

I moved around to the back of the store. It had a secluded rear entrance with a simple pad lock. I took a careful moment to pick the lock so it would remain intact. Sometimes a show had to be preserved for another time. I moved the lock with my mind so that the dust would not be disturbed. The door stuck tight so I gave it a mind shove to open it. Telekinesis could be very awesome.

Once inside, I set down the lock and looked at the space I had to work with. Mostly empty there was a lot of space and not much to work with. Many old fixtures were left, but not much beyond that. I strolled through to get an idea of the layout and familiarize myself with the space. I walked through slowly, checking all the exits and windows. I had made a wonderful choice on the location. This would work perfectly.

I walked through for an hour and a half before I fully decided what all I intended to do. It would take me another hour or two to lay everything out before I had it all the way I wanted. Did I mention that my job can be a lot of fun sometimes?

The sun was still up when I finished my preparations, but not for much longer. I left the store, carefully locking the back door again before walking back to my car. I sat down and put my sunglasses back on. Here I just had to hope, because the transfer would look odd to anyone watching. If he were using a screen to see from my point of view, then I may have blown the whole thing. I tried to make it look like I was taking them off to clean them before putting them back on. I got out and walked to the store making sure to look around so that the path was apparent. My shadow might be stupid and I did not want him getting lost now.

I walked around back to the door. I used my mind now to split the lock and then I kicked open the door. The show must go on. I glanced inside and then walked back to my car. The path should now be in my shadow's mind. Now I needed some time and to see just how this would play out. The thing about these plans is that there is no way to plan for the exact nature of everything. There were many ways I could be approached. I mostly wanted to have a home field in which to have an advantage.

I drove to a small Italian place in town for dinner. Once I got there I took my sunglasses off. Anyone who wanted to know should be able to track me. Why dinner? Well, I needed a public place where a meeting could happen if that was the route he chose. Also, I was mostly hungry and the cheap gas station sandwich sounded terrible in comparison. I ordered a rigatoni with cheese bread and a side order of meatballs. It had been a while since my last meal. I sat and waited for a sign.

My first sign was my food arriving. My stomach took this to be a wonderful portent of things to come. I sat quietly and ate. The pasta was good. The sauce was a bit too sweet, but I am not the kind of man to discriminate against food just because it was made this way. Sweet sauce needs love too. The meatballs were exemplary so all worked out well.

While I ate my sugary repast, a man dropped into the seat right across from me. I ignored him and continued to eat. Of course, I kept a careful watch of him with my mind to catch his emotional state. I continued to ignore him once I realized how much it annoyed him. Was it possible to ignore someone harder? If so, I must have managed it because his anger grew rapidly. He waited as long as he could hold out. A tough guy would not let me get on his nerves. He would have known not to act out of anger. This guy was tough enough for three minutes.

"Hey! Asshole!"

I continued to eat. I didn't even look up as I grabbed another slice of cheese bread.

"Are you deaf or just stupid?"

"Hungry and you aren't helping," I said with a mouthful of bread.

"Look, fucker, I have a message for you and you better pay attention cause I'm only gonna say this once."

"Good. I'm sick of your voice already. Can you just text me?" I looked him right in the eyes and he paused for a moment. My intense look must have temporarily seized his mind. That or I may have had sauce on my face. Who can say?

"Tonight, at ten o'clock you're to meet my boss at the park next to the war memorial. You got that?"

"So tennish around the playground equipment?"

"Ten sharp at the war memorial, you fuck. Got that?"

"I knew I could make you repeat yourself."

"You think you're so funny. Laugh all you can now. Boss will change your tune tonight."

"So, do I need to fill out an RSVP card? Do I get a plus one? What is the dress code? I need details."

"Laugh it up, just be there," he got up and walked away.

Well, aside from being annoying, this wizard was fast. I had about three hours until ten and less until I actually met this guy. He knew enough to stack things for him, but not allow me time to prepare. Meeting a hostile wizard is a very tricky proposition. Though I do not use magic myself, I do know a fair amount about how it works and have seen it up close many times. Wizards were very tough customers.

In general, a mage was quite powerful, but given time to prepare that threat grew exponentially. It was also very difficult to gauge a wizard's capabilities before you actually got to see them. Mortals with access to magic manifest their abilities according to the make-up of their mind. Everyone perceived the world in a way that developed for them over time and this included magic. It was an extension of how the brain was programed to filter everything through the memories people already had.

When someone was quite religious, like a staunch Catholic born and raised, this person was likely to see magic as divine power that would be best accessed through prayer and careful rituals. A Wiccan practitioner might draw power from circles and a connection to nature or their personal totem. A scientific minded wizard would probably skew toward alchemy or quantum theory to manipulate the world around them. That was the basic formula for magic use. It then splintered off even more according to each individual's strengths, weaknesses, fears, culture, and so forth. There were basic concepts, but there were many paths to use the same forces in the world. I have even seen a few use magic to imitate my abilities, though I have never met someone who used their mind the way I can.

For tonight the particular mechanics of this wizard's magic were not all that important for me to know. There was one thing that seemed to be universal across all forms of magic: the need for concentration. All of these other methods served to focus a mind so it could concentrate enough to actually manipulate the forces of magic. The best way I have ever found to directly fight a wizard was to break his concentration. Of course, any wizard worth his pointy hat knew that and practiced concentration intently. I had to be better.

I knew what I needed to do and where I needed to do it. I was left to wait for a bit so I could show up at the right time. I couldn't appear to expect too much. Maybe this didn't have to be a fight. Maybe we could talk and reason with each other like civilized people.

"Yeah, and maybe Rob Liefeld draws realistic musculature and feet."

CHAPTER ELEVEN

I left the restaurant and drove for about half an hour or so to allow a little time. I didn't want to seem too eager. I then headed for the department store I had prepared. I found a spot to park that was about a block away to protect my car. I sauntered casually to the back door, pushed it open, and quickly shut my eyes.

A bright light flashed and the room then glowed steadily.

"Welcome my friend," a voice said. "In a moment you will be able to see me, but trust that I still have the situation completely in my control. I am Daniel Davis. I was the one who had you summoned. Stay calm. I know you are perplexed as to why I am here now and not our agreed meeting place. Well, to put it simply, I have been following you. I know everything you do and have done. Make this easy on yourself; acquiesce to my demands and you will not have to face the true nature of the immense power at my command."

"Take a breath there, Danny. Did you go to the Chris Claremont School of Villain Dialog? Quick! Tell me your nefarious plan or were you sick on Ian Flemming day?"

"You impudent fool! You have no clue as to what I can do to make you suffer."

"That's good. I also would have accepted 'how dare you mock me?'"

He paused for a moment and chuckled, "no matter. Give up this job you have been hired to perform. This woman must pay for her crimes."

"So, there is a plan to kill her. Thanks, Gabby."

"Yes, it matters not that you know of her fate soon to come. Leave now and you will live the rest of your miserable life."

"Really not good for my career prospects, though. Not many clients want to hire a guy who was run off by a cheesy silver age comic book villain. I do believe that my union requires that I claim incidents like that somewhere. I'll have to check with the shop steward."

"Enough! I will simply end this and you now then go about my business."

Just because he was goofy didn't mean he wasn't legitimately tough. I was taunting him and massaging his mind to get him to blow his cool. Apparently, he tended toward the melodramatic. Big surprise for a wizard. I worked to amplify what he was feeling and that was the route he took with it. Another unfortunate side effect of mind tampering. Before he could get his footing, I flashed his mind. This was a trick I had developed for fights with wizards to break their concentration. It was similar to what he tried to do with my eyes. I assaulted his mind with information. The human mind spent a lot of capital organizing and understanding all the stimuli entering it at any given time. With practice people could learn to do this very quickly but most simply stop paying attention to much of that stimuli to save effort.

I had to find a way to counteract the practice mages put into concentration. I found that I could send quick one-way transmissions into someone's mind forcing them to receive instant information. The more types of information that entered the mind at once, the harder it was for that mind to catalog. This process put them off for a few moments, thus allowing me time to get the upper hand. With wizards it also broke spells and whatever effects they were maintaining.

In this case I chose to flash three complete episodes of The Simpsons instantly into his mind.

He paused for a moment, the light went out, and I took my chance to move. I bolted toward the front of the store along the outer wall. Moving quickly through the space I kept my mind's eye on Daniel. He recovered well and turned to deliver a bolt of electricity at the wall where I had been just a moment before.

As his first offensive move, he had gone big. He either had a lot of juice or needed to end this quickly. Possibly both. I knew in which option my hopes lay.

Unfortunately for him I had positioned myself with one of my cerebro-mines between us. This one was fairly simple. It used my mind and a positioned mirror in the store to reflect someone's malicious intent and energy back onto them.

He didn't like lightning any more than I would have and barely got a partial shield up in time to reflect some of the blast. It struck all around me, knocking me to the floor. This guy meant business.

He stepped toward the wall to get a clear shot at me. Staying down along the floor I slid along the front wall away from him. With fights like this distance could help either of us so I couldn't simply extend the space or close right away.

He drew up his hand and I felt power beginning to well up around him. I took another chance. I threw a mental fishing hook into his mind in an attempt to pull forward a painful memory for him to experience. This was a jab in a fight like this, but any good fighter knew that a stiff jab could win a fight. It worked to some degree as he paused and tears came to his eyes. I have no clue what he experienced.

I stood up and bolted down the aisle in front of me to bring cover between us. I dove behind a pillar a moment before a ball of fire shot past me and collided with the wall. Great.

I checked and there was still a solid forty feet between us with no easy path to traverse. I was realizing that distance was to his advantage in this fight.

Fuck.

Improvising, I telekinetically flung a couple old paint cans at him from across the room. His shield reflected them away with ease. I took the moments to move closer to him. He stood in what had been the big main aisle of the store and began to draw in power again.

I was still in front of him in the aisle to his left. I tugged on his foot telekinetically. He faltered a moment, but did not fall. I didn't have a good position for this and my traps were laid for me to be in a different location. I had planned to run further on but his electric bolt had cut off my path by starting a fire.

I shifted to the main aisle, but immediately had to throw myself to the right as yet another spear of electricity shot past me. What little of the store that was left was singed or on fire now. This couldn't last much longer. He'd finish taking out everything I was hiding behind. I would have to take another route to finish this off if I wanted to win. He stood in the aisle and drew himself to his full height as he was collecting power.

I moved down the aisle slowly. I had about twenty feet still between us both. I reached up above him and pulled down the light fixture with my mind. He moved from its path but lost his chant. The power dissipated. I took that moment to turn and rush him, but I took a burst of force in the chest that threw me back. I landed hard in front of him with nothing else between us. He threw his arms out and force shoved back the fixtures and debris around him, thus clearing the space between us. It also took away my places to hide. He was better than I had expected.

Damnit.

I fished again in his mind for a familiar voice. I used that as a skin over my words and made him hear it as if it came from behind him.

Daniel! He should have heard in whatever voice I managed to grab.

It only managed to work partially as he tilted his head but stayed focused on me. I think he realized that it was me doing the talking. The danger in causing hallucinations was that someone could see through them or could ignore them. I waved my hand and threw telekinetic force toward him in a wave. It was a clumsy attack and he deflected it easily and laughed.

I stood up and positioned myself right in front of him. I threw another wave at him. The force was slow and aimed at his chest. Again, he was able to shrug it off. This time he laughed hard at me.

"Is that all you have? I was warned to be careful with you because you were dangerous."

"Well, I do better with a full house and a laugh track."

I waved my hand again, sending out yet another wave at his chest. He stood with his hands on his hips and waited for this one. At the last second, I bent the wave down and gave it an additional push at his stiff legs. Both of his knees broke completely backwards. He screamed and fell to the floor. I rushed forward as he hit the floor and delivered a boot to his head knocking him unconscious.

I bent down to move him to a better position and restrain him when both of his eyes shot open. They were entirely white. He smiled then and spoke to me in a voice not his own. It sounded like it was coming from a voice modulator.

"I knew this wouldn't go well. He will still be useful to me."

His hand rose up and small points of light appeared on his fingertips. One began to grow. It swelled up to the size of a softball and launched toward me. I rolled as it came and I was tossed onto my back as it continued to the ceiling. There, it erupted as flame and caught additional parts of the store on fire. The next ball grew and shot out. I ducked it and got to my feet as it hit the front bank of painting supplies and rubbish. More fire erupted as the third ball grew.

I saw what was coming and I got to my feet and ran for the back of the store. The third ball collided with a mine I had set, but didn't use. The back of the store where I was headed exploded with fire and force blowing out the glass in the front and bringing in a rush of air. I quickly created a telekinetic cushion of force in front of me. The force from the explosion hit that and threw it and myself through the now shattered front windows.

I hit the pavement hard as I saw the forth ball hit another trap. I lost track at that point of what was going on specifically. The whole store was engulfed in flames. I got up and started to walk off so I could avoid talking to anyone about this whole business. As I walked away, I felt for the possibility of Daniel surviving, but his mind was completely gone. Of course, his chances of surviving that conflagration were low. I got to my car as I heard the sirens drawing closer. This was the second time something connected to me in this town had burnt down. I was beginning to think I might be a menace.

As I sat in my car I thought about the voice that came from Daniel at the end. I had no doubt that whoever that was did not die in that fire. Before I drove off I placed my sunglasses under the rear tire of my car. I couldn't be sure that spell had originated with Daniel. As I backed out and felt the crunch of my glasses I wondered to myself when the last time was that this town was so busy.

CHAPTER TWELVE

Back at the hotel I started the process of getting cleaned up. As I went through it I took account of my clothes that were too damaged to keep. Burns, tears, and rips meant that not much beyond my coat were worth keeping. As each article came off I discovered sore spots and the like from the fight. In the heat of battle most injuries go completely unnoticed. Usually, aside from a major injury, it wasn't until later that I would find cuts, bruises, or pains. My body seemed to be far more interested in surviving than saying ouch. I climbed in the shower and let the hot water run over me. I generally prefer higher water pressure for the massage quality, but hotels seem to maintain a pressure slightly above gravity drip. That would have to do.

Once the physical pains were tabulated I checked my mind. Here, there were rarely injuries beyond fatigue. There was a serious tax to pay for the use of mental powers and that tax usually took payment physically. My energy seemed to run off me with the water. I felt myself begin to shake slightly as the adrenaline drained from my body. My thoughts grew foggy and muddled so I decided to think back on the fight then before my mind became too tired to do any serious work.

The fight, as I went back over it, seemed to be fairly manageable throughout. I had a few shaky moments, but I was never too close to death. That was until the very end. Suddenly that guy grew far more capable to harness vast power when he delivered his final strike. The voice I heard was obviously not his own, so the power might not have been either. There was some level of possession involved. Usually any possession would be fought bitterly by the person being affected. A human mind would naturally fight against any invading force and it had home field advantage. This time the invader seemed to have full control. The reason most of these events end with some weird cryptic words was that almost nothing else could be managed. This force could sling magic.

Of course, it was possible that the fight made it easier. I considered that I might have knocked him out, but that usually ends possession. The target's mind was needed to control the body to some degree. Maybe there was a spell cast before that created the doorway through which the invader entered. It had not seemed like a willful act, however. I was beginning to see why Alan thought I might have found this one interesting. I would have to watch myself.

After I finished my shower I began to lay out my clothes for the next day. I wanted to be very prepared for this party. By that point I was assuming that the invader was involved in this and might be there. Someone wanted me out and I had no intention of giving in. Of course, Alexander wasn't going to make it very easy for anyone to crash his daughter's wedding. There would be some very serious power in attendance with a strong interest in protecting itself. I still didn't want to depend on anyone else for my safety or the safety of my client. I knew very little about the intentions of the attacker aside from going after Clara and myself for protecting her. That made this all much more difficult.

I knew that I had to watch out for possession as well. If the invader could take over different people as easily, that would make obfuscating their presences so much easier. I might end up searching minds or having to fight in them. I would have to watch Clara very carefully. I laid out the only suit I had. Fortunately, my suit stays in my car on trips like this. I used it more as a costume so I wanted it to be available. I also laid out my holster that best hid my Rhino in that suit. Sometimes banal weaponry turned out to be the best available. There was a reason guns were used so often. I sat down and began to list out things I needed to do before I arrived. The more I considered it, the more I wanted Alan to be nearby when all of this was going down. His help could mean a world of difference if the situation went pear shaped.

I'm sure Alexander would have competent security both conventional and magical. That could, however, just make more fodder for this wizard. I had to assume the wizard knew the field better than I would. At times like this I cursed my lack of magical knowledge. I might better know the threat ahead of me if I was more capable of assessing the abilities of the opposing force. I knew how hard it was for me to control someone's consciousness and I knew what I could do to overcome those. I really had no idea how the spell making this possible worked or how powerful it could be. Maybe it took everything the wizard had to do it. Maybe it only worked on that one man. It took me a lot of concentration and it was not a very efficient use of my power. That might not have been true of my counterpart in this situation. If I had more time I would've liked to have talked to Alexander and get his thoughts.

Of course, there was another possibility.

Alexander could be on the wrong side of this whole thing. If he really did blame Clara for the attempt on his life he might be fairly cavalier about my conundrum. It was even possible that the wizard could be working for him. Alexander was immensely powerful. It was certain that if he knew a way to achieve it, he did have the power to pull off that possession I had witnessed earlier. Of course, if Alexander wanted me off this detail, he would most likely have asked me to leave it alone at least once when we spoke. He did have a very strict code and he would have extended me that respect. At least I assumed as much.

So, with further thought, I probably wouldn't have asked him about this to begin with. That, once again, leaves me with only my knowledge and abilities. In situations like this trust could be a hard thing to come by. If only Alan had the knowledge needed. His deductive mind was amazing and I was sure he could provide insights I just couldn't get otherwise. No sense whining over what I couldn't have.

As I continued to work through the knowledge I had and prepared for the next day, I began to fall off into sleep. I realized I was completely spent and needed rest. Since I had to leave by ten tomorrow morning to pick up Clara, I decided that the prudent action would be to get some solid rest. Good sleep was every protector's best side-kick. Wow! I must have been tired if I was coming up with cliched shit like that. As I pulled the sheets off the bed an astral form appeared in the room. The image was quite amazing. If not for the fact that I could sense no mind in the room I would probably have had my gun drawn.

The figure was cloaked with a hood that shrouded the

face entirely. I stood in front of the image looking for any clue to its identity for a moment as it floated there silently. Finally, it spoke directly into my mind.

"As you can see, I can find you anywhere you choose to go."

"Impressive, but I prefer juggling chainsaws or flaming corgis."

"Your flippant attitude will not help you. I have come to offer you one last chance to give this up. You have no business involved in this and I have no desire as of now to harm you."

"Funny that. Tonight, you seemed to try pretty hard for having no desire."

"That was just-"

"Stuff it. You tried and failed to kill me and now you're on to desperation tactics. Whatever you have planned has less of a chance if I'm there tomorrow. Forget it. I'm going to be there and you won't succeed."

"You pose no threat to me. You impressed me tonight and you have earned this last offering. If you choose to deny it then I will deal with you tomorrow along with the woman."

"Yeah? And my little dog too? If you're so omnipotent why are you floating there giving villain speeches and not dealing with me now? Here I am."

"It serves my plans better tomorrow."

"Sure. That's a nice way to say you can't. You don't have the chops to take me on in my playground. Why don't you just take your little sideshow and fuck off?"

I pushed with my mind just slightly to gauge the apparition's strength. It shifted but it was strong.

"Believe what you will but tomorrow will be my day entirely. Show up if you like, but you will meet a terrible end."

"Really? You float there and actually missed your chance to say, 'meet your doom?' Go back to villain school."

"What does Monty see in you? I guess I'll have no choice but to end you. He'll be upset, but I can live with that."

The specter dissipated with those final words. Once it was gone I threw up a solid mental wall to block any invading intellect. I had been so wrapped up that I missed that earlier. That was a huge mistake I would need to fix. It was the kind of sloppy move that could get me killed in this line of work.

With my wall up, it was definitely time for sleep. Tomorrow would be a very interesting day. There may have only been one wedding, but there could be many funerals if I wasn't ready.

CHAPTER THIRTEEN

I woke up at eight on Saturday. I was still very tired from the night before. That kind of energy expense does not return quickly. I would have loved nothing more than rolling over and hitting my own internal snooze button, but I had to meet Clara at ten to take her to the wedding. I figured it best that we arrive together and in sync. I was not expecting much to occur during the wedding proper. There would be a lot of rage and power to face down if someone were to ruin Jessica DesChanes' ceremony. The reception would pose a much more enticing time for some kind of attempt.

I called Alan first to make sure all was well on his end.

"So, have all of your plans come to fruition?"

He sighed louder than I thought necessary. "All is fine. What do you want?"

"I figured I'd check and see if you had any plans to be at the wedding and maybe we could discuss strategy and tactics like the bad-ass professionals we are."

"Really? There's a wedding? Yes, I have already staked out a position for myself. All is well. Again, the less you know the better for all involved."

"This is wearing thin. Why won't you talk to me about this? I'm not a child or your employee."

"Look, Trevor, I know this drives you nuts, but you do trust me. You need to be ignorant here. Please, just let me do what I'm doing. When this is all over you can tear me a new asshole."

"Fine, but you're pushing me, baby."

Alan hung up with no response which made me more nervous than angry. What kind of plan could he be working on?

I put all of that aside to prepare for the wedding. I got the basic showering and shaving out of the way. Somehow, I figured that Clara would inspect me very carefully before we attended anything together. I put on the suit I had laid out the night before. There had not been an instruction to wear a tuxedo so I had planned to avoid that like the plague.

The day was very bright but still cold. The party was set as an outdoor event so I would get the great benefit of wearing my black duster and wide brim hat. A suit coat is good to conceal a gun, but the coat worked so much better. The hat worked often to obscure my eyes and sight-line. I also brought along a snub nosed gun strapped to my ankle. I had not used my gun yet, but maybe that was because I was not carrying enough of them.

At over six feet tall and broad I looked very imposing in my duster and hat. I liked them for both their intimidating appearance and near complete rain protection. Now that I was all clean and spiffy I could think of no other reason to delay this day. So I headed for my car to go meet Clara. As I walked I scanned for minds following me. At this point I figured that there would be no more attempts to scare me so anything from here out would simply be an attempt on my life.

I drove out to Clara's place. I kept my mind out for menacing figures while scanning the city on this cold morning. I didn't like this town. Nothing here ever felt honest or genuine. Something was always below the surface. I arrived at Clara's unmolested to find a large black limousine parked in front of her house. I guess the plan was to travel in style. She was walking out of her front door when I pulled in and parked to the side. She stopped and waited as I approached.

She was stunning in her black and silver dress. Instead of blunting her height she dressed to accentuate it. She looked and moved like a jungle cat who owned this patch of land. The colors of her dress were not the wedding colors, but were close while showing her defiance. A small protest was my guess.

As I approached she addressed me very formally. "Good morning. I had assumed you would meet me there."

"There have been incidents now and I would be remiss in my duties were I not present for this journey as well."

"Well, that sounds reasonable and one of the most professional things you've said to me during this whole situation."

"Thank you. I've been rehearsing that on the drive over. I won't burden you with the options I decided against."

"Good. Now, get in the car and let us get this travesty over with. I have no desire to dwell on this day."

With that she slid into the limo with ease and grace through the door her chauffeur held for her. He maintained no eye contact and a straight face through it all. He turned his head toward me once she was in.

"Sir," his voice a smooth baritone.

"I'm impressed. Never once did I see you try to look up her dress… or down for that matter. Do you have a system of mirrors that does that for you?"

He glared at me and said nothing. He didn't have to. The simple act of releasing the door and stepping back told me exactly what he thought of me. This town had a sever lack of a sense of humor. I slid into the car with none of the practiced grace of Clara. I was beginning to understand that entering and exiting a limo in a short dress without giving the world a peek was quite a skill to be learned. It was all I could do to keep from bashing my head into the door frame.

The chauffeur did not close the door for me. I closed it myself and thought about how I would stiff him were I covering the cost here in any way.

The interior of the vehicle was deep, rich, and lush. The surfaces were all leather and wood. The interior was quite large and dark and there was a wall up between the driver and the cabin we were in. A long seat ran down one side and a bar on the other. I had no doubt that the bar was well stocked. It probably had booze older than most everyone I know and worth more per bottle than the suit I was wearing. I was tempted to try it out, but my hostess did not so I followed suit.

The limo began to move and our silence stretched on. Clara finally broke it out of curiosity.

"So, there have been incidents?"

"Yes, someone seems to want me out of the picture."

"How melodramatic."

"True, though. I'm beginning to think something serious might be planned."

"I think I told you that already. I don't know if this is connected in any way, but someone broke into my house yesterday."

"Was anyone hurt?" my nerves flared. Had I already missed my chance to save her? "Was anything taken?"

"No, I'm fine. No one in the house has reported any

injuries. Some things were moved around and I think my diary was read."

"Really? How can you tell?" I tried to suppress my smile.

"Do not mock me. I have a pressed rose petal in it. The petal was on the wrong page when I checked last night. I was feeling nostalgic so I was reading entries I wrote about Victor when he was younger. The petal was on the day after Mother's Day that year. He found a rose the day after and thought I would like it. The thought meant so much more to me than the present his father had bought for him that I saved a petal on the day after."

"I see. So, have you ruled out Victor or the help in this regard? The book could have fallen and the petal moved."

"The maids do not open my drawers to clean and Victor would know well what page that petal belonged on. Though I doubt that he would snoop around my things. Someone must have broken in and went through my things. Could you find him?"

"Honestly, for work in that vein either Alan or the police would be vastly better than I am. I'm a terrible detective. It's why I never went into that line of work."

"Could you please? I think it may be connected to the rest of this. Please. I would feel much better. At least keep it in mind as you go about the rest of this."

"Let's see how today goes and we can discuss the rest after. Maybe things will clear up soon."

The limo came to a stop and a small opening in the wall dividing the driver and our cabin slid down.

"We have arrived."

"Fine, Gerard. Get the door please."

After a moment the door opened. I stepped out. Gerard was emotionless. I would have said something biting, but I glanced around me for a moment. All comments stopped in my head. I was not prepared for the sight of this wedding. Not at all.

CHAPTER FOURTEEN

As I stepped out of the limo my mind was assaulted by the sheer mass of mental activity transpiring around me. I have long built a habit in which I open my mind as I exit a vehicle or door to avoid something that I could not see resulting in tragedy. This time my habit resulted in something I could see all too well resulting in tragedy. Good grief.

The grounds around Alexander's home were expansive. I had seen them mostly empty before and the well-manicured lawn and gardens only accentuated how large of an area his mansion occupied. Standing outside of the limo the sheer volume of space informed me of how many people must have attended this wedding. They were not packed in like a protest march. Instead, there were attendees moving and flowing almost everywhere. The only places they did not inhabit were protected only by the valiant efforts of caterers, decorators, and ushers creating lanes for food and people to move. Never in my life had I seen such a collection for a private, exclusive event.

As I stood by the limo and watched, Gerard helped Clara from the car. She appeared at my side observing the same throng.

"To think, this is what Sica referred to as 'a small wedding of close friends.'"

"I keep expecting to see TV cameras here so that all of her subjects can witness the royal wedding."

Clara laughed. She genuinely laughed at one of my jokes. Time to put together that comedy special.

"Yes, I'm sure that's exactly how she sees this situation. Her father is the king over the wizards of this world making her the princess. That would explain a lot about her attitude."

I had really only been joking, but Clara did have a point. In many ways this was magic royalty. Here was the great and powerful daughter of the king marrying a commoner who had no talent. I'd bet there were a lot of young men who would have loved to see Victor fall hard.

As we stood and watched, I began to see a pattern form in the motions of the attendants. The whole crowd seemed to flow toward the back of the house. From above I imagined that it looked much like a human river. Within the current were eddies and even tidal pools with people flowing in and out of them. I lost myself in observance of the crowd for a fairly long amount of time.

Without a spoken word, we started to move with the river and immediately we were caught in the flow. For a time, we moved with it. It was soon evident that we stood out in this river. Clara was stunning. Graceful and tall her defiance shown like a beacon for all to see. I seemed more of a dark blotch that no one wanted to notice. People seemed to turn their heads just before they would look directly at me. I felt like the dark spot on a shiny apple or a cold breeze on a warm spring day. Couldn't have done better if I had tried.

As we flowed toward the back-yard and the eventual promised land of this wedding we spotted a small eddy around Alexander. The flow of people seemed to split and moved around him. Nothing pushed him against his will. He grasped my hand as we moved and pulled me into his protective space. Clara stopped as well, seeming to slice through the crowd. He then turned toward Clara, took and kissed her hand gently.

"Mrs. Edwards, soon we will join our families. How are you on this lovely day?"

"I am well," though I felt the chill in her mind and thoughts, her words and demeanor were warm and pleasant. "How're you holding up under this army of workers?"

"I find the activity pleasant and I am more than a little excited for my daughter. She has wanted this for so long. She is, of course, scurrying around with anxiety beyond compare."

"That's the state of young ladies on their wedding day. Has my son been comporting himself as a useful young man?"

"I fear that his power is spent weathering the storm that surrounds him. He has a look in his eye that is not dissimilar from most young men on their wedding day. Yet I am confident that he will prevail."

"That's good to hear. Is there anything I can do to assist?"

"Milady, I suggest that you relax and take in the day. All is in hand."

"I will find my son, and ask him then."

Alexander face flashed with rage for but a moment. He quickly came down. Most would never have seen that bit of rage.

"As you wish. A mother should see her son on the day he is to take a new woman into his life. Trevor, get her a drink and see that she does not meet any undue stress.

This should be a joyous day."

With a slight bow he moved off to meet a caterer quickly slipping into a discussion about the reception meal. They were lost in the river of humanity. I turned toward Clara to find a look of shock on her face.

"Are you okay? You suddenly look ill."

"I just had a moment." Her face lightened with the skill and acumen of one adept at faking joy. "I was hit with the reality of my son growing up. I knew it would happen, but it seems so quick now. Does it move slower for other mothers?"

"No, I don't think any mother's ever truly ready for that realization. This is the kind of event to cause that feeling." I thought she wasn't telling me the whole truth about the cause, but there was no benefit to arguing now so I just let it go until another time. I had a feeling I knew what was really going on.

We moved with the flow toward the rear of the house. As we walked we finally caught a glimpse of the setup for the actual ceremony. There was an area lightly ringed with trees that served as the location. There were easily over three hundred chairs set up in the clearing. The aisle created by the two symmetrical grids of seats was draped with a thick blue satin carpet on top of a hard-wood path. The rest of the area was meticulously manicured grass cut to an exact and uniform height. The grass was almost unnatural it was so green. The dais and alter at the end of the aisle were marble. Both must have weighed hundreds of pounds. They had both been draped with blue satin and lace and were carefully decorated with flowers in intricate arrangements. An arch of wisteria grew over the spot where the couple would say their vows. The vines were carefully wrapped around each other coming together in a knot at the top. The usual white flowers that would be hanging from the vines were now blue to match.

The entire setup dripped with the impossibility that only magic could create. There had been a lot of physical and magical effort expended to make this look the way that it did. I could feel the power course through the air from all the enchantments resting on the area. I now came to the realization that Alexander employed magical gardeners. That would allow him to have the absolute best of everything. Of course, that was the only way it could be when his only daughter had her wedding.

During the time before the ceremony the guests were allowed to mill around, talk, and be impressed with what had been created. Waiters moved through the crowd passing out finger foods and flutes of champagne. One of the waiters caught my attention. He looked familiar, yet unexpected.

"Excuse me, Clara, I need to check out the area and people."

"That's fine. I believe that I'm somewhat obligated to speak to people. My son is the groom after all."

Having excused myself I moved off to speak with the waiter. He deftly moved through the crowd offering some kind of food on a tray. He appeared not to notice me as I approached from behind. I reached out and put my hand on his shoulder.

"I don't think you belong here, sir."

Without turning around, he spoke. He showed no signs of surprise.

"Remove your hand, Trevor, unless you want me to remove it from your body."

I pulled my hand back as Alan turned to face me.

"Risky, isn't this?"

"Less so if you weren't going around acting like I'm any different from any of the other servers here. None of these people know me by sight."

"How did you get in?"

Alan sighed, "I simply applied and got hired to serve. There are always openings for temp help when a huge event like this happens. Easy and straight forward."

"Watching it all from the inside, huh?"

"It's usually the best view. Now, take one of these and move away. I'll contact you soon. I have some information to open this thing up."

"I hope it's better than your food," I said as I took one of the odd goop covered crackers that he had on the tray.

"You have no appreciation for fine food."

"I figured it would be cocktail weenies and cheap champagne."

"You're hopeless," he said as he walked away into the crowd.

CHAPTER FIFTEEN

I found Clara standing by a wall of floral arrangements that almost sparkled. She had managed to find and trap her son for some time. She was talking at him and he seemed about ready to gnaw his own arm off to escape. Some aspects of mothers were the same through multiple generations. I smiled as I moved into the fray.

"Mom! Would you chill out."

"No, and you have no right to expect me to. You tell me that your bride expressly forbade my involvement and then you ask me to 'chill out?' That's the most ridiculous thing that has ever been requested of me. This whole thing is just ridiculous. It's absurd."

"What's the problem here? Should I be working to protect Victor as well?" I advanced in against all reason or sense of self preservation.

"I've been forbidden to help. His bride fears that I will sabotage it all somehow," the venom that dripped from the word bride made it hard not to see Sica's point of view. Clara turned back toward her son. "Why would I do that? Answer me now. Why would I ruin a major landmark day that you have already chosen to ruin through your own stupid life choices? Huh? How could I make this day any worse?"

"Because she is a mage, mother. Who knows what you might do."

"Is that all you think I care about? Do you see no possibility that I want to help with my son's wedding? I bet she wants me out of your life right after the ceremony, too."

"Well, she does want to avoid you."

"Why?"

"Why, Mother? Really? Maybe because you tried to kill her father."

Clara's hand was a blur of motion as she slapped Victor hard across his mouth. He stood dumbstruck. It was obvious that she had never struck him before and that he didn't know how to react to it now. Clara was breathing rapidly and looking as if she might do it again.

"Whoa! Hold on a moment. Let's calm down before things get said or done that will cause any more damage."

They spoke simultaneously in the same cadence and tone as only a parent and child truly can.

"My mom just slapped my face and you dare say calm down?"

"My son just accused me of attempted murder."

In a knee jerk reaction, I flashed both of them Martin Luther King Jr.'s famous "I have a dream" speech. They fell silent. There are many things I have kept memorized just for such occasions that might arise. With my abilities it just makes life easier than shouting over people.

"Now, you're both very emotional and getting each other further worked up isn't going to help anything. It doesn't take a telepath to see that. However, you both need to take a step back for a moment. Clara, your son is a ball of emotions as any young man is on an occasion like this. His life's changing rapidly and he has all sorts of feelings to sort out. His future's both opening and closing rapidly.

"And before you feel too high and mighty, junior, your mother's equal parts elated, anxious, depressed, and terrified. You cannot expect her to simply roll over, after raising you for all these years, and be kicked from your life. Why would you even want to do a thing like that?

"Before either of you say or do anything else that might create and irrevocable rift in your relationship, maybe you need to retreat to your corners. Victor, why not go get your mother a drink while I have a word with her?"

Victor moved off sheepishly toward the waiters and I turned to fully face Clara. She seemed to have calmed down some. Suddenly she began to tear up and flung herself upon me. She wept hard. Her whole body shook and rattled with her sobs. I stood and held her while remaining silent. I figured it was not the time to speak. I could sometimes figure out when that was. Sometimes. She finally calmed enough to hold herself up.

Clara stepped back and cleaned her face carefully. After she got her control back she decided to speak to me.

"Why is he marrying her? Why couldn't he just find a nice girl? I wouldn't care if she was poor, homeless, or anything. Why'd he have to find a mage?"

"Clara," I stroked her back as I spoke. "Many children find some way to rebel against their parents. Many mothers hate the girls that their sons marry. Most likely there's a lot about Sica that is similar to you. You're the most powerful woman in his life and it's likely that he found someone with at least something similar to that strength. Have you taken any time to give her a chance? Maybe, under that magic, she's a nice girl and good for Victor."

"She's never given me a chance to know her. Of course, I've tried. Why wouldn't I? I don't want to lose my son. At every juncture I have tried and she finds some way to block my efforts. She wants nothing to do with me. She won't attend meals or family outings. I always invite her and she always refuses. She won't even say more than a few words to me when we do speak. She's hiding from me and no good girl would do that."

"Maybe she is scared. She does have reason to think you hate her and would never accept her no matter what. On top of that you are strong and forceful. Maybe she doesn't want to bring the inevitable conflict."

"I've tried to extend an olive branch. I know there's reason to be scared, but if she would speak to me maybe we could get past it. And to make it worse Victor just takes her side in every conflict. Any time she does anything he just waves it off or argues her side. He never seems to understand how I feel about any of this. She's stealing my only son. The only person I have left."

As she spoke Victor returned with drink in hand. He also brought one for himself. I was left out in the cold. He handed her the glass and they both took a moment to drink and get control of their feelings. Both of their minds swirled with emotion. I stayed out of it all. I tried to give everyone privacy when possible. Victor seemed to recover first.

"Mother, I know this is hard and that you and Sica don't see eye to eye. Most of the people around her think that you and your group are monsters. They think you're dangerous, but I know that you're my mother. I've been working hard to show her that you're my mom, and that the woman who raised me couldn't possibly be a monster. It's been hard but I think it's working and that in time I will succeed.

"But you have to understand that I love her. She loves me, too. Purely. Not like the other girls I've met. There is nothing for her to gain from me, but me. I have no magic for her to learn. She has more money and worldly connections that I do. She's beautiful, smart, and fun to be around. There's no selfish reason to have me around except for my love. The fact that she wants to marry me is proof that she truly loves me for who I am."

Clara moved close and cupped his cheek with her hand. For a moment all I saw in her was a mother who cared for her son.

"Victor, honey, I know you feel that way. And I understand how you feel. I can see it in your eyes every time you say her name. Why else do you think I've tried to be closer to her? However, there are things you don't see. There are things you don't know. You're still so young. I know I can't stop you, but I pray that you open your eyes and see her for who she truly is."

Victor sighed and his head drooped into his mother's hand. They stood that way, silently, like a pair in a painting.

"I'm sorry, mother. Maybe this whole thing's been a mistake. You've always been so strong and I see that in Sica," he lifted his head and looked directly into Clara's eyes. Tears fell down his face.

"You don't even realize it. Sica wanted you here. I thought she'd fight me over it. I was prepared for a massive fight. Not only did she not fight me, but she made me promise that you would attend. She brought the whole subject up before I did."

"Wait," I chimed in. "She insisted on Clara attending?"

"Yes. She was so adamant that my mother be here. I was so happy when she asked me. It felt like it was finally time for the two of them to make progress. My arguments had finally had some effect. This will finally be the first step in bridging our families."

Something about that struck me. I didn't know then why it seemed so odd. I stood quietly for a moment and reached into Victor's mind. He had that memory very close to the surface since he was recalling it in the conversation so I did not have to dig. I could simply float there and watch it. Watching a memory play out was a lot like a movie. The events flowed with the time and editing was done by the person who was remembering it. There was always editing and it could never be trusted entirely, but it was a better window than having him tell me and create another layer of editing. The whole process really took no time at all, but it always felt like being there in the event itself.

Victor and Sica were at a very chic restaurant in Miami on vacation. The lighting was low and moody but I could see that this was a private room. Outside of the room the lights were bright and festive. They were already in the middle of discussing plans for the wedding when this particular memory sets in. Memories are framed in a bizarre way. People rarely remember the whole event as one memory. Instead, they tend to break it up into episodes for easier consumption. I was seeing this through Victor's eyes.

"Honey," she spoke forcefully. "As to the guests attending, do you suppose that your mother will be there?"

I could feel the apprehension of the moment. He truly was gearing up for a fight.

"Now that you mention it, I would really like her to be. I think she would like that as well."

"Good," Sica smiled broadly. "I do really want her to show up."

The emotional elation and relief were amazing. In this Victor was being completely honest. There were markers there in his mind reliving memories. From his emotional state I figured those to be memories of fights they had had about Clara.

"Really? Frankly, I had expected a fight on this one."

"No, no. We must bridge the gap sometime. You have been asking for this for so long. I don't trust her, but you love her. I'm open to trying, but please assure me that she won't do or say anything to ruin it."

"Great! Of course. My mom may have her own ideas about wizards, but she would never ruin my wedding. She wouldn't want to make a scene in front of so many people. That would be social suicide." His emotional state was extremely high. Had she wanted anything from him he was completely willing to give it to her then.

"Please assure me that she will show up and that she won't do anything stupid. I am putting my trust in you."

"I'll ask her and I'm positive that she'll want to, but you still seem very apprehensive about this."

"No, I really want her to be there, I'm just so anxious about what she might do. It just won't be the same if she doesn't attend."

"Well, I'll see to it that she knows she *is* invited."

Sica's face hardened for a moment. It must have been harsh. His memory was distinct about how her face looked.

"No, I must be sure. Please make sure that she attends," she lightened up. "It simply won't be the same for you if she doesn't show. I'm afraid you'll resent me forever.

"Never. I'm just so happy this is so important to you. I promise you that I will ensure her attendance. I love you so much."

Sica seemed to calm with his assurance. They continued to discuss things, but this particular memory faded out there.

As I came out of the memory Clara was still speaking with Victor.

"-I am here. Tell her that she always gets whatever she wants."

"Mother, it's a good thing. This could be the start of a real relationship between you two."

"You tell her, and I want you to quote me on this, tell her 'you'll get your day. Just as you planned.'"

"I don't understand. I don't understand what your problem is."

With a dismissive wave and a sigh, he walked away. I looked at Clara for a moment. I let my mind rest easily on hers to get a feeling for her surface thoughts, but she was hiding a lot and working very hard to do so.

"You just do your job and be sure you stay out of my head."

"It would all be easier if you'd just tell me what's going on. What is it that you're so sure is planned for today? What do you know that you aren't telling anyone?"

"Oh, the plan is over. The deed is done. You just be sure to stick by me and do your job."

She walked off and left me standing there. I was beginning to see more going on here, but I could only see around the edges. I couldn't help but feel that key information was being kept from me by the exact people who most wanted my help. At that point my best hope lay with the information that Alan said he had. I decided that it was time to mix a bit with the other guests and ask some questions. Maybe it was time to search a few minds. Maybe I needed to take what no one wanted me to have.

CHAPTER SIXTEEN

I did a quick bit of mental work with Clara before I let her walk too far away. I didn't tamper with her in any meaningful way. I simply created a mental thread that ran from her mind to mine. It connected to the emotional centers of her mind and acted as a spider's trip line. If she had felt any particularly strong emotions I would be alerted. That way I could keep track of any danger she might encounter while I would be free to search and find out more on my own.

I meandered off and allowed my mind to flow with the currents of thought in the crowd. I was searching for specific thoughts about Clara, as well as malicious intent that might be leveled in her direction. It is easy to imagine that weddings would generate a lot of general ire and ill will. Most of it was leveled at the bride or the groom with a healthy chunk aimed at the families of each. Jealousy and anger could create quite a storm of emotion, but there were also eddies of regret, remorse, and loss. This atmospheric disturbance of the emotional climate made my search quite difficult.

Many of the girls in attendance were split between jealous anger at the bride and mild depression toward their own current status in society. Too many of the men were on the hunt thinking of who they could get and who they had already had. What it was like to be twenty-one. That was only eight years ago for me, but it seemed such an alien state of mind. So many facades were here. One boy was trying to fill a card in his mind with the girls he had slept with. It was so obvious to me that he was trying to compensate for his lack of any real relationships. He broadcast his longing for love from his parents like a college radio station. I tried to move my mind forward as I kept seeing lives such as his.

As I walked I lightened my touch on the surrounding minds. I realized that I had been delving a bit too deep. I forced myself to think back to what Clara had said about the deed being done. What had she meant? What was done? I could tell that there had been a touchstone event for her recently, but I could not see it without pushing and she wasn't talking. Maybe she was just being melodramatic. Some people were always in a state of emergency. If that were true than she was going completely method. Her mind was convicted when she was on that subject. I didn't think she was that good of an actor. So, that brought me back to the major question: what deed? That was the core of my thoughts when a mind reached out and found me.

"Hello there."

The thought was clear and directed. This was someone who was both powerful and practiced with mental magic. I walked slowly through the crowd scanning for location as we had our mental conversation.

"Hi. I would shake your hand but that is a weird image for two brains."

"Yes."

"Well, you called this meeting of our minds, what can I do for you?"

"Such confidence. You really can't fathom someone being a challenge to you on this level. I can feel that."

"Well, it's really just a show to get you to talk. Seriously, what do you want? Are you just showing off a new power you learned? Did you level up recently?"

"You've been looking for me. I see the connection you made to that bitch. I can tell, even now, that you are trying to find me to protect her."

"Oh, I see what is happening now. You want to give me the villain speech. Okay, let's see what you've got."

I continued to search in real space for the source. The voice was right about that. I could tell that, like before, the broadcaster was using an intermediary to transmit. It was working very well to mask the identity of the speaker. My best hope would be to find the transmitter and then work back from there.

"You're so sure that you have the upper hand. You don't even see how out-classed you are. I'd pity you if you were worthy of my pity."

"Well, if you're so vastly more powerful than I am, why not tell me your identity and your evil plan? Then you can claim all the satisfaction and you have nothing to fear from weak little me."

"You know that is a good idea?"

"Really?"

"No. What kind of fool do you think I am?"

"Can't blame me for trying. Had it worked my life would have been much easier."

"True, but you're going to have to try much harder than that to outsmart me."

"Damn! So, what is the point here? You keep yammering on but you haven't said anything. Are you a teenage girl? Should I picture little hearts dotting all of your I's?"

"Bastard! I had wanted-"

"No, wait! Don't tell me you wanted to convince me to work with you?"

There was a moment of silence.

"You did!" I projected with a laugh. *"You were going to give me the speech about joining forces. How cliched!"*

"Don't you get it?" I had come to think of the source as a young girl now. She was obviously angry. *"I have already won this. You cannot change the outcome. Your only hope is to join with me."*

"Sorry, Honey, but I just can't see myself sending thoughts in Hello Kitty print. You'll have to go this one alone."

"Fine!" there was a cold edge to the emotions now. No more fun. *"Oh, and say goodbye to your link."*

The thread I had tethered to Clara went slack so to speak. Somehow, she had cut it.

"How did you do that?"

"Arrogant fool. Do you think you know a trick that I don't?"

"I can pee standing up."

A loud noise came through. Or maybe it was a bright light. It is hard to describe things in the mindscape to those who have never experienced it. Either way it hurt a bit and she was gone. I took a moment to search for the broadcast source to no avail. Her mind broadcasting worked very well. I would need to find a way to track that back to its source.

She had obviously spent a lot of time working with mind magic. In fact, she was probably forced to innovate many new processes as it was a field that so few wizards bothered to follow. I had managed to glean a few clues as to her identity, but not nearly as many as I had hoped. She was correct about having a high level of skill and power. This would have been a great time for Alan to have found me with wonderful information to crack this wide open. I look to my left and then to my right. No Alan.

Shit! I'd have to find him on my own.

I really didn't like detective work. It was incredibly tedious and often required long hours for very little progress. I had the patience for the waiting. That wasn't the problem. I simply had trouble waiting when there seemed to be no forward momentum. The problem with all of this was that I have never been good with the deductive side of the work, so I could rarely tell if forward momentum was being made. Alan was vastly better at that side of the business. He was a professional.

I still had so much information to find out. Who was behind this? What was her plan? How did all of this involve Clara? When would it happen? How many licks did it take to get to the center of a Tootsie Pop? Life was bombarding me with the fact that I knew almost nothing including how long I might have to figure this all out. On that note I was running with the hypothesis that there was little time left.

CHAPTER SEVENTEEN

I spent the next half hour mingling through the party and quietly trying to find Alan. It was high time that we compared notes and he told me what he knew, whether he liked it or not. As I moved through the party I also searched minds for someone who resembled the girl I had spoken to earlier. I figured it was a bit of a long shot as she was probably using a surrogate again. Maybe, having had two encounters with her now, I could pick her mind out with the qualities both had in common. Unfortunately, none I found fit the bill.

Of course, the whole time I was also searching those minds for Alan. In that case I was fortunate enough to find him multiple times, however at those moments there were so many guests around that I could not chance an actual meeting. I wanted to avoid mental speak if possible. Most people did not handle pure mental speak very well. Most initially felt anger at having someone invade their mind with a small number physically fleeing the vicinity. I've even seen one man scream like a Looney Tunes character "get out of my head" while running and pounding one ear to knock the voice out. He lasted only twenty yards until he hit a tree and knocked himself out. Even the best people have a bad tendency to speak out loud or to, at least, move their mouths when they spoke mentally. I did once use that reaction to trip a man up who was lying to the police, but that would be a story for another time.

As time progressed to forty-five minutes of searching and waiting, with one very weird discussion about magical sex spells with a lonely house wife, I had reached my limit. I decided that one concise message with all the information I needed to send that required no response might go over better than a conversation. I moved around a little more, I only needed to touch his mind enough to transmit.

"Alan. This is Trevor. Meet me by the main food table in ten minutes. Do not reply to this message."

I waited a few beats but received no response to the message so I walked over to the food table and began to inspect the fare that had been laid out. I picked at the food a bit with little actual interest in eating anything. I was closely inspecting a shrimp puff when Alan slid up to me. He was, as always, silent like ninja.

"You do know how weird that is, right?"

"Yeah, but coming from you that has no meaning. Look, we need to share info. I need to know what you know."

"Trevor, we don't have that kind of time. Simply bringing you up to code of food taste alone would take weeks."

"Can it, jack-ass. Seriously, I need information that you have."

"Fine." Alan quickly glanced around. "Let's move toward the house so we can get a little privacy. It will look like I am showing you toward the restroom."

We walked away while he recited some basic information and directions for anyone who might be listening. We got around a corner and found enough space to have our conversation.

"So, what have you got?" Alan got straight to the point. I filled him in on the voice and the conversation that we had earlier. I gave him my basic conclusions with only the minimum jokes required to be sure he knew just how witty I was. He listened patiently taking in all the information. He didn't laugh once. Alan never rushed things. It seemed that every part of a story had meaning to him.

"I think this girl is the one behind it all. She might be taking orders but if she is a pawn it is unwittingly. I also think she plans to make her move today at this ceremony."

That was my big explosive end to show him just how much I had figured out.

"Well, that is something. I agree with you about the ceremony, but I think she is working with someone. One attempt has already been made magically. I think today's will be physical."

I was floored.

"Why do you say that?"

"Well, if magic failed once why not try another method? One that had worked for centuries? Magic is not the only answer."

"How do you know that one attempt has been made already?"

"I've done the job you asked by spying and detecting. At this juncture I would prefer to leave it at that."

"Fine, have your secret. Why didn't Clara tell me an attempt had already been made? That would have strengthened her case greatly."

"That, sir, is a really good question. She has a lot of information that she is not telling you. So far, you have been terrible at getting that information from her."

"Yeah, I think it's time to start asking her some hard questions."

CHAPTER EIGHTEEN

So, I knew that an attempt had been made on Clara's life. That also led me to think that she not only knew about it, but where it came from. Since I didn't know where Alan had gotten his information I could not say for sure who knew what, but I had already suspected that Clara was hiding a lot from me. It all seemed to keep coming back to that. If she wanted my help why was she lying about all of what she may know. If she did know who or even that the method was magical, I could start trying to track that back to a source. At that point I had to assume that she was keeping information from me for some purpose.

I stormed my way toward Clara. Wedding guests seemed to part for me like the Red Sea as I walked through. When I am in a foul mood people in general moved away from me. I'm not sure what I was projecting, but it worked very well. I would have hated to move them physically.

I found Clara with ease. Despite what the voice thought, I knew a few tricks that she didn't. At least I assumed that to be the case. It was always possible that she knew them too and purposely left my backup alone so that she could bolster overconfidence in me. That, however, was getting into the realm of paranoia and didn't help the whole case move forward at all. I also found that idea hard to believe. So, I moved forward with the idea that she knew nothing of the small imprint of Clara's mind I kept in mine running like a short video. It really only gave me a glimpse of what she was immediately looking at, so it was not nearly as useful as the tether, but a great low power backup.

Clara stood talking to a woman that I did not recognize. As I strode up with purpose the other woman physically jumped and found a quick excuse to leave. Clara turned to look directly at me. Even she appeared fearful as I cut my swath through the crowd. Seeing the look on her face, I realized how angry I was and worked to rein in my thoughts. Her mental and physical state eased as I got myself under control. I stood quietly for a moment before her for both effect and a chance to cement my control.

"Clara, we need to talk."

"I gather it must be important by the way you approached. This event seems to be agitating you."

"Yes. There's a lot that you haven't only failed to tell me, but have purposely held back. I can't protect you in any way when I don't know all the pertinent information. Information, for example, like previous attacks."

"What? There hasn't been any previous attempt on my life. There's only the one that I've hired you to prevent."

"Are you standing there telling me that there's not been any previous attempt to kill you?"

"Of course not. I'm rich and powerful and wizard filth exists. There were two previous attempts. The most recent was over three years ago. That man was caught and is going to spend many more years in prison. I'm sorry if I failed to give you my entire history. Should I start back at losing my virginity to make it interesting?"

Clara's emotions were flaring now.

"No, that won't be necessary. Just to be sure there has been no attempt on your life recently through a magical method?"

"That's what I am beginning to regret paying you to find out."

As I watched her mind many different things were playing across it. I was sure she was still lying about something. Most people were at any given moment. She was, however, very convicted about this very subject. She very strongly believed what she was saying to me now. Even as a telepath there was really no good lie detector. People still have a belief in many things and have the power to convince themselves of almost anything. Lying was nothing more than saying something that you knew to be wrong. The problem has always been that people could tell the truth, but still be very wrong. I could have ripped her mind apart for more information. Many things lay deep in the mind; but pulling them out rarely went well for anyone involved. Memories worked oddly in the human mind. They changed over time and people tended to believe their memories.

"I still don't think you're telling me the whole story. What else do you know?"

"Well-"

"If everyone could gather the ceremony will begin shortly," a voice boomed over the whole event. I checked the time and it was ten till.

"Well, let's get to all of that later. Today, my boy is getting married."

Damn!

CHAPTER NINETEEN

As the guests took their seats for the ceremony, I had to narrow and then close my mind off almost entirely. Had I tried to keep it open to the mass of humanity that was streaming into the seating area, their lives, past and present, would have flooded my mind like water from an open fire hose. I never would have been able to sort out any specific ounce of water. I still tried to focus a mental beam as I looked around, but there was just too much noise from the mental conversation.

People's minds were picking up information all the time. Any time there was a meeting of two people in close space there would be some information passed through mental currents. Those people simply had no clue how the information was being moved. With so many minds gathered in one place the connection became a giant echo chamber, each mind picking up a bit, adding to it, and sending it along to the next. I have never had to question how mobs formed or how mob mentality worked. I have witnessed it all too often first-hand.

Even here with a wedding, there was a specific structure that began to bend the minds present into a recognizable pattern. Simple rules existed: be quiet, sit still, turn now, stand, sit, gasp, etc. Remember how you were taught these things by your parents? With these commands in place, people never fully realize how they collaborated in unison to make certain events work the way any culture had decided they should. Even thoughts as to who looked good in her dress and which groomsman was sleeping with which bridesmaid tend to flow through the crowd. The current was slow and heavy so it tended to leave ideas on the attendees like heavy silt on a river bed.

Taking my own seat, I was quite unhappy with my placement in the crowd. The groom's mother sits up front, but it was intrinsically difficult to spot danger coming from behind the viewer's position. I took the set-up time to look around and get the lay of the land. The ushers were working hard to seat all the guests as they funneled in. There was a large archway denoting the beginning of the bride's walk and each guest was entering through it and grabbed by an usher at the other side. There was a small army of them pulling guests like ants. I decided that the arch was just the spot I needed since it was located at the rear and the highest place with a good view.

I sat quietly for a moment and went to work. This was the kind of thing that Clara was paying me to do. I slowly split a small fragment of my mental functions off and set it to process sense input from another physical source. I then had to move a portion of my senses to the top of the archway facing the wedding party. I couldn't fully explain how this process worked unless someone had experienced it as well. It felt like an advanced form of closing your eyes and trying to hear something more accurately. As I focused I felt my mind slowly open something similar to another screen sourced from a different camera. I then slowly tuned in to the frequency of that source. It was possible to attach many senses but sight and sound would be enough. I did a bit of mental fine tuning which allowed me to record to my memory.

All that hard work, and it was hard work, allowed me to have eyes in the back of the room, so to speak. Now, not only could I see everything from another angle, but I could also watch my own back. Alan was around, and I trusted him entirely, but he was not always able to act and may not understand a magical threat if he saw it.

I turned back forward and took some time to see how good the view was and what blind spots I might have. Not a bad job really. I could see the entire platform up front and the majority of the guests behind me. I located myself just to be sure. I could zoom to an extent. Like real eyes it was possible and this even worked a bit better. Then I had to deal with the sound. That could be more difficult. There would be two different, but very similar, sources which could confuse even my formidable mind. I had found it easier in the past to allow myself to switch sound sources instead of blending them. I had made the mistake once before of using an owl for this trick. The view was amazing and no one ever suspects the wise old owl. It had been perfect until he started hunting. I was taken for quite a ride that day. Caught the mouse though; good for him.

As everyone sat the wedding proceeded. The band off to the side played a series of old love songs that I was sure were carefully compiled by someone older than the bride but working for her. After the ushers finished carefully seating each guest according to a hierarchy decided by the bride's and groom's careful judgment of each individual's merit, the groom and his party filed to the front. With the groom came four very handsome young men clad in tuxedos, each worth more than my car. The groom stood, steely, trying to hide his nervousness. He gave a very capable performance, but it did not take a psychic to see how nervous he was.

With each groomsman came an attached bridesmaid. While the groomsmen were handsome, the bridesmaids were gorgeous. Each came clad in a dress made by designers whose names are heard on red carpets during awards shows. The colors were shining emerald green and silver. I came to think that each dress may have incorporated actual gems and precious metals. The crowd was appropriately awed by this spectacle.

With the wedding party gathered and the crowd hushed in awe the music shifted deftly into a new tune. The standard wedding march did not play as all had expected. A collective shock shot through the mental river as a different song began to play. Haunting and beautiful the new tune began to wash over the crowd. It felt like an old song. No, older. The song itself seemed to have had the cobwebs blown off during the first few notes before it could truly be played correctly. Despite its powerful sense of age, it felt familiar. I sat for a time as it played trying to place where and when it came from. There was an ethereal quality to the music that made it play directly through the soul of the guests.

After a time known only to its composer, a choir of quiet voices seemed to rise from the depths to join the instruments. Slowly and carefully the choir grew louder and more forceful. As the almost inhuman voices rose I was set on edge. Looking through the crowd I could feel the effect replicated in the guests as the choir neared fortissimo. The effect was not overt enough to alert the individual person. It simply created an anxiety about what was approaching with the voices. Anticipation drew nerves tight awaiting the heralded event they were coming to fear.

Though this all seemed to draw on for hours, it was truly no more than two minutes. Right as the true climax drew near, the music shifted to something of awe as you would expect for a lord of a faerie land. At this shift in tone the bride actually appeared from smoke. As the cloud cleared the audience broke wedding etiquette and, fueled by pure adrenaline, roared with applause. Their fear had broken and Sica was the hero who had saved them from the dread faerie lord.

I watched from my vantage point above the bride on the archway as I allowed the mental river to flow past me. I caught the ebbs but never allowed the full flow to hit me. I could feel most strongly the relief and fading fear that had cause the explosive response. Sica did not seem upset by the break in protocol. In fact, she seemed to revel in her new position of power over their emotional state. This was her element. A coy smile grew on her face as she took in the state of her wedding and her guests. Her dress excluded her from the natural world with its magnificence as she stood and soaked in the energy in the clearing.

With my view-point set as my own eyes, I took her appearance in. Even I marveled at the craftsmanship on display before me. I cannot say for sure what materials comprised the dress. It seemed to have real ivory, silver, and emeralds worked into a fabric too finely woven to be of human hands. The crowd had also taken full notice of this fact as they were now entirely quiet as if their volume alone might tear the delicate fabric. Even Clara could not help her gasp as she was taken aback by the resplendent view in front of her.

Finally, the music, having never actually stopped, seemed to fade back onto the material plane of our existence only moments before Jessica began her walk down the aisle. Of course, Alexander accompanied her. Alexander wore an impeccable tuxedo and carried himself with the same quiet grace and elegance, but he was entirely overtaken by the storm that was his daughter. No girl who has ever dreamed of her wedding day from queens to paupers, storybook princesses to Hollywood celebrities could have wished up a better moment with an army of fairy godmothers at their beck and call. I knew at that very moment that Maleficent herself, with all the powers of Hell, would have stood aside for this procession.

As the two of them walked the slow stride toward the groom, the audience began to relax. This was what they had come to expect of events like this. People do not like to be removed forcibly from their comfort zones. As many times as people beg for surprises and originality, they crave it only within the general stage of their comfortable lives. A new act is good, but not a different play entirely.

Jessica finally reached the alter and everyone took their assigned places. Victor fought with all his might to keep his expression to a mere boyish grin as he saw his truly gorgeous bride for the first time in her wedding attire. At that moment he appeared to be completely bulletproof. Clara stood next to me amid a torrent of mixed emotions. Her son was so happy that she beamed with pride, but that was cut with fear for the threat she perceived. She wanted nothing more than to protect him from the happiest day of his life. The conflict raged within her as a tsunami rages against a shoreline. Clara's will stood strong against the primal forces. Her face only showed a sad longing and disappointment.

The arcane priest began the ceremony as any good performer. He played his role brilliantly managing to chew only the scenery in his efforts to conduct the proceedings. I was impressed at his restraint. The crowd settled in with the excitement over. Their thoughts and feels returned to the gentle ebb and flow of the proper river for an event in this vein. After a long and flowery reading, it all came to the climax of any wedding: the reading of the vows. In this case the couple chose to read their own vows as was the only fitting option after everything that had preceded. The groom started. Leave it to Sica to demand the parting words for impact.

He spoke eloquently of love and peace, riches and destitution, health and all the right things a groom should. I had trouble focusing on his exact words. Watch any sappy romance and you will hear most of them in a similar order. There was an obligatory pause before Sica answered.

"I do."

Something told me, after this show, Sica would not be nearly so trite in her word choice. I was quite curious what she would choose to ask her groom to swear.

After a proper dramatic pause, still holding his hands, she spoke. Her voice was calm, but forceful. She seemed to press her words into the very fabric of reality so as to leave an imprint. She knew how to perform.

"Victor James Edwards do you swear to
Stand with me against those who oppose us
Forsake all others before me
Your heart to my heart
Your blood to my blood
Give me of your strength when I need
Together stand forever and a day
Woe to those who stand to make this union fall
May fate cut the thread of she who stands to unravel

ours?"

A moment passed before Victor recovered from her pronouncement.

"I do."

A spark struck in Clara's mind. That moment had come and nothing had stopped it. Her thoughts darkened. She was taking this very hard.

The priest stepped forward and spoke again, "with these vows do I pronounce you man and wife. You may kiss the bride."

Victor lifted Sica's veil and kissed her passionately. The crowd erupted once again and so did Clara. She stood and took two steps into the middle aisle. She then dropped to her knees and thrust her head forward, eyes bulging and mouth agape, as a crimson blood fount erupted from her mouth. The force pushed her to her hands and knees on the wooden path as more blood vomited from her mouth, nose, and even her eyes. Trickles flowed from her ears as she convulsed. Stunned for only a moment Victor rushed forward to catch her as her muscle gave entirely. He turned her to face him. For a moment they locked eyes tightly before she expelled the last of her life's blood onto the front of her only son on this, the happiest day of his life.

Unflinchingly he held her tight as the light passed out of her eyes. The crowd was aghast. Some were running and many were screaming. None there that day seemed to hear his feeble pleas for his mother.

"Wake up, Mommy, wake up. Little Vic needs you. Please wake up. Please... don't go."

CHAPTER TWENTY

I have never had any special knowledge of the human soul, its existence, or what may happen after people die. There were almost as many ideas about death as there were people on Earth. Personally, I have never spared much thought on the subject at all. Living life has always seemed complicated enough without stirring up thoughts of what happened after the end. That having been said, there was a lot that happened in a person's mind when they died. I knew this because when I had a strong mental connection with someone I saw and felt what they saw and felt, even when they died.

There really wasn't any kind of life flashing moment during death in general, but I have seen a mind take refuge in a pleasant memory when death came. It seemed that there was a part of the human mind that needed to be coddled, protected from the harsh realities that filled the real world. The conscious part of the mind that people lived in needed to be sheltered like a child. That was the part that would get offended, felt rage, pain, joy, and had pride to hurt. The other part, the much larger part, dealt with the mechanical and basic functions of life itself. This part acted like a parent in death and wrapped the conscious mind in a warm blanket of memories and hope to quiet it while the stronger part tried like a rabid beast to hang onto life for a few moments more.

The weaker part was really just the chief executive of the mind. It was a tiny part, but was the one in charge of all the decisions, except only as those were framed by the rest. That wasn't the only part of the human mind I would connect with, but it was the one I would usually listen to. While that part remains protected, I did see that view almost like a movie being played on a screen. The rest of my connection was with the stronger part and that was a terrifying thing to witness. The rest of the mind fought like a demon bitten by a radioactive spider to hold on to life for even one more day.

That all happened, of course, only in the event of sudden demise. There were other kinds of death that both portions of the mind handled very differently, but those were not pertinent here. So, when Clara died I was taken for the entire ride through her fight. Her mind and will fought the situation as strongly as I have watched any mind fight. She grasped for every trick possible to counter what was happening to her, but her mind never fully understood what was happening so it could not fight properly. This reaction of her mind was my biggest clue that what had killed Clara was done by a magical method.

There were signals going to many parts of her body the whole time, but the loudest klaxon was going off in her stomach and blood. Her mind reacted to that klaxon by trying to expel what was causing the alarm. That was why she vomited out blood. Her body detected a toxin in her blood and the fastest way to remove it was to remove her blood. So, to save herself her body evicted all the blood in her body as rapidly as possible to remove the unknown toxin. The kicker was that it worked. The deadly agent was completely removed. Of course, the next problem her body had was finding a way to live without any blood. It never had enough time to figure that one out as she had died first.

So, that showed me in blaring neon light that she had ingested a magical poison. I wanted to get right on this new information and try to find the person who murdered Clara Edwards, but I had an immediate problem. My mind, having been unprepared and attached at the moment of her death, also thought it was dying and I was in severe pain. I had to get my mind under control before I could do anything productive at all. My mind had to be convinced that I was not dying. So, instead of doing some heroic awesomeness and catching a murderer, I lay on the ground almost comatose.

This turned out to be a great time for my recording rig in the back of the group. It stayed where I had put it and continued to do what I had set it there to do. I did not get the live feed as I was taking a forced nap, but the audio and video continued to be recorded in my mind for later interpretation. Sometimes I actually managed to do things very correctly.

So, I continued to lay there moving slightly in pain but I was later able to fill in the gaps with what was recorded in my head. Jessica had rushed down to help Victor as he cradled his mother's body. Victor was weeping uncontrollably. Alexander, having presence of mind, had his security form a protective barrier around them as more of his people moved the guests away from the scene in an orderly way. One of his people must have called emergency services as it was not long before both police and EMT's were on the scene. The police corralled guests and made sure that the scene was as controlled as possible while the medical crew attended to Clara. It took a moment for Victor to realize what was happening and relinquish her to the professionals.

Shortly after arriving on the scene the medical crew pronounced her dead. Well, they loaded her into the ambulance, but my recording overheard them saying there was no hope. It was a pretty simple investigation when they found no blood in her body. Two of the medical crew moved toward me, but Alexander waved them off saying I would be fine. The police spoke shortly with Alexander and debated questioning all the guests. Alexander informed them that now would be a bad time, but that he had a thorough list and would provide it for later questioning. The police really seemed to be looking to him mostly for assurance that waiting would work out. His money and influence won out and they left after giving him their contact information.

Having loaded Clara into an ambulance the medical crew left with Sica and Victor following behind them. Sica convinced Victor to allow her to change quickly out of her wedding dress. He was already so blank that she mostly led him like a puppy. He was moving through the world now on autopilot leaving any decisions to his new wife. She seemed quite at home in this position as she cared for him and got them going rather quickly and efficiently. Victor seemed, for now, to be in good hands. I saw on the recording the last of the people move away from the area. My own senses returned just as Alexander was walking toward me again. He stood over me and just waited. He was neither impatient nor annoyed. He simply waited.

His standing over me gave me a concrete thing to anchor my senses on and helped me completely regain consciousness. Finally, I sat up and turned toward Alexander. I managed a weak smile and said, "the rumors of my death are greatly exaggerated."

"You were only mostly dead so I waited," Alexander spoke dryly as I got up and into a chair.

I pulled the extra part of my mind back as I sat there seeing no reason to maintain the effort. I had a few more moments as the information came into my mind and combined into a narrative. Alexander continued to wait patiently.

"So," I spoke up finally. "It seems like quite a lot has occurred."

"Yes. I am not fond of such events transpiring at my personal residence. I am especially upset when those things occur at my daughter's wedding."

"I can understand that. I can see that I have my work cut out for me."

"So, you intend to continue with this as an investigation now?"

"Yes, before I was trying to protect her. In that I failed miserably. Now I'll work this as an investigation into my failure so to speak."

Alexander smiled slightly as he said, "I did not think you the type who would stop when he was beaten once. Thank you for proving me a good judge of character. Should you need anything do not hesitate to come see me. I want this taken care of quickly and completely. I will not have this incident tarnish me, my house, my daughter, or my new son."

"I understand. What should happen if my investigation should point towards one of those you have just mentioned?"

Alexander's eyes narrowed and grew hard. His voice lost its friendly tone entirely.

"Are you now making an accusation?"

I stood to my full height to hide how taken aback I was by his complete emotional shift.

"No, but investigations go where they go and you and I both know that the mostly likely suspects are those closest to the victim."

"I suggest you look first toward the people she chose to ally herself with."

"The Humans First Coalition? Of course, I intend to speak with them, but they do have one thing going for them."

"And what might that be?"

"None of them are here or were. You saw to that personally. I assume that I can trust that?"

"I will overlook this disrespect as you have lost a client and your current state, but I suggest that you leave now."

"I think that might be for the best," I spoke turning to walk away with all the dignity of a man who had been out cold moments ago.

"Good bye, Trevor."

"Thanks for the wonderful party, Alexander."

There I was again saying just the right thing to get me banned from further murder/weddings. I walked around to the front and found all the guests gone. Gerard had seen what took place and waited.

"I never leave a job unfinished. She left, but my other passenger's still here. I'll take you back to Ms. Edward's house."

"Thank you. That is very kind."

"Fuck kind. She's hurt so I guess you failed. I'm a professional. Get in the damned car."

I got inside. He was in the driver's seat before I was in the car. He took me straight back to Clara's place with no more chatter. This might be how the rest of the case would go. No one seemed happy with me. I decided that it was time to head back to my hotel and get some rest. I also needed to contact Alan soon. Hopefully he would have more information that he could now share with me. It was possible that he might still like me too.

I drove back to my hotel and picked up a pizza on the way. It was always advisable to eat before or while thinking. The body likes to feel helpful in situations like this. Eating allowed it to be busy digesting food while my mind attempted to digest murder most foul.

CHAPTER TWENTY-ONE

In the morning I awoke heavily and slowly. I must have fallen asleep some time during the night while I was thinking. I had spent much of the night trying to search the situation for a good starting point that I could grab hold of. In the end all an investigation became was grabbing hold of threads and following them to the very end. I had hoped, in some small way, to prioritize those threads and get a touchdown on the first try. I simply could not pull out which threads looked more promising and I had wasted most of the night in that futile action.

This was one of the things that Alan excelled at doing. He could look over a situation and discern threads and starting points rapidly and accurately. Of course, knowing this I had spent a lot of time last night trying his number and getting increasingly angry when he did not answer. I finally came to my first great investigative conclusion: Alan was asleep because it was late. I was very proud of myself for my great strides in logical deduction. I never had trouble staying awake when I needed to, but I couldn't expect the same from everyone else. I'd finally stopped calling and complaining after I could think of no other original complaints. I came to another conclusion: I would have to do this myself without Alan. The nerve of that guy.

I checked the clock in the room and found it to be 9:37. At least I hadn't slept all day long after staying up most of the night. I decided that I would give Alan one more chance to prove he was an upstanding guy and help me. I would contact him in a bit, right after I woke up myself and got ready. In fact, I would surprise him by showing up at his office. That would make not answering his phone far more difficult for him. Before that I would get some food and wake up fully. I took a shower singing some new pop song I heard on the radio by an English girl that was extremely catchy. The song seemed to be completely stuck in my head ever since I had heard it. This was how cults started.

Afterward I got dressed settling on jeans and a casual shirt. No reason to go all formal when I didn't even have a plan. Formal dress was for well thought out actions only… and weddings. I still wore my duster to help conceal my Rhino. No sense taking unnecessary chances when there was someone out there obviously willing to kill. Especially when I could reside firmly in the loose ends category to be tied up.

I left my room at about ten-thirty feeling clean and ready for a productive day. As I stepped outside the front doors of the hotel, I was immediately met by two men. Both were fairly young wearing similar casual suits. They didn't look the same but they were probably playing for the same team. One stood about two inches shorter than I do. His hair was sandy blond and a bit long and unruly. It wasn't really wild just the kind of hair that seems to actively fight being combed. His face was stubbly giving his whole appearance that of being slightly unkempt. However, his eyes were what truly drew my attention. They were focused, unwaveringly, on me. Clear blue, bright, and unblinking I couldn't help but see the intelligence and energy behind them.

His partner was a few inches shorter still, but built heavier. He had the body shape of a fire plug or an orangutan. His dark hair was straight and rigid having been meticulously put together. I was hit with a strong air of military rigidity and training. Both men moved in well-practiced synchronization. They split off to either side of me so that I could not fully see both at any one time.

I quickly split my mind to view them both at the same time. I had a few tricks too. Instinctively, I faced the blue-eyed man. There was a quality of a leader that shown from him.

"Trevor Harrison?" he asked.

"Only when I'm not playing Thor on the big screen. You have to keep the two lives separate."

"Real funny," the shorter man said. "Look, for once, can we just do this the easy way?"

"Fine. Yes, I am Trevor Harrison of the Vermont Harrisons. Now what? You finally decide to carry through on your threat from the other day?"

"I'm Detective Wall and this is Detective Galante," the blue-eyed man said. I was still looking at him. "That was personal, now you have me interested in an official capacity. I told you not to fuck up. We're here to talk to you about the wedding you attended yesterday."

"Wow. You guys work quickly. I figured this visit would take place a day or two from now."

"Well, we figured that maybe we should speak to the guy hired to protect the victim first." Galante took pleasure in bring up the subject.

"Somehow I think that is a jibe at the competency of my services."

"Well," Wall smirked. "One client and one murder

victim. You have a perfect record. From a certain point of view."

"Fair enough. So, do you want to speak here? What've you got?"

Galante spoke first: "When did you meet the victim, Clara Edwards?"

"Here it is. It was Wednesday night when she first hired me."

"Did you know of her before that night?"

Wall seemed to pull back a little and watch as his partner did the questioning. He seemed to take it in and quietly watch for an opening that needed him.

"I had heard of the Humans First Coalition, but I didn't realize that she was a member until after I'd met her."

"So, you are aware of her role in that group. Does that bother you?"

"Well, yes, to be honest. I'm generally opposed to hate groups and tend to judge the people who belong to them harshly."

"Aren't you a magic user, Mr. Harrison?"

"No."

"No? You are saying that you do not use magic?"

"Correct. I do not use magic." I could guess where he was going with this line of questioning. I just had to wait for him to get to his destination.

"So, all we have been hearing about your mental power is just a lie told by who, your enemies? People trying to get you work?"

"No."

"Okay, now this is pissing me off. This all makes no goddamn sense."

"I'm a psychic, yes. I do have mental abilities, but I have no talent at all with magic. You can probably cast as many spells as I can."

"Really? Are you going to stand there and split hairs about the damn wording used and tell me that you don't use magic? Are you just embarrassed to have been hired by a woman who hates you on such a fundamental level?"

"There is a big difference between magic and psionics. I could try to explain it to you in a technical way but it would be very dull and difficult. I would assume that Clara disliked me less than a wizard, but more than any other human but she never showed it. She must have seen the difference as enough to prefer me to a wizard."

"So, Mr. Harrison," Wall spoke up. "Do you have an explanation for what happened at the wedding?"

"I do, but you won't like or believe it."

"Well, I'm all fucking ears," Galante practically hissed.

"She died from a total loss of blood from her mouth and face. The autopsy should show that and I assume it will also have no way to explain it."

"Okay, do you have a reason for this total loss of blood?"

I could tell from a casual glance at their minds that the autopsy did indeed show what I had described. I also saw that both of them thought I would make a great suspect for this whole business. I knew the real cause, but not the who or why. I decided that now was not the time to give them vague ideas and hypotheses.

"I would say it was caused by a recent viewing of a Kurt Wimmer directed film. You might want to stop him now before he can kill again."

Galante's face turned a deep red. His mind was filling with thoughts of violence and I tended to be the subject of most of them. I really did have to give him credit, though. I was expecting him to go through the roof but he kept his composure quite well. Military training rears its head.

"Okay, asshole. You're a real fuckin smart guy. You have any serious answers to give?"

"Calm down," Wall spoke up again. "He knows more than he's saying. If we keep our eyes open we might find out what. Isn't that right, Mr. Harrison? Don't bother denying it. You do what you feel you have to. We'll go about our business. We'll be seeing you again and I may not be nearly so kind next time."

Wall turned neatly and walked back toward their unmarked car. Galante stood there looking at me trying to find any reason he could to get violent. I had never turned to actually look at him during the entire exchange. Failing to come up with anything he finally stomped off to join his partner.

I've never liked the moment when the police get involved if I was not the one bringing them in. I could talk and tell them all the things that had happened to me, but I had no illusion as to their belief of any of it. Without my conversations with the voice I really had very little information. If I stayed quiet and worked on my own and failed, then the consequences fell on me. If I could convince them of what I knew, they did have more man power and resources than I did. They might have been able to crack it. However, they would have most likely taken me off the street. No matter how this went down I thought it would go better if I was involved. I decided to roll the dice and see how things would turn out.

This could get very ugly. I needed to find Alan.

CHAPTER TWENTY-TWO

I drove to Alan's office and knew right away that he wasn't there. Well, I knew that his mind was not functioning there. It was most likely that he wasn't there, but it was also possible that his body was there and his mind was not functioning. I dreaded that thought but with everything that had been going on with this situation, I couldn't assume that everything was well.

I walked into the building keeping my mind open to threats and messages. I also kept my Rhino in my hand and at my side. A mental blast was a very useful tactic, but there were problems that could occur with using it. Sometimes a gun could get the job done quickly and cleanly... so to speak. Magic or not a lot of threats would think twice about anything when staring down the unblinking barrel of a .357 magnum. I had to wonder how differently Harry Potter's trials would have gone had he carried a pistol.

I took the stairs to the third floor encountering no one along the way. By the time I reached his office I was mostly certain that there was no one else in the building. I had figured that Sunday would make it slow, but Alan loved to use his office to think. He had said before that he felt different in his office. With this case I had hoped he might be there thinking.

I stood outside of his door and scanned his office. No one was inside and thinking. Of course, bombs have no mind to scan for. Maybe I was getting paranoid. Why would someone show up in Alan's office today and plant bombs to kill me… or Alan? This case seemed to have gotten to me more than I had thought. I holstered my gun and mentally arranged the tumblers in his lock.

Despite expectations that there was a bomb, or a shielded assassin, or some unthinking monster inside that I missed, there was not. His office was empty and very clean. I wondered if he had someone come in and clean it over the weekend or at night. Everything was arranged for him to come in on Monday and get right to work. I walked over and sat in his chair and looked out his window like detectives in old movies.

"I was looking out the window wondering how I could pay my rent. That's when she walked into my life. It was always a dame."

My narration felt hollow and alien. I did not belong here or in that line of work. More importantly, this was getting me nowhere so I picked up Alan's phone and called his cell.

He answered on the first ring.

"Well, I never expected this call. But, then, you know that already. Well, future Alan, what world ending disaster must we team up to stop? Or is it a warning that you have come back to deliver? Must we fight to see who the one true Alan is?"

"Wow, and here I thought I'd seen too many movies."

"You have seen too many movies. Remember, you showed me most of the movies I've seen. Why are you at my office?"

"I couldn't reach you last night so I thought I'd pay a

visit to you today."

"I see. And you just assumed that I'd forget that this was a weekend and go in to work?"

"After yesterday, yeah, I did."

"Why? Your client died. Your job ended. Your job that was yours and never mine."

"I still need your help on this."

"Damnit, Trevor! She's dead. You think this is wonky wizard shit, but maybe it isn't. Let it go. Let's get together and get a burger before you leave town. Or we can order a pizza and watch whatever new flick you think I should see. I'm down to see you, but this case died with Clara Edwards."

"I can't leave it at that. You know that. This is wonky wizard shit and I was hired to protect her and I failed magnificently."

"Fine," Alan sighed loudly. "Can we at least get that burger?"

"Sure, when and where?"

"Twenty minutes at the Downtown Diner. I'll drag myself out of my reverie and go back to work… for free… you jackass."

"You love me."

"Fuck off."

I was waiting in a back booth when he arrived. I had weaved a small mental pastiche throughout the restaurant to obfuscate our conversation. It was not invasive. It would have the effect of making people want to turn their attention away from what we were talking about. This made it easier for us to discuss things and watch for any true eavesdroppers.

Alan came back and sat across from me in the booth. Because Alan knew me so well, and he was actively looking for me, he could see past my mental trickery. He ordered a burger and a cup of coffee while I got a turkey sandwich and an unsweet tea. For some reason I really enjoyed the taste of iced tea with no sweetener. We made small talk until our food arrived. I had to open the mental cover so that the server would realize that we existed.

"Why isn't there a term for unsweet tea?"

"There is. You just said it."

"No, that still has the word sweet in it. Half the time I order tea that way the server only hears sweet."

"Okay, have you tried saying something like plain tea?"

"Yes, actually. It was assumed that I wanted no flavor. The result has been both a question as to the level of sweetness or just giving me sweet tea because that is seen as the norm."

"Well, it sounds like you have a real problem on your hands. Maybe you could create a new term."

"Sure, but then I would have to spend all of my time explaining it and it would never get enough penetration to stop that. Maybe if I had a TV show I could try some shit like that."

"Well, I would say that you have two cases that are none of my business to worry about."

We got quiet for a few minutes after that until our food arrived. After the food was laid down and I gave him the signal that my shield had gone back up he started in.

"Okay, why? Give me a good reason for us to continue. Better yet, give me a great reason for me to continue."

"I was supposed to protect her and I failed. Plain and simple. I can't live with that. I need to figure this out. You and I both know that you are a much better investigator than I am. I don't think I can crack this without you. Please."

"I don't need this. Look, you were never supposed to protect her. You were just there to witness this whole charade. That's all."

I resisted the impulse to probe his mind right away.

"What?!"

"You heard me. This whole business was a farce."

"She's dead, Alan; how is that a farce?"

"Do you want to know? Do you really want the answer?"

I took a moment to think about that. Alan never acted like that. Something must have had him extremely worked up. This was the guy who was always calm and logical acting like he was barely holding on. If something had him this fired up maybe I didn't want to know. Maybe I should simply finish our meal and drive away.

"I have to know," I finally spoke.

"Fine. I found her diary the day before the wedding."

"That was you? She said someone had. I thought she might be paranoid."

"Yeah, it was me. I found a passage about being poisoned weeks ago. Some magical thing that was supposed to kill her without a trace. You were meant to see this. She was setting you up to tell the story she wanted told. You would read it at the trial and validate it leading everyone down the road to her obvious killers. Of course, she never intended to die. She would barely survive and be shocked that Alexander tried to have her killed. It would achieve so much more than the previous assassination attempt.

"She would be around to help with the public outcry. The wonderful woman who was a victim of this insidious attack. Magic would be run into the gutter. Maybe she could even get laws enacted if they could move quickly and strongly enough. She would be a sympathetic victim and all the while you would be there to validate her stance."

"But she was poisoned. And she did die."

"Yes. She had expected it to hurt but she would ultimately survive. Her colleagues in the HFC thought that a martyr was far more useful that a living victim. They killed her so that it would all appear even more real. She could never turn on them. If you back their story then you win. If you decry it you are painted as a mage sympathizer. They can just lump you in with the murderers and go after you as well. The best you can manage right now is to walk away. There is nothing to prove. You didn't lose a client; you watched a show. Walk away. Your job is over."

I was stunned. His story made a lot of sense for a convoluted plot. He had uncovered tons of information in a very short time in ways he did not want me to know. However, something just didn't seem right. This did not feel like the full story. I knew about the poison. I knew what I felt when Clara died. Was there a physical toxin that worked the way this toxin had worked? I needed to find out some tough answers.

"Where did you find all of this?"

"Aside from the diary, I spoke with a few of her cohorts and a few of my contacts. The only thing I don't know for sure is the identity of the toxin, but the coroner should come up with that at some point. She allowed herself to be poisoned; this is toxic for you, Trevor. Your only play here is to leave. Just walk away."

"It still doesn't feel right. There are pieces that don't fit."

"Damnit, Trevor. Why can't you accept that there is no way for you to win this? There is no good outcome. Side with the HFC and Alexander comes after you. Side against them and they put you on their hit list."

"It just isn't right. The toxin was in her blood. It had been there for a while."

"And you know this? You can prove it in court that it was there before that day?"

"Well..."

"Exactly. You will feed the beast with your conjecture. You'll muddy the waters of a hot debate and some of that mud will splash up on you. There's no win here. You have no play where the hero walks away victorious. Be realistic. These are murderers on both sides. None of them are clean. Just leave. Let them fight and take each other down. Walk away... now."

CHAPTER TWENTY-THREE

Alan left after a bite or two more. He never said another word. Really, he didn't have to. His case was rock solid and air tight. There really did seem to be nothing for me to gain by hanging around and I stood to lose a lot. The more I thought about that, the smart action did appear to be walking away right then. I sat there in a booth with no one in the building paying any attention to me and tried to convince myself to do the smart thing for once.

I thought about packing my bags. I could load my car fairly easily seeing as I did not have much left after the fire. The rental property could be cleared up by Alan; I'm sure he'd do that for me if I left. There would be a few problems but he was good with those and he would feel better knowing I was gone. I assumed that I had no pay coming to me and that seemed the right way for it to be. I could consider returning what I had already gotten. I hadn't managed to earn anything, not really. My car was gassed up so I could drive for a few hours before I had to stop. I could be in another state well before then if that would help. Alan would make any excuses and explanations that were needed after my flight. I had no roots here. In the end my decision came easily. There was only one choice that would serve myself and everyone involved well.

I would stay and figure this whole thing out.

I got up and left enough money to cover the check and a nice tip. For some reason the server forgot to bring the bill. I strode out with purpose. I had a mission now that only I could accomplish. I needed a plan of action to go along with this great purpose. Both Alan and Clara had mentioned her diary so maybe that would be the best place to start. Alan was brilliant but he would never recognize magical hints like I would. If I could get my hands on the actual document then I could tear this whole thing wide open. That would make things better.

I walked out into the last of the morning sun and stood looking at my Buick. As I said before most people would not consider it beautiful. It had the angles of the 80s in spades. The nose is long and square like an old-time boxer, though this one showed no sign of having been broken. With the black finish clean and shining I had no trouble seeing why people tended to call it Darth Vader. The imposing look was good, but the engine was even better. It had real power and speed while still having weight. In a car chase weight was at least as important as speed. I never wanted to be sliding all over the place and it was nice to be able to take a collision if called to.

Also, it was nice having the leg room of this car. At my size I could not imagine packing myself into a Volkswagen Beetle.

I stepped into the beast and fired it up with a roar. Turns out I was wrong about having it all gassed up. I would have to fix that. I tried to check these things as often as possible as that kind of mistake can lead to disaster. Running out of fuel in a chase or when following someone could destroy a ton of work or even lead to death. A quick stop would fix that and allow me to grab a cup of coffee and maybe a snack for later.

The station down the road had quite a good business going. I found an open pump and began to empty their tanks into mine. My beast was quite thirsty. I could tell that people were watching me. The other side of being intimidating was that people watched you when they thought they safely could. I had mostly gotten used to the effect. Children were especially bad about staring at the huge man in the black coat and hat. After taking all the fuel I could, I went inside. There, I got a large coffee that would taste terrible and a pack of small donuts that would be stale. I paid for the whole lot and never once got a smile from anyone. I did not seem to be garnering any good-will here.

A light scan of the building revealed that stories of the wedding were already spreading around and I tended to be attached to those stories. This was probably not going to help my mission any at all. Not that I could do anything about it. The rumors would grow and spread. I had no way to control how I would appear in those stories. I was used to that. Fortunately, I was a stalwart and courageous individual.

As I drove off I began to think of how to go about getting the diary. Chances were good that I would be persona non-grata with the Edwards household. Victor might not have even wanted me to investigate this at all. It should not have come as a surprise if I was seen as quite the villain. I might be required to use some advanced persuasion to continue my course. No matter what this should have been a very fun visit.

Again, I felt out of place in Clara's neighborhood. I had always gotten by; I even did pretty well for myself all things considered, but these people were wealthy. My beat up and functional clothes and car didn't belong there at all. I should have probably been entering through some back entrance like the hired help. Well, joke's on them, I've never been any help to anyone. I pulled into the drive and slowly followed it to the house. I carefully parked so that even were I to be blocked in I could still exit through the yard. More of that preparation that was simply required to do a job such as mine.

My scan revealed the help going about their duties normally, but there was definite evidence of a fugue hanging over the whole household. Hopefully I could use this to my advantage if things started to go sideways. I walked up to the door and put on a careful expression to not appear out of place. I continued to scan. This was a fairly hostile zone so I had to keep my defenses up. A man opened the door with a most sour look on his face. Despite his pressed suit and shirt there was an air of disheveled about him. The whole household was missing Clara. It was also obvious that he had no desire to deal with me at that moment.

"Hello," was all he said. So friendly.

"Hi. I'm very sorry for what you are all going through. I was hoping to check a few things and ask a couple questions to clear this all up quickly and easily."

"Clear what up? Those filthy hexers did this. That much is obvious, isn't it?"

"Well, I think there might be solid evidence inside and I want this locked down. I want the right people to pay for this before they can find a way to weasel out of it."

"That is what we all want. I guess that it wouldn't hurt if you intend to actually help."

He stepped aside and let me in. I quickly moved past him and to the room in which we had talked before. I did not want him to change his mind. A little mental massaging had helped but nothing serious would have worked in this situation. His mind was very set. I hoped that she might keep the journal in this room. I had no good reason to think that aside from Alan's assurance that she had wanted it to be found. A search was so much easier when you knew what you were looking for. It took me about five minutes to find her journal. It would have taken less, but I was being careful to not wreck the room.

It was a thick blue book bound in leather. The only thing holding it shut was an elastic band so she must not have feared its being opened. Inside I found a very careful penmanship and well-organized thoughts. Some sections had headings and all her thoughts were laid out coherently. This was not a stream of conscious journal like most people kept. I flipped through the book and skimmed a few passages to get an idea of time.

"You did what?!" I heard from outside the room. Instinctively I closed the book and slid it into one of the pockets of my duster. Another great advantage of a big coat: deep pockets. I turned to face the door just as it burst open.

"You goddamn bastard," Victor stormed into the room with all the force he could muster.

"Hello, beautiful. How does the last of this morning find you?"

"Shut your fucking mouth you son of a bitch. You have a lot of nerve showing up here. What the fuck do you want now?"

I paused.

"Oh, can I open my fucking mouth now?"

"Bastard. Answer me when I am talking to you," Victor's facade seemed different. I knew he had been spending some time with Alexander recently, but I didn't think he would try to simulate his ways so soon.

"Sorry, I still have three weeks of etiquette class before I get my certification. I swear I'll pass this time."

"You dare take that flippant tone with me… in my house?" He moved toward me but not too close. This was all still a bit new to him.

"Well, you ignored my invitation to the stag party. Where else can I talk to you in this flippant tone?"

"Get out! Get the fuck out right now before I have you arrested. Never come back here again, you hear me? And don't think you're getting one fucking dime from me. I told mother you were a goddamn mistake. I knew it then."

"Fine, I guess I won't be getting a thank you note or this year's Christmas card either. You can keep the juicer. It's what kept Jack Lalanne healthy for so long."

I walked out past him as he tried to stare daggers into me. I simply smiled and moved smoothly out as he followed me all the way to my car. His mind radiated rage and nothing more. I really couldn't blame him for that. It was a good thing he kicked me out when he did. I was about to break out the "do you kiss your mother with that mouth" comment. I had gotten what I came for and with it I could, hopefully, end this whole business. Victor provided my escape plan.

I waved happily as I got into my car. A security guy in a golf cart followed me to the gate. He looked very tough so I didn't spin my wheels as I left. I would not want to be on his bad side.

CHAPTER TWENTY-FOUR

I drove to a park I had seen when driving through town earlier. I was not yet ready to be cooped up in a building, but I needed a quiet place to look through the book. I had to get what I needed before anyone realized that it was missing or who might have taken it. The park looked to be mostly empty but I scanned it just the same. It was almost perfect. I found a spot to park with an easy escape route. It was becoming clear that I was pissing off people who did not like being pissed off. There was not much time before someone would decide to take a run at me and I had to be prepared. I had no back up on this one.

With mental assurance that there was no hostile presence I exited my car and found a bench under a tree. Even a tough guy likes a bit of shade. Once again, I wove the obfuscation net around me. Though few people were around I wanted to avoid as much casual interference as possible. I pulled the book out of my pocket and felt the weight in my hand. It was about the size of a paperback aside from being very thick. I opened to the beginning and started reading. I had to assume that some part of this was a real document and the beginning seemed the most logical. If parts were forged, changed, or added for this incident I needed a baseline to be able to compare. It was much harder with writing as that changed with time anyway, but I no longer had her mind so I had to use what I could.

As I started, it hit me right away that this might be the only journal she had ever kept. The first entry was about Victor as a baby. Early on there were fairly simple entries that were mostly factual. The starting place seemed fairly reasonable so I didn't think the whole book was a plant. There was a bit about her emotions but it really seemed to recount her time with Victor. As I read I learned very little about his father. Somehow, I didn't think that theirs had been a marriage of deep love and passion. I found the entry about Mother's Day with the dried rose. It was the day after as she had said.

The book continued throughout his childhood without anything very interesting coming forward. I was certain that she loved her son. I found where her husband died but she was far more concerned for Victor than her own feelings. She did not write a bit of her joining the HFC four five years later. Lori had either gotten her years wrong or was blaming Clara for everything. From the journal I took it that the HFC had had a presence in Marksboro for years before she joined. She never really mentioned her hate for wizards being very strong. She seemed to distrust them, but not hate them… yet.

Finally, I got to the portions when Victor went away to college. This was five years before the wedding and things became more detailed and interesting here. She gave details about his school and dorm room and then said, "I felt lonely as I drove home." At first, she visited a lot and as she did she also focused more on her feelings. Her emotions were finally taking center stage. There was no entry about a therapist, but I could almost feel the influence of one. I guessed that maybe she had a friend or started casually dating one.

During the first year she seemed to take his absence hard and sought out companionship. She began to increase her time with the HFC, treating it as almost a social club. It seemed to help for a while. She seemed lighter and happier. She gave Victor more space and did things for herself. There was little to no mention of what the Coalition did in these early entries. Maybe she didn't really buy into the whole foundation at that time. I would have to ask some people at the HFC about this. She never wrote about any inciting incident, but as the pages continued her hatred grew stronger. She began to refer to wizards as "hexers" and other choice terms. I began to wonder if this growing hatred pushed Victor into Sica's arms. Damn! I wished I had more minds to search for this information. An interrogation would make this so much better.

I kept reading, skimming at points for pertinent information. When I found an interesting passage, I would peruse the pages around it for clues. I finally reached the point when Victor told Clara about his relationship. It did not take her long to get him to tell her the girl's name. He should have known his mother would pick up on his attempts to conceal that information. Her hatred hit a new spike when she heard who he was with. I guessed that Sica and Victor had been together for months at that point and he was finally forced to let the cat out of the bag. Clara's involvement in the HFC increased rapidly from here. Her rank and standing increased rapidly as well. I noticed then that she had been steadily rising in rank before that as well. I wondered if the HFC had their eyes on her money and wanted her close.

I had been at the park for a while at this point. The

journal was quite an engrossing document when there was a mystery to solve. The intrigue of searching a dead woman's inner thoughts for clues to her death made me feel like the protagonist of an old movie, maybe a Hitchcock or Orson Wells flick. There was an interesting voyeuristic feeling sitting in a park reading a woman's diary that I had stolen. It did not have a strong effect on me but I caught a tinge. Playing in people's minds must have dampened those kinds of feelings. Funny, though, I could not remember having ever felt them.

I hit a solid wall that was a tone shift in the writing. The words here became tight and very careful. Before there was a flow that sounded very natural, but now it lost that entire conversational feeling. Now it seemed more a log to be read by someone else. There was a formality that belied being read by someone else. She was discussing Sica and Alexander. There was mention of the wedding and her feeling about the union. She was careful to call it "ill advised" and "unsustainable." The hatred was gone in word, but not in tone.

I continued to read very carefully now and reached a passage about a meeting between Victor, Clara, and Sica's family. This was the passage that Alan had told me about. She described the whole event in a very perfunctory manner. She kept from calling them wizards or mages or even magic users, though I am sure each was. It was probably a dinner party, but Clara gave it a tone much closer to the dinner seen between Michael Corleone and his father's would-be assassins. She spoke of a moment when Jessica pulled her to the side and spoke of their relationship. Jessica gave her an "odd tasting" drink. Jessica wanted to "smooth their relationship" and made sure to toast the wedding. Clara was certain that it was at that moment that she had been poisoned.

At this point the tone returned to a more natural one. She called Sica many words that needed not be repeated and turned the page blue with hate and bile. She also included multiple ideas as to why she was poisoned. Most of them involved dirty mages and many old ideas of stealing her son. As the passages continued and she remained alive, she began to write about the "magical element" that must have been in the poison. She held strong that Sica was killing her but changed the way it must have worked. I did not know for sure how much of this was actual knowledge and how much was conjecture. I would assume that the HFC had people who knew enough about magic to work a few things out, but that was not certain. This mostly created more questions for me to ask when I finally spoke with someone from the HFC.

An odd presence entered the edge of my perception. I continued to look at the book but began to actively scan the area. Someone was trying to find me. It wasn't Alan; I knew his mind too well. There was a hostile tinge to the mind but that did not eliminate the source being a police officer or simply someone who didn't like me. I had not made any friends so far on this trip to Marksboro. I closed the book, stretched, and stood up from my seat. I wanted to appear casual as I looked around trying to see the person whose mind I felt. Though I saw people walking around there was no one who synced up with the presence I was feeling.

I began to walk. I didn't move directly away from whoever it was. Instead I moved further into the park. If possible, I didn't want him to know that I had caught on to him. I slid the book back in my pocket as I walked, best to not be a stable target no matter who it was. I didn't go to my car because I needed to know who would have me followed. This could be the best way to crack open my whole investigation. Further into the park was also the less populated areas. If things were to get ugly it was best not to have people around to get involved or witness things. As I walked I glanced around only as much as I could get away with. I couldn't place a part of my mind somewhere to watch as I was on the move and any work like that would leave me vulnerable for a bit as I concentrated to split my mind. I kept his mind in my mind and tried my best to locate him.

He kept following me showing no sign of fear that he would be discovered so I knew he intended to show himself eventually. I decided to have it happen on my terms. I moved back to an area that used to be a small island in a pond. The island was round and possibly twenty feet at its widest. It was shaped almost like South America with trees on the north and east sides. The water was all gone so it was easy to get out to the ground in the middle. I figured from the island he would be forced to show himself as he approached. As I stood there and watched I knew something was very wrong. The mind was moving closer but I could still see no one.

He was on the small island with me so I had little time. There were two possibilities as I saw it. Either he was a false image of a mind meant to scare me or he was using some kind of magical cloaking spell. I was banking on the second because it was hard to believe that anyone could create an image that could fool me with this much close scrutiny. I focused on the mind and began to try and open it up. Maybe I could break his concentration.

I heard a soft grunt and he rushed forward. I must have hurt or surprised him, but before I could capitalize on it he was on me. I still couldn't see him. The magical cloak must have been quite good.

I stepped to the left of where I thought he was rushing and brought my hands up. This was going to be rough. He was near me but I could not get more than a hazy idea of his location. The spell was cloaking his mind some as well. I felt a blow to my stomach and realized that he was strong. It hurt. I slid to my left to stay moving and kept my guard up.

I felt him move in quickly and took my chance throwing a jab. I missed entirely as he connected a right and a left with my body. I took a stiff leg kick to my left leg that I did not properly block. Without a target I could not keep this up for long.

I had never fought an invisible opponent before and I was not doing well. I flipped out another jab but only barely grazed him. He had both skill and surprise. Shit.

I moved backwards to make him chase me. My only hope left was that I had reach on him. Not many people are as tall as I am. I began flicking jabs out in the hope of keeping him at bay, but he came in under and I felt another right to my body.

As I stepped back he caught my leg again. He was trying to take my speed and movement from me. He might succeed. I kept a hold of his mind but the magic made it feel slick. I was also feeling more pain.

Two more shots under my ribs and my breathing was getting tight. Thinking fast and desperately I rushed forward and flung my arms out. I was just hoping to grab any part of him. If I could grab him I could better control some of this one-sided fight.

He was ready, however. All I found was his leg and I went down on my face. He would have had me if not for his only mistake. He jumped on top of me to end the fight. Fighting invisibly must be fairly new to him. I rolled under him to my back. He had mount but I now had my hands on him. Sight isn't as important on the ground.

I reached up and grabbed him high and bucked my hips hard. He fell forward and I slid out to one side keeping hold of him. I drove my elbows into his side multiple times. He attempted to get to his feet again realizing his mistake, but I grabbed his leg and rolled.

I had an iron grip on his right leg and wrapped my legs around him. Gripping his foot under my arm I rolled hard to my left executing a heel hook. I felt his knee break under the force. He screamed out as all the tendons attached to his knee snapped.

I stood up for a moment. He could no longer walk, so I assessed the damage I had taken. I hurt but nothing was broken. He was screaming in agony over his now useless leg. I knelt down next to him and waited a moment. I wanted him to conclude that he could no longer walk.

"Hello. You never should have gotten so close," I couldn't help being a bit pedantic after winning.

"Fuck you."

"Excellent point. Now for the trite part. Who sent you?"

"Fuck off."

"Come on. No one can see you and I'm dampening the sound in this area so no one is coming to your aid. If I don't get you help you won't get it. Who sent you? Why?"

"Shit. I ain't telling you shit."

"Ugh. I can get it. I can peel your mind apart like an onion and take what I want, but while your leg can be fixed your mind will never recover from what I'll do. Just talk to me and I'll get you to the hospital so you'll be able to walk again after months of therapy."

He moaned for a while longer and swore a lot. Finally,

he spoke up.

"Fine. Victor. Victor Edwards sent me. He said that if you didn't leave town I should give you a good reason to leave. Fuck, man, I can't walk."

"I know. Just Victor? No one else was involved?"

"No," he hissed through his pain which was mounting. "Come on, man. I told you."

"True. Do you control your invisibility spell?"

"No."

"Then who does?"

"Some guy Victor knows. Probably connected to his wife."

"Okay." I searched for the mental connection to the magical spell. I found a thread going out to someone else. I thought about tracking it but it was a fine thread and a well-crafted spell. Chances were it would not lead directly to someone before they could break it. I concentrated on the thread and attacked it with my mind. Not being a magic user, I did not have the best tools for this, but a wrecking ball could still shatter a window even if it isn't the right tool for the job. The thread snapped and my assailant came into view. He was a short guy writhing on the ground with an obviously broken leg.

I got up and started to walk away.

"Hey! You said you'd help me."

"I have. There are people coming this way. They can see and hear you now. One of them is sure to call an ambulance... and probably the police."

As I walked off a couple ran to him. I saw the woman take out her cell phone to make a call. I had already shrouded myself again to avoid view as much as possible. I didn't want to be involved in all of this. I walked back to my car calmly and got inside. So, Victor wanted me to leave. That made sense but who wove that magic? I was not buying "just some guy." Victor could not have done such a precise job. His wife could have. Maybe it was time to talk to her soon.

Of course, with both Victor and Alexander angry with me a conference with Jessica might be a bridge too far. There were a few other lines of inquiry ahead of me. Maybe if I went to the Humans First Coalition the other side might calm down a bit. I had a feeling that at least some of what Alan had said was correct. Maybe all of it. He was good at finding things out, I thought he was only lacking some important information. The more I thought about talking to Sica, the more I realized that the only path to that meeting ran through the HFC. I did have a few serious questions for them as well. With my decision made I started my car and pulled away.

CHAPTER TWENTY-FIVE

Fortunately for my search the HFC had an office in Marksboro. This probably had something to do with the rich, high ranking officer who lived in town, though it had existed before in a smaller way. Well, had lived in town. The organization was very open and proud of their efforts so they made themselves easy to find and join. Unfortunately, it was Sunday so the office was closed and I could not walk in and start pissing people off. They had to wait until tomorrow for their turn.

I could have called Alan to see if he had any connections that might be able to get me in. However, with no additional information, he would have probably told me to go away again. I needed some evidence to get him interested. Were he curious then he would have assisted me if only to answer the question himself. I had to find another way to meet with the HFC. Waiting seemed like the obvious answer, but I did not want to spin my wheels. I also had a feeling that I needed to move quickly on this before things could completely shake the ground underneath me. I did have another idea but, like most I had lately, it was probably a bad one. I continued to drive shifting my direction a little.

Minutes after birthing my idea I was pulling into

Alexander DesChanes' drive. The afternoon was cool but warmer than when I had arrived in town as it was closing in on night. Workers scurried around the yard cleaning up all the decorations from yesterday. The police must have delayed the clean-up for the investigation. This probably angered Alexander even further. More evidence still that this plan of mine was not a good one. I might have done better to pass on the one-yard line. I drove in slowly all the way to the front door to allow the servants to give Alexander ample warning of my approach. I figured that, as a courtesy to Alexander, I would give him plenty of time to decide how to tell me to fuck off.

As I stepped out of my car, Alexander met me. I closed the door and turned to meet his eyes and felt a weight push me back. While his gaze did carry the weight of power and authority this was an actual force pressing upon me. Alexander was applying a magical pressure to push me backwards. Many people attempted to push me around both magically and physically, but very few could actually achieve it. While I was not paralyzed, I was going to have to expend a lot of energy to act normally under that force. Considering the circumstances, I chose to stand still and see how this all played out. No sense in looking for trouble, right?

He walked slowly and deliberately in my direction. To any outside viewer he was as calm and purposeful as he ever was. Alexander did not get out of sorts, not over some hired protection. His mind told another story entirely. His emotions roiled darkly in his head as he walked. There was no way this could be a good meeting. I had my work cut out for me.

"Trevor Harrison, why have you come here today?"

"Good afternoon, Alexander. I had wanted to ask you a few questions."

"My new son's mother died yesterday and already you come to cast aspersion and accusation over my household. Tell me why I should not crush you where you stand?"

"You can try that if you want, but you don't have the power."

To drive my point home, I stood tall and made an effortless step forward. No reason to show him how hard that had been. His mind recoiled for a moment. We had never truly tested each other this way.

"You come here to test me? Others have tried and failed to get anything from me but pain."

"Look, I said questions. I have no desire to get into a dick measuring contest with you. At least not without some shots and attractive women watching. You might hold on until you hear what I have to say."

"Victor already told me that you broke into his home and searched it. Suffer no illusions as to your ability to do the same here."

"Jesus! I was allowed in there by his help and I came here to talk to you. We can stay right here if you'd like. When did I become public enemy number one around these parts?"

"Fine," he said reducing the pressure. "What do you want?"

"I have questions about the HFC and their involvement. I thought with all the dealings you'd had you might be able to give me more background. I have no contacts within the Coalition so I can't get in. Since their office is closed today I can't just waltz in in my usual friendly manner."

"I see," his mind relaxed and the pressure was lifted. "What can I tell you about the people who want me dead?"

"I know about the propaganda and all the things they

claim to stand for and want to accomplish. I assume there's another side, less public, that's more important to this situation. I could spend forever dancing with their propaganda arm getting nowhere. I need to know about the other. Who could I talk to who is involved with the more shadowy side?"

"Well of course they do not speak publicly about their more violent side. Victor might know more about them but he may not even know what he knows. From what I can tell he had nothing to do with them aside from some social events. Besides that, he wants nothing more to do with you. That bridge is burnt."

"Who do you think were the people behind the last attempt on your life? There's a good chance they'd also be involved here."

"Ah, yes," Alexander responded. "That whole messy affair. To be honest we had come to the conclusion that Clara was one of the highest names involved with that business. I had tried to handle interactions with her civilly until I knew for sure. I do not, however, wish to speak ill of her now."

"I understand, but you say you actually had evidence?"

"Not the kind that I could take to the police or show in a court of law. I am sure you understand that."

"Certainly," an idea began to form in my mind as we spoke. "You would have turned that in to the proper authorities had you had it. I had assumed you had clues that made you so certain."

I began to lightly touch his mind. Whether or not he believed he was telling the truth could give me a lot of information in this situation. I increased my hold as I worked. I did not want this information to stay hidden from me. I had to be sure. Also, I may have still been a little upset about his magically pushing me around earlier.

I did not like to be shoved around even by a man who had every reason to do it.

"Well, yes. Some of my people had contacts who said that the plans came from the HFC. I have agents in play who could get warnings to me about attempts made against myself and the Neolithic Consortium. I have always found it better to have information than not."

"Of course, I've found the same to be true. But why Clara specifically? Just her rank?"

"Well, at first I had suspected Victor. Who better to get close than the fiancé of my daughter? I kept an eye on him for a while and even began to track his movements. Jessica found out and we had a terrible row. It was grand and theatrical as only a young wizard can make it. I'm sure you have seen already her penchant for theatrics."

"I have indeed and can only imagine what that fight must have looked like."

"Keep it that way," I had managed to loosen his mind enough that the information was flowing now. "A young wizard adds much to the hormones and stupidity that is youth normally. Afterwards she saw that the most effective course of action before her was to clear Victor's name. She was the one who dug in and found emails linking the attempt to Clara herself. That made sense for most of the same reasons that Victor made sense. Clara was only a step farther away from me. It also allowed for a step more of cover that Victor would not have. The logic was solid. I was also aware of her rank, which gave her access to the power structure needed to make the attempt."

"So, it was Jessica who was able to actually pinpoint Clara in the conspiracy. Were you planning to take any action against her in particular?"

"Ah, I never reveal actions not taken. Seeing as we were to be family and I had agents in place I was not so concerned about further danger. I decided that watching would be more useful than action in this case. The evidence was still tenuous and there was no reason to escalate."

"So, you're still investigating the whole matter?" I asked.

"Of course. Always gather information when possible. The emails were one line of proof but a corroborating source would solidify the whole thing. The safest state of being is always to know as much as possible."

"But now that she's dead you have no real reason to continue investigating her involvement in the case, do you? It can just be wrapped up quietly."

I could see from his mind that he believed what he was saying. There were dark patches where he was holding some information back, but that was to be expected. Some of the methods were probably shady and he did not want to give anyone's name up to me. He had no intentions of telling me what he would have done. He probably was lying about not retaliating, but I had no desire to keep digging. I had what I really wanted to gather from his mind. I could also see that I had pushed a bit hard and it was starting to cause him pain. To his credit it never showed on his face.

"Well, I would like to clear her if possible, if only for Victor's sake," Alexander spoke almost reflexively as I massaged his mind.

"But you don't seem to be expecting that outcome. You seem pretty convinced of her involvement."

"Sadly, yes. The facts line up very well and it is not hard to believe."

"So now you have very little reason to truly dig into the

information that Sica gave you to check it. You can allow all of that to stand as it is."

"What are you saying? It sounds like you now suspect my daughter to be involved in all of this beyond it being her wedding."

Alexander tried to shut down his mind but I was already in deep. He brought up the pressure again against me but I fought back. We began walking toward the house as I pushed. I found a choke point in his mind and clenched it tightly. For the moment his will and magic halted. The pressure was released entirely again but I did not let go.

"You know, Alexander," I continued to step forward as I spoke and he walked backwards as if we were dancing together. "You started this little contest of wills absolute in the knowledge that you could win. Maybe you should be more careful who you try to push around."

His back hit the exterior wall of his home. He had both hands clenched on his head. The pain was obvious on his face now.

"Do not test me. I'm a reasonable guy but I can become very unreasonable very quickly."

I grabbed his head with both hands and got nose to nose with him. I made sure that we were staring into each other's eyes. Alexander continued to fight and kept my gaze strongly.

"Do not think me a fool. I may be relaxed and fun but I'm neither stupid nor weak. Go to war with me if you want, but I will crush you."

I let go of his head and he dropped to his knees. Blood dripped from his nose and his eyes were red. I walked calmly to my car and did not release his mind until I was driving away. I was right, that wasn't pleasant.

CHAPTER TWENTY-SIX

I decided to drive for a bit and think about the information I had. So far, I had not really stopped for long enough to compile anything and I had a lot of facts bumping around in my head. I set out further west of town and simply drove for a while. Marksboro was a fairly small town so I was outside the limits and in the countryside as soon as I left Alexander's. I found that driving was very conducive to thinking and getting myself straight. My body needed to be doing something while I thought or I became restless and my mind could wander. Walking also worked really well but I had run into a few problems recently. I didn't want to be too easy a target for the numerous people who wanted to stop me.

As I drove I tried to connect all the dots I had. This would all be much easier for Alan but he stood as one of many allies I had managed to push away during this whole business. First, I had the journal. It contained passages that lent credence to a magical attack toward Clara from Jessica DesChanes. That worked with what I had experienced at the wedding through my link to Clara. The poison seemed to check out in that line. Then there was my discussions with Alan and Alexander. Both pointed very strongly toward a plot from the HFC. Both had evidence of a plot against Alexander and Alan added the motivation used to kill Clara.

I then laid out what I knew for sure. Clara Edwards was dead and it was caused by a poison. I knew that this poison triggered her to expel all the blood from her body. I did not know for sure when she ingested it, but I knew when it took effect and that she had been expecting something to happen. That much was apparent by her hiring me to protect her. I knew that Alexander had protected his own both at the wedding and when we spoke later. I also knew that he had proof that led him to believe that Clara was the person behind the attempt on his life.

Additionally, I knew that people had been sent to scare me off the case. There was the phone call that had come first, then the guy who followed me early, the wizard who tried to kill me, and then the guy who tried to kick my ass. The first three never told me who sent them but the last said Victor. He was different in that he was not a magic user but more of a target of a spell. I also did not have proof that the phone call came from a magic user. Add to all that the Voice at the wedding who I had come to believe was behind the first three men. She was smart, powerful, and very capable. It was hard to see her as the mind behind the invisible assailant. That last one felt too clumsy. Why was she sending henchmen at me like a dime store hood when she obviously had the power to attack me more directly?

On the other side, Alan had all the evidence he needed to blame it all on the HFC. He must have had very solid proof for him to be so convinced. He was the best investigator this side of fictional detectives I had seen. I couldn't disregard his conclusions easily without strong evidence that I didn't have. I had told him of the Voice and what I knew but that did not seem to sway him. His one failing was his strong disregard for what magic could do. He was not accounting for a magical poison.

I needed to eliminate things. I could assume that Victor as not involved in the actual magic that killed his mother. He had no real talent. He had dabbled some but that powerful and intricate of a spell would take someone far above his pay grade. Someone like the Voice. I could not try to track the poison in any reasonable way. I lacked a sample, the science, the time, and the knowledge to actually discern it. If it was as Clara wrote, and it had been given to her earlier, then the spell used to trigger it might have been an easier spot for me to focus. Dormant poisons with magical triggers were not unheard of.

I would never have been able to show proof of the toxin the HFC might have used. With all of Clara's blood on the ground contamination became the problem. Some might have still been in her cells, but the magical toxin probably made her expel most of it and since the dose makes the poison there was too little to prove it was really there at all in any concentration. That left me with little help coming from the coroner or the police. They could only chase down what they could prove.

The Voice I had met lead me to believe that there was a mastermind here and that she was a wizard of some sort. I could not buy that the HFC was behind it all. I thought of the Voice as a woman but I did not know that for sure. She had always used intermediaries to hide her presence and that through off my abilities enough to make me unsure. That assumption, like any, could prove disastrous if I allowed it to color all my decision and was wrong. However, I could not shake the certainty of that much of the Voice's identity. Add to that that the Voice wanted me to leave at first and then switched to asking me to join her. Why the change?

Was it possible that there were multiple people behind the Voice? Maybe it was all filtered through a young girl giving it the feeling I was connecting to. That would have been a lot of work. Even more work would be required to make the multiple people seem so similar in everything but motivation. Probably made more sense that she changed her mind. Did she fear my involvement? That would stand to reason if I posed a threat. She didn't seem to bother Alan at all. Maybe she was unaware of his involvement. No, that was too dangerous to assume. She seemed to know so much that I had to assume that she knew about him as well. She may not have been concerned with his involvement. He was a human detective. He could be below her view.

Maybe Alan was needed. With what he found out, he could have created a very convincing argument to the police. He was the person contacted first. Alan chose to bring me into the whole thing. Maybe I wasn't accounted for. Wait! No, Clara approached Alan. She couldn't be the Voice. She also had no talent with magic and she simply hated them too much to use one. She didn't even seem very happy about using me. I didn't think the Voice hired me for this job to try and scare me away.

None of this was making any one coherent line so I had to start thinking that there were multiple lines in play. This could all have been a convergence of threads creating what appeared to be one big conspiracy but was, in reality, a twine ball. Maybe the biggest in all of Minnesota. I had to think that the Voice was attached to the murder itself. She had immense magical power, as well as a shocking control of mental magic. That would make her decide to try and get rid of me at first. I was the only one who could play her mental game. That made sense.

Of course, with time, magic would probably be the conclusion people reached because they would not be able to explain the method of death. It was reasonable that the true toxin would never be found so circumstantial evidence would be all they could use. So, to protect herself the Voice would want to detract from the magical conclusion. Unless... Maybe she wanted magic to be blamed but she wanted it to be Alexander's magic blamed. If magic were the conclusion then he and his people would be an easy step to make. He had evidence that the victim had tried to have him killed. That was a powerful motive. In that case a magical investigator would be useful to help prove this and maybe she considered me a magical investigator.

There was another possible way the mastermind might have been able to escape detection: the HFC. If Alan had it right and the HFC was planning to kill Clara, and the Voice knew about it... It could work. The two sides would be working at cross purposes but with the same means. Alan had the proof and it was hard to believe that someone pulled the wool over his eyes. I had to believe that Alan was at least partially right. The HFC was probably involved in the whole deal. It was even possible that there were multiple parties involved. I would have to figure out the extent of their involvement tomorrow. It was getting too late and I didn't think a breaking and entering job on their office would be advisable yet.

On the other side, it did appear that the venue of the murder may have been chosen to cast dispersion on Alexander and his people. It seemed likely that someone was using this incident to pit the two sides against each other in a war. That would be incredibly destructive. I had to find out who would benefit from a war between the

Human First Coalition and the Neolithic Consortium. At that juncture I should find the Voice.

That was a very simple place to be, but not an easy one. Once I nailed down the HFC involvement for myself I would have to find out the identity of the Voice. Of course, the only way I could think to do that was to become a big enough threat that she had to come after me again. Of course, she would probably try to kill me again but, fortunately, I was about as good at surviving assassination attempts as I was at pissing people off. I figured I could manage both fairly well.

CHAPTER TWENTY-SEVEN

I decided that I had caused enough trouble for one night and decided to return to my hotel for a little relaxation. I would make a nice night of it since I had the time. I bought a cheap DVD player and some beer at Wal-Mart and before I picked up a pizza I stopped by the video rental store in town. I was a bit surprised that one existed, but very thankful because hotel cable was always shit. This seemed like a great way to spend a night before I started rattling more cages trying to get someone to come kill me.

Being self-employed now and the complete master of my fate, I decided that I could stay up late, drink, and watch a couple movies. Now if only Billy and Timmy could come have a sleep over. I laid out the pizza on one of the two queen beds and put the six pack into the mini fridge provided. It took a bit of work but I did manage to connect the DVD player to the TV and change the input. So many hotels made that as hard as possible.

I sat for a moment contemplating my options. I had chosen two Cary Grant movies that I loved to fill the night. I deliberated and ended up picking Hitchcock and Eva Marie Saint first to be followed by Ralph Nelson and Leslie Caron. I thought that suspense followed by comedy would aid my sleep better. So, I put in North by Northwest, grabbed a Red Stripe, and sat down by my pizza. Felt like home.

After a couple hours, three beers, and half a pizza, I switched to Father Goose and sat back to laugh. Cary Grant never failed to make me happy in all his roles. He could be funny, serious, debonair, or whatever else was asked of him. Hitchcock was easily my favorite director for film though North by Northwest was not my favorite of his films. That honor belonged to Rope. Both the suspense and character work in that movie were amazing. North by Northwest did have one of my favorite costars, however. Eva Marie Saint was given a lot of space to play her part and she runs away with it. Throughout the movie the audience both loved and hated her. She was hauntingly beautiful while still being that classic Hitchcock type. He was more than a bit of a pig.

Father Goose, on the other hand was one of Grant's funniest and most out of step films. He played a drunkard slob who didn't get along with anyone well. I never failed to laugh just from the basic premise alone. Leslie Caron was tough, beautiful, and hilarious. Her timing with Grant was spot on and the two meshed very well. I fell asleep trying to debate the virtues of both Eva and Leslie. When I faded out I think Eva may have had a point up on Leslie.

I had not set any kind of alarm the night before. There was no particular reason to start early. The offices of the HFC opened at ten. I had enjoyed myself the night before and managed to wake up at ten-thirty. I still saw no real reason to rush. I got myself together and dressed for the day and out the door at eleven-forty-five. My plan today was to go to the HFC first. Maybe I could use lunch as a time to meet with someone out of the main office. Everyone has to eat, right?

Their office was on Broadway a few blocks east of the main downtown area. The building was old and used to belong to one of the many fraternal orders that people joined to drink and play BINGO. They had taken over the space and managed to use most of it by also being a fraternal order where people went to drink. Life worked in mysterious ways sometimes.

I walked into the side door and entered a small waiting room with a glass window like a doctor's office. Seemed a bit odd, but the flow was what I was going with today. I figured that maybe I could try to get information the nice way today before I started trying to get killed. There was a woman sitting in the room behind the glass window. She looked annoyed as only a receptionist who was expected to do way too much and was paid way too little could. I guessed that this woman was the life's blood of this whole building. I wished I had picked up a good cup of coffee for her. This was why prep work was good when you wanted to do it right.

I waltzed up to the window, made sure I had a nice smile on my face, and waited patiently for her to finish the form she was filling out. She dropped it into a basket on her desk and glanced up toward me. I could tell she took a moment to decide how she wanted to deal with this quite large individual who was smiling at her. I sometimes worried that my size works against me in some situations.

"Can I help you," she said with a lack of interest matched only by Janine Melnitz.

"Hi, I was hoping that I could talk to someone in the office about the Coalition."

"Are you a reporter, law officer, bail bondsman, or

politician?"

"No, I am quite certain that I am none of those?"

"Are you a domestic terrorist, magic user, or woman wanting a paternity test?"

"No, no. Still none of those."

"Are you trying to film an expose on magic and its uses within society and here trying to besmirch a high-ranking officer by spreading claims of hate crimes ending by throwing a bucket of cold fish guts at three of our officers?"

"That is amazingly specific. Do you get that often?"

"Three times last month," she smiled at me as she slid the glass to the side. She set a clipboard on the small tray there with a pen attached by twine. "If you would be so kind as to sign this visitor list I will see if anyone can help you. What is it you want to inquire about?"

"I would like some background information about the group in general and I have a few questions to ask as well. Mostly it is a conversation."

"I see. That sounds highly suspect," she eyes me for a moment as she spoke. I feared for her children because she had quite a piercing gaze for a non-magic user. "I'm not sure I should let you in. You may just be here to cause trouble."

"No, I assure you, I just want to chat and learn more about the whole organization. I have heard a lot on both sides and want to understand."

"That sounds like a reporter, but I don't give a fuck. I've asked the questions. You've got a nice smile, pretty muscles, and these assholes just dumped a week's worth of paperwork on me and want it done today. Serve them right if you are a reporter."

"I… don't know what to say. Thank you?"

"That'll work. Now sit down. I'll call you when

someone is ready."

I walked over to the two available chairs and sat down. That was why it paid to treat everyone in your organization well. I almost hoped that I would have to cause some trouble, though it would probably make her life harder. Somehow, I got the feeling she could handle herself no matter who caused her problems.

I waited there for about ten minutes before she buzzed me through. She smiled at me again as I walked into the back and met with a man who was fated to be a used car salesman. He even had on a checked suit with fucking suspenders. I had to fight every urge to laugh as he strode up to shake my hand.

"Hi there, Trevor. I'm John, John Calvin. How the heck are you?"

Jesus Christ. He was a fucking cartoon character.

"I'm fine, John. How the fuck's life treating you?"

"Great! Now, you want to learn more about the Humans First Coalition, huh? Let's go back to my office and see if we can get you the education you need."

We walked through the halls, but most of the doors were closed. I would guess they were closing up in the time I as waiting. I sensed minds behind most of the doors. The place was hopping today, but to my vision it was a ghost town.

"Not many people here today, are there?"

"No, we are slow here in the office. Most of our people are out in the field right now. One of our charter members died over the weekend. There's a lot to do," he spoke as he motioned me into his office. He closed the door and walked around his desk and took a seat. "But you knew that, didn't you Mr. Harrison?"

"Yes, I did."

There was a hard turn in his demeanor. His mind

remained the same, but he had put on a great show for anyone without my power.

"So, what can we do for the man who failed to save Clara Edwards from some fucking filthy hexers? Hm? How can I make your life better, you fucking son of a bitch?"

"Okay, so pleasantries are over? Fine, I want the ass of the people who killed my client. I'm going to find them and nail them to a wall. Now, would you like to help me find them or just cause me more problems and get nailed to the same wall next to them?"

"Okay okay, calm down. I just had to see what you were planning. We know a little about you, Trevor, but you're a bit of a mystery to us. So, you actually want to get the people who did this? That's really your intention?"

"Of course, I do. I take my job seriously and these fuckers made me look like a fool."

"True, they did do that. Well, we've been investigating this as well. We've got a pretty good idea that the whole thing was done because Alexander DesChanes thinks we tried to kill him. He still tries to spread the lies that we're a hate group trying to kill wizards. Nothing could be further from the truth, and if we can get enough evidence we'll put his ass in prison where he belongs. That'll show these unnatural monsters we mean business."

"So, your big goal with wizards is to wake people up and get them to oppose magic? Or are you hoping to affect law?"

"Well, of course we want to educate people as to the actual danger of magic and those who use it. We want Americans and all people, really, to see them for what they are. As far as our other plans maybe you should talk to Chuck. He knows a lot more about our long-term plans. I'm really just a bridge to the outside world. Gotta be careful who has access to the chain of command, right? Follow me."

He got up and walked out the door. A few other doors were open now but most of them were closed still with people behind them. We walked down the hall and he stopped and knocked on one of the closed doors. I could sense one mind behind it and that mind was not happy.

"What?" the question rang out before the door was fully open. "What dooya want?"

"I wanted you to have a word with Trevor, here."

Chuck turned to me for the first time and his face turned significantly sourer. He snapped his head back toward John. I recognized his voice but could not place it right away. I was upset that he hadn't spoken from behind the door a bit more. He was probably going to be mad at me soon enough so I could get another chance from behind the door.

"What is he doing here? I don't want to talk to this fucker. I'll have your ass for this, John."

"You're breaking my heart, Chuck. Any more talk like that and I might think you don't like me." I smiled big and toothily.

"Look, you may be tough shit around your hexer friends, but I thought very highly of Clara and I'm not all that excited to talk to the asshole who got her killed. You get me? I knew hiring you was a mistake the moment I heard about it."

"Chuck, wait man, he wants to investigate the involvement of magic in her death. He was hoping for some info from us to help put these guys away."

He looked me in the eye closely. He had to look up and that did not help his demeanor at all. I lightly touched his mind to try to smooth over his conscious thoughts. Maybe I could make him think a little higher of me.

"Yeah? Maybe, but I still don't like it... or you. Come on in."

He stepped back to his desk and waited for us to step inside. John closed the door and motioned for me to have a seat. The office was similar to John's but better furnished. John's office was all faux surfaces and cheap filler. This office had real wood and glass. I could tell almost immediately that rank here was important and rewarded. John's acting like a small dog around his obvious superior was also evident. These guys were constantly comparing power. Clara must have seemed like a god to them.

I sat down and looked at Chuck. There was no reason left to deal with John. I was obviously above his clearance level now. I kept trying to remember where I had heard Chuck's voice before. As I sat there I felt the weight of my gun under my coat. I was surprised that no one had checked. I wondered if anyone else was carrying here. Considering the power struggle, it was probably a perk to be allowed to carry.

"So," Chuck folded his hands at his desk. He must have seen that in a movie once. "What do you want to know?"

"Well, I want to prove what happened to Clara. At this point I don't give a shit who did it, I just want to crucify them and clear this all up. At this point I'm just trying to understand what you guys even do so I can find motive for why she was killed?"

"Well, that seems rather straight forward. Are you working from the story that Alexander DesChanes tells about Clara trying to kill him?"

"I've heard that story, but I don't have the evidence he

claims to have proving that story. I'm not going to move forward with an assumption unless I have to. I was hoping you guys could clear that up as well. I don't even really know what Clara did here. Surely she wasn't head of assassinations."

"No, she didn't arrange murders. I can tell you that. Clara was this chapter's connection to the main office. She rose through the ranks to hold office at the central HQ. One thing she was really good at was PR. Clara could work a crowd like nobody's business. She was good with all the protocol stuff. She also helped with planning and strategy."

"Planning and strategy for what? What do you people do? You still haven't told me."

"One of her biggest projects was trying to lobby for a government group to oversee magic use. That's the project I'm now trying to continue. She felt passionate about controlling magic use. Many here would rather see it banned, but Clara believed that was impossible. She thought a regulating body would be the first reasonable step. I think she wanted a ban, but she wanted to try to achieve it in steps."

Chuck had obviously read her files and notes. I had trouble believing he even understood many of the words he was using. I had no clue why he was continuing her work, but I couldn't believe it was out of faith in her project.

"Really, all the stories and you guys are just a grassroots political group trying to petition for a new regulating body? I'm surprised because I haven't seen a university student here yet. Where are all the hippie vegans? Or the young college conservatives with their rhetoric and organization? How have I not heard about any of this yet?"

"Well, maybe you just aren't as smart as you think. What? Did you think we were some crime organization trying to have wizards killed? Watching too many movies maybe?"

"No such thing. I just find it hard to believe that you're making all of these political moves and yet you aren't making the rounds on the Sunday shows and CNN. Maybe you'd prefer Fox, but either way where's all the debate on this topic?"

"Well, most of it died Sunday. Clara was the one getting the ball rolling on all of that."

"Okay, so, outside of her completely altruistic political work, what else do you do? The entire organization existed before Clara Edwards and will go one after her. Did you all just drink beer and jerk each other off? Was there an asshole orgy today? It that where everyone is? Sounds like Clara was the only one who got anything done around here."

"You shit-head! Did you just come here ta fuck with us? That was a bad idea. Did that hexer scum send you here to find out what we were doing? I'll fuckin' kill you myself if you try that shit."

"Now it's coming out. Why are wizards so bad? What do you really want here, Chuckles? Did a wizard not suck your dick correctly?"

"You fucking prick!" Chuck stood up and started across the desk. I scooted back and stood in one motion just outside of his reach. John fell out of his chair. He was not ready for this reaction. Neither of them could possibly know that I had been slowly trying to raise Chuck's anxiety level. I wanted to see what came out when he was mad. I was getting nowhere with his stump speech.

"Calm down there, Chucky. Voodoo can only make you so powerful. It won't make you a real boy. I just wanted to get past all your bullshit."

"You fuckin' asshole. Get the fuck outta here. You just wanna stir the pot so's these magic wanks could get away with killing one of our own. This is just the kind of hatchet job I expect from your kind. I know you're one of them. It shows. I can smell it on you. Get the fuck out now."

"Well, I can tell when I'm not wanted. Thanks for all the southern hospitality. Maybe one day your fairy godmother will let you go to the ball." It hit me in the face suddenly where I had heard that terrible grammar. "You planted that phone in my place and called me, didn't you?"

"The fuck're you talkin' about?"

"You tried to scare me off first. You didn't want me looking into any of this from the moment Clara hired me. No wonder I couldn't connect all the people who had tried to scare me off."

"If I'd tried that you'd be gone. Believe you me."

"Sure. Just tell yourself I'm running scared now instead of tired of looking at your ugly face."

I turned and walked out of the office as John held Chuck back so that the cops would not have to get involved. I walked down the hall slowly back toward the exit and felt the emotions around me. There was a lot of concern that I might have found something out. They were definitely hiding something, but I could never get it out of them without a lot of time and hurting a few people. That might have to take place, but not now. Maybe tonight would require a little breaking and entering job. I opened the door to the outer offer and came face to face with the receptionist.

She slapped me hard across the face and grabbed my coat for a moment.

"You lying fuck. Get out of here."

"Yes ma'am," I said putting a hand on my face where she had slapped me. I walked out the main door into the sun and got into my car. I started it up and drove a couple blocks away and parked in a spot on the street. I reached into my pocket and took out the slip of paper she had dropped into it. Her legerdemain skills were quite strong. I wasn't entirely sure that I had actually felt that drop.

I unfolded the paper and read the very simple message she had written.

Mac's Uptowner
8 pm
Pool side

Seemed simple enough. I guess planning my little B and E job could wait to see what this was all about. I pulled out of the spot and went in search of the lunch I never got.

CHAPTER TWENTY-EIGHT

I drove in search of some lunch and a place to think. Apparently, Miss Melnitz was not entirely happy in the hateful land of Oz and wanted to talk. Good news for me. I decided on a Mexican place by the hollowed-out husk that was this town's mall. Most of the people in town traveled to do any major shopping, so it did not pay for any store to pay the exorbitant rent asked. The whole mall experiment in America had mostly crashed and burned. There were still a few decent ones around but they tended to be in the bigger cities where people were migrating to shop anyway.

I was seated in a booth on the one side of the restaurant with customers. Possibly the best part of coming to one of these restaurants was that chips and salsa were brought to the table right away. I was too hungry to wait for my food. I tore into the chips while I waited for my Corona to arrive. The menu was mostly the same as every small town Mexican restaurant. The dishes consisted of the same foods but some places named them differently. Occasionally there might be a real authentic place. When those places could be found I made sure to eat there. Places like this, in my mind, were serving Gringo food. I figured that there was a joke played on those who were too stupid to know any better. Well, joke's on them, I still really liked this food.

The server returned with my cerveza and I ordered el pollo ranchero. It was one of the many combinations of chicken, cheese, rice, and beans. Here they left off the red sauce I had found on similarly named dishes elsewhere. That was fine, I didn't really like the sauce. Outside of that it was about the same. As I drank and waited for my food, I tried not to think of the morning's events. I hadn't really achieved much aside from pissing those guys off. Maybe Janine would have some great information, but if not, I really hadn't gotten anywhere. I knew they had a political agenda and that they really hated wizards and me.

That wasn't entirely true. I did find out that Chuck was the one who called me the first night at my rental. He might have had information about who burned it down as well. In fact, if the HFC were involved in that fire, proving that he knew anything might have been beneficial to this case as well. That would have to be one thing I kept in mind as I continued to unravel this knot.

My food arrived and I ordered another beer. It was exactly what I had expected and tasted fine. Maybe it pays to not know any better than a Gringo sometimes. I tried to form some kind of plan while I ate and drank. Mostly it consisted of waiting to meet tonight and hope Janine cracked this open for me. Otherwise I would continue to piss off everyone involved until someone tried to kill me. My methods were exciting as well as crazy. I knew how to hit the whole spectrum.

Halfway through my second beer I had a great idea; why not hit the library and do some research? Maybe this was the step I usually missed. I might have been better prepared for my meeting this morning if I had known more going in. I didn't really understand much of the HFC's history. I didn't even know when they actually started. Yeah, dull leg work was the part of the process I never read about that must have made it all work. To celebrate my genius, I ordered another beer. If two helped then three could have solved all my problems. Either way it did make my chicken taste better.

Paying my bill and leaving after my third Corona, I had to leave some problems for the world to solve, I had to follow my brilliant idea and go to the public library for the research. My brain was firing on all my high school cylinders. I could search all those sources that were supposed to lead me to great conclusions. Marksboro had a library near the downtown area that was old but still in fairly good condition... from the outside at least. I figured that would make a great way to pass the afternoon before I went for my meeting. Maybe I could even have some better questions to ask when I met her.

I spent the next few hours going through magazines, history books, and the Internet. The HFC had an overactive PR arm so there were a lot of articles and interviews to be found. I tried to avoid the rabbit holes of on-line conspiracies, but some were so fun. They had connections to aliens, ancient gods, the Illuminati, and the Masons of course. They held many old spell books of true power and kept them out of the hands of evil wizards. They also held books of ancient power that would cure disease and end all evil on Earth. They were both the best and worst people on the planet. The Internet was almost useless for any real information.

The magazines were better. Those were where I found a lot of articles about their history and interviews about their goals. I even found a few interviews with Clara. One was about her involvement in the attempt on

Alexander's life. She held her innocence and that of the HFC. Most of the rest of the article was fluff. Jesus! The interviewer actually asked her how she would dress to attempt an assassination. My faith in these magazines was waning as well. It was sad that Wikipedia seemed to have one of the best accounts of the base history of the group. Too bad I could not be sure about it either.

After hours of running and rerunning leads I had, what I thought to be, a pretty solid history. This information could be the key to better understanding in this case. I finally did something correctly on this case. The librarian had been softly trying to push me out for about ten minutes when I finished. I had a feeling she would stop being soft shortly. I packed up and took off. There were still a few hours until my meeting, but I wanted a chance to case the place first. I didn't want to walk into a trap if she was not on the up and up. Her slap was pretty damn hard.

I ended up closing the library plus twenty minutes. No wonder the librarian wanted me out. I drove east to a tiny town outside of Marksboro. I had to search for the bar she had named and it turned out to be a tiny dive bar in Trilna. As I drove into town I almost missed the bar and the town. Actually, the bar would have been harder to miss than the town itself. It was the largest building in town and the center around which the town was built. I pulled into the lot and sat for a bit watching. It was early still as I arrived at five thirty-seven. There were five vehicles in the lot but considering the size of the town that could be a large crowd.

The vehicle breakdown was three trucks and two bikes. That seemed to be a pretty reasonable group judging by the look of the place. All three trucks were beat up and older. My guess was local farmers avoiding their wives. I liked to think of the world in very stereotypical ways. The bikes were both Harleys with bright chrome. They were very well maintained. I watched the lot for a while but there was not much to learn this early. No one else entered and none of the occupants left. Finally, it was time to go in myself to see how it looked.

The building was bigger than a dive bar needed to be, but the note made me think there were multiple divisions inside. I scanned the lot and inside and found eight different minds inside. Maybe the farmers brought their wives in this town. I might have needed to update my old time thinking. The general feel I got from the collection was dull and normal. No one seemed to be expecting anything different to happen. I took this to be a good sign. I just hoped that laying traps for newcomers was not a normal activity for these folks.

As I sat scanning I kept my second pair of sunglasses on and kept my left eye closed. I expected the bar to be dark and I wanted to adjust as quickly as possible. I locked my car and trekked to the front door. As I looked back I realized that my car fit right in here. Not sure I liked that. Inside did not disappoint me. It was quite dark considering that the sun was still out. I switched which eye was open and closed. I could scan the room fairly well even without depth perception. There was a long bar across from a wall covered in old tattered booths. Behind the bar was a small collection of neon lights for American beers. The tap was small as was the girl near it dispensing beer. I saw a door past the bar that looked to lead to another part of the bar.

I walked to the bar first. I could see five of the minds I had sensed here. The others seemed to be on the other side. The girl behind the bar appeared to be just old enough to sell booze. She had a nice smile and a fair collection of tattoos showing on her bare and well-muscled arms. I revised my original opinion. She was not small, I would say lithe. I would wager that she had more strength in her than most people expected when looking at her. I stood and waited for her to acknowledge me. She walked over.

"What can I get for you, stranger?" She sounded friendly, but her mind showed that she was checking me carefully. I would guess that she spotted my gun in less than thirty seconds. I was quickly being classified as dangerous, but her smile never changed.

"What do you have on tap?"

"Bud, Bud-Lite, Miller and Lite, as well as Guinness."

"Really? Guinness seems very out of place here."

"Sure, owner likes it. What can I get you?"

"I'll have a Guinness. Thanks."

She walked to the tap and began filling a glass. She was quite deft and knew well how to pour a Guinness to get just the right head and the specific bubble flow that people like. Young as she might look she had real experience at this job. She sat the glass in front of me.

"Five bucks."

"Seems high for a town this size."

"Locals pay three but I don't like you. Five bucks or get the fuck out."

I pulled out my wallet and fished out a ten.

"Keep it. Now, why would a girl who's never met me and rides a sweet Harley have a problem with me?"

"You some kind of stalker?" She was eying me hard now.

"No, I just saw your tats and figured you weren't driving one of the beat-up trucks. I don't know which bike is yours, but both looked pretty sweet."

"Yeah, one of them is mine. I hope you don't think a cold reading's going to warm me up to you."

"I guess not but I'm no good at magic tricks and I could never juggle."

She tilted her head like a cat and chuckled.

"What the fuck's wrong with you, stranger?"

"If I could answer that question three therapists would go out of business and the economy is too bad for me to do that. Besides they're good people with bad student loans."

She actually laughed.

"Okay, maybe you aren't a complete asshole, but don't think I missed your gun or the way you cased the place. If you want to rob me go ahead and try. I've had five attempts so far and the three that survived had broken bones. You want to take a shot?"

"Fuck no," I took my first drink of Guinness. "I like my bones whole and enjoy living."

"So, you're just an NRA nut here to support your right to carry? I could ask to see your concealed carry. Cops may be interested."

"You don't like cops. We both know that. I don't want trouble. I know that. Sometimes I need to convince people that giving me trouble costs more than they want to pay."

"Aren't you intimidating enough being pro-wrestler size and dressing like you're going to shoot up a high school?"

"Sometimes that just invites people to try. We can't all be small and stronger than we look."

"That would be rough for you," she finally smiled and I felt her relax a bit.

"I'm supposed to be meeting someone here later but I always like to get a look at a place first. Never know what could happen."

"Sounds a bit paranoid to me."

"Sure, like you don't have both a gun and some kind of beat stick under the counter just for guys like me."

"Never said I wasn't paranoid, just said that you are."

"Fair enough."

"So, why's a scary motherfucker like you in this shit-kicking town?"

"I rolled in town for the cute kitten convention and the guy at the desk said this is the best place to get a beer. You must be paying him well."

"Fuck you."

"Would you believe someone brought me in town for protection?"

"That sounds far more reasonable. I don't need to know any more about whatever business you're in. Just talking to you is probably going to make me have to talk to the cops. Thanks for that, by the way."

"I aim to please."

She walked down the bar to answer another patron's request for booze. I sat drinking my beer and thinking. Some of the most interesting people were stuck in places like this. I wondered what her goals were. She could probably achieve most of them out of sheer tenacity. I would not enjoy being between her and whatever it was she wanted.

I finished my beer and motioned the girl to come by.

"You want a refill?"

"How about a Bud? I never really liked Guinness to be honest."

"Neither does anyone else, really. The owner just uses the bar to cover buying it as a business expense."

She walked back and poured me another beer I don't really like but would drink anyway.

"So, what do you plan to do with your life?" I asked as she poured.

"Excuse me?" she set the glass down and looked at me.

"You're young and this is a pretty good job, but I bet you have the will to do whatever you want."

She laughed. Hard. It surprised me entirely.

"Oh, come on. Don't get predictable now. That line is so weak."

"Line? Oh, shit. No, no. I just figure you have goals and wanted to chat a bit."

"So what, tending bar's not a respectable profession? I must want something else? And, let me guess, you can help me achieve it? No need, brother. I got everything I want right here. This is my bar. I own it. I also own both those bikes out front. I'm doing just fine."

I paused. Way to fuck up a simple conversation.

"Sorry, I got no excuse. I guess I assumed that you were too young to be that far along. You were right about me being an asshole. I guess it just comes natural. However, I had no intention of offering help. I figured you can do it yourself. I was just curious what it was you'd do. I guess now I know."

She posted her hands on the bar just past shoulder width. She sighed and looked me in the eye.

"Well, you wouldn't have been the first. People usually approach me trying to tell me how strong I am. I don't need your compliments or praise. I can take care of myself."

"Let me guess, after you shut them down the next question is about your sexual orientation."

"You know it. I've been called a dyke so many times I'm considering trying it."

"I can't advise it. Being with women is just as bad as being with men. Either way you have to deal with shit. I suggest you find a nice imaginary friend. Can't go wrong there."

"Stranger, you don't know my imagination." We both laughed at that.

CHAPTER TWENTY-NINE

As we were laughing Janine walked in. I watched her walk back to the door and to the other side. I'm not entirely sure she even saw me there. Her mind was scared and focused. I watched her go and then looked toward the door for a moment before turning back to the bartender.

"You might want to be careful bout that one, Stranger. She's got big ties to a local group of assholes."

"Do you mean the HFC?"

"Yeah, she's in the local chapter and, from what I hear, pretty deep."

"That's actually what I'm hoping. She's here to talk to me about the whole thing."

She took a step back and looked at me a moment.

"I didn't have you pegged as a wizard hater, a creep sure, but not hater. I would have guessed you were a user before some supremacist. I don't need shit starting in my bar."

"No no. I'm looking into a recent murder and I need some info about the HFC. I have no intention to join."

"You talking about that Edwards chick dying at her bastard's wedding? I heard about that. If you're wrapped up in all that I don't need you. Keep your shit short and get out."

"Wow. I can't seem to keep friends anywhere. Thanks for the drinks."

I pushed back from the bar and followed the receptionist. With my ability to turn people off I should start working for politicians I didn't like. Through the door was a separate room with pool tables and high-top tables. I glanced around and found the other minds playing pool. I also found Janine in the back area by the bathrooms. She was seated looking around the room nervously. I walked back and sat down across the table from her. I was facing a back wall so I kept my mind trained on the room behind me. I did not want any surprises here.

"Hi. You're early," I kept my tone light as I spoke.

"So are you. Done hitting on the bartender?"

"Why does everyone think I am trying to pick up everyone else?"

"You're a man."

"Oh. I had forgotten. That explains it, then. Do you want a drink?"

"Rum and Coke, please."

"I'll be right back."

I went back to the bar and leaned watching the bartender. She walked down to me after a moment.

"Look, maybe I was a bit rough on you, Stranger. You can stay."

"Thanks, you're all heart, but it's probably best that you aren't connected to me. I seem to bring trouble along with me."

"How cliched. I guess I should say something like 'I know how to take care of myself' or 'I like trouble' or some such drivel."

I liked her.

"I would go with 'trouble is my middle name.'"

"How old are you? That line's barely surviving on life support. Try a trope from this century."

"Damn! You're a fucking harsh critic. Give me another Bud and a rum and Coke."

"I can't help it if you are stuck in the 80s," she smiled and started making the drinks. "Maybe you should watch a new flick once in a while. You'll still be a hack, but you'll be a modern hack."

"Can I help it if cinema peaked with *Back to the Future*?"

"What's that? Some movie from before I was born?"

"I don't think we can be friends anymore."

"Well, try not to sleep with your mom too often, Mr. Klein."

"Just give me those," I smiled and put a ten on the bar. She set down my drinks and took the bill. Grabbing both I walked back to the back comfortable that my friendship with a woman whose name I didn't know was intact.

I sat back down at the high top and handed the woman I thought of as Janine the drink. She took a sip and set it down. I drank some of mine and waited. In an interview silence could be a very useful tool. I wanted to see how she handled a few moments of silence. I still couldn't be sure that she was trustworthy. This could all still be some kind of show or trap. Maybe I was a cliched hack.

"So," she broke the silence after another drink. "What do you want to know?"

"I am trying to find out about Clara's death. I had to check out her partners."

"Don't call them partners. Clara was a much better person than any of those assholes. She built the chapter here and Chuck is just jumping for joy at the chance to take over. It was a complete joke before she joined. My dad was a member when I was a kid."

"Okay, so they didn't like her?"

"Well, no. You think guys like that like being under a woman? Not like that. They hated that she had more power and influence than them. They all said that her money was all she had and that she climbed the ladder on her back. Typical fuckers. Anytime a woman gets far in the world she must have had it handed to her by men that she slept with. You probably wondered that too."

"Hell no. I met Clara. That woman wielded power too well to have not taken it herself. I would find it more believable that some of the guys tried to sleep with her for power."

She smiled at me.

"Maybe you do actually understand something. Not that she slept with any of them. They were below her. She had far more refined tastes."

"Fair enough, but did misogyny cause someone to want her dead?"

"Not only misogyny, but it was part of it. She had planned to fake a poisoning to discredit Alexander DesChanes. She would get really sick and blame him and his wizards. She thought it would be very effective. She even hoped it would keep her boy away from that wizard. Chuck and his weak pussies thought they could take advantage of it and actually kill her. They really poisoned her and the authorities need to find out. I want those assholes to pay."

"So, how do you know all of this?"

"John Calvin is such a weak douche. He wants to brag about anything he is being included in. Chuck only had a few people he could trust would do as he said and John was one. People didn't like Clara but they were afraid of her. John knew everything and tried to use his new position to pick me up. What a fuck," she was almost crying she was so mad.

"You loved her, didn't you?"

"What?! No, I…" she could not hold back anymore. She started to weep quietly.

"I understand. She was an amazing woman. Did she reciprocate at all?"

She nodded her head slightly. I waited for her to get control of herself again. She looked up at me with red eyes.

"Yeah, we had spent time together. You could say we were dating even though that word doesn't seem to fit a relationship with Clara Edwards. I don't know that she would have stayed with me, but I enjoyed the time we had. She was an amazing woman."

"I'm sorry that she invited me to the wedding and not you."

"She never wanted anyone to know. She would go out with John Wall once in a while so no one would find out. I was fine with it until she died. You're lucky I just slapped you."

"I'm sorry I failed. Now I want to end this for the people who did it."

"I do too and I have information. I can help you take Chuck and his group down."

"I'm sorry, but they didn't do it. I think a friend of mine stopped them. What killed her was a magical poison."

"Bullshit! How do you know?"

"I'm a psychic, for lack of a better term, I was connected to her mind when she died. A magical poison killed her. I'm going to find a way to stop the people who did it."

"Then why are we even talking?"

"I knew there was a kind of plot against her in the HFC. I had to try to find out if someone in the HFC worked with the wizard involved."

"Not Chuck or John. Those assholes hate too much to do it. They're also too stupid to figure out a deal that would make them look clean. They're just too dumb to pull it off. So, it really was a wizard?"

"Yeah, I'm so sorry for your loss. Can you talk to Victor?"

"No, he never liked me. He knew a bit about our relationship, but I don't think he ever admitted his mother had real feelings for another woman. I think he thought I was a gold-digger. He refused to acknowledge my existence. Clara and I had not been together long either way. I wasn't very connected to her family. I think she liked having a place to go to escape family. I was safe and fun."

"So, you can't see any way they would have worked with a wizard? How about anyone else there?"

"No, Chuck was running the whole *Get Rid of Clara Club*. Maybe someone from the head office could, but I don't know anything about them."

"Okay, thank you. I'm sorry that I couldn't take these guys down for you."

"You should be far sorrier that Clara is dead. I had high hope that you would save her. She was not comfortable using you, but I told her it would be worth it if she lived. Maybe I should have advised her to just tell the cops."

"The cops couldn't have saved her. Not this time," I stood up. "I'm sorry for it all. She played in a dangerous game and it got her."

"You fucking asshole," she came around the table and slapped me again. The sound drew attention from the pool players. They all watched as I stood there and she walked out. I walked back to the bar with the two drinks in hand.

"That sounded like a strike out, Stranger," the bartender said as she walked over to me. She picked up the two empties and poured another beer. "On me."

"Thanks. Don't blame her, I failed to save someone she loved dearly. That slap was a gift from me to help her feel better. She can't get to the people who really deserve it."

"Well, aren't you just the sweet, selfless knight?"

"Yeah, knight in a black duster. Thanks for the beer, my name's Trevor, by the way."

"Heh, I know," she shook my hand. "Dani, of course I heard about you already."

"Of course, you have. Who hasn't? Glad to meet you Dani. Is the word on me pretty bad?"

"Depends on who's talking. Well, I guess they all speak poorly of you, it just depends on the specifics."

"Oh, great," I took a long drink. "Glad everyone hates me."

"Well, you got yourself involved with some big players. Can't expect people to like you. You're on the wrong side no matter what side you are on."

"You sound like a friend of mine. He thinks I should just get out of here."

"Yeah? You gonna do it?"

"Hell, I'm too fucking stupid to get on the right side of this, how could I be smart enough to leave when I should?"

"Yeah, that's what I expected. You seem that kind of dumb to me."

"Thanks," I smiled and continued to drink. I set down the empty glass and looked at Dani. She got it and poured another.

"You going to be good to get out of here?"

"Yeah, might need a little time and another couple drinks. I'm still a bit thirsty."

"Well, keep that seat warm while you do."

She walked off to check on a few other people. Seemed to be getting a bit busier in here now. I sat and thought about Janine. This seemed to be the right time and place to do that.

CHAPTER THIRTY

After another hour and another beer, I decided to go back to the hotel. I had no more will for fun or trouble causing after that night. I said goodbye to Dani and went on my way. I thought about picking up another movie, but decided that I just wanted to think a bit and go to sleep. Miss Melnitz made a strong case for the HFC trying to kill Clara and for them being unwilling to work with wizards. The whole HFC lead seemed to have hit a solid wall. Tomorrow I would have to return to the plan of trying to get the Voice to show up again.

The problem was not getting the Voice to show. I could make most anyone yell at me. The problem was that I still didn't have a very good method to identify the Voice once she spoke again. That left me with trying to get someone to try and kill me. Seemed like murder was on the docket. I would have to make sure I was ready for whatever the Voice tried. She had proven herself to be quite imaginative and powerful so far. Who knew what she might bring if she no longer had to go after Clara as well.

I kept thinking of Janine. The look on her face was terrible. Not only was her loss terrible, but she would not even be allowed at the funeral. It sounded like Victor wanted nothing to do with her and he was running the show now. Jessica would be with him, but she was not going to invite someone her husband hated that much. The people from the HFC that had planned to kill Clara could end up being more welcome than her lover. That was some very cruel bullshit.

I was getting depressed the more I thought about it all. It was definitely time for me to get some sleep before this got worse. With my mental powers my mood could also flow out and effect those around me. This was a bad time for me to be in public. That was a lot of the reason I left the bar. I had seen moods like this cause fights and other problems when I wasn't careful. Best if I sat in my room and got some sleep. I could start tomorrow with a whole new plan. Maybe I could even find a way to get Alan involved again.

I woke up at eight-twenty with the sun shining bright through my window. I felt fairly well considering the depression that had been sinking in the night before. I took a long shower just to wash off the smell of the bar from the night before. No matter that smoking was banned in bars there was always a distinct smell from spending a long time in one. It tended to linger and announce to anyone where you had spent your time. I got cleaned up and put on some clothes. I would need to either shop or do some laundry soon. Since most of my bags were burned I was running short on clean clothing.

With my coat, boots, and hat on I was ready for the day by nine-thirty. I dressed fully today since I would be trying to intimidate and piss off as many people as possible. I now had to try to make other people act and that was always a shaky proposition. As I made sure I was ready to go, I was working out who to talk to first. I wanted to hit the right buttons hard and quickly. The police were going to get involved soon. I was angering powerful people and my rental had burned down. Those facts alone would draw a lot of attention but then when my dead client was added it became only a matter of time.

I needed breakfast. That was what could kick this whole process into overdrive. No investigator should face a day of questioning without a solid meal. This was feeling like a whole steak and eggs day. Time to find a good diner. I opened the door and stepped into the hall to run directly into detective Wall.

"Hello," I was not ready for this.

"Mr. Harrison. It seems that you are still here."

"Before we dance I have a very tough quandary ahead of me and I was just about to get some breakfast. Would you like to join me or are we heading downtown for a more formal meeting?"

"Our station isn't downtown, but I'm only here to talk. Let's go get that breakfast. Maybe I can even help you with your quandary. I do know a thing or two about investigation."

"Great, I'll drive."

We walked to my car and got in. The beast roared to life as if it resented being silent overnight. I pulled out of the lot and headed once again for the diner. I could think of no other place better to eat greasy diner food.

"So, what's this conundrum of which you speak?" Wall seemed genuinely interested in the problem at hand.

"Fancy words for a cop."

"What can I say, I have been known to read a book on occasion."

"Well, I have spent two nights now bogged down by the comparison between Eva Marie Saint and Leslie Caron. Both are amazing and I just can't decide who I would rather spend a day with."

"Damn! It's too early for a question like that. Let's warm up with an easy one, like who shot Kennedy?"

We bounced ideas around for the drive to the diner. It continued as we enter the Diner and took a booth in the back. I was searching the menu for its steak options when the server approached. She was quick today. We both ordered coffee. I ordered steak and eggs while Wall ordered eggs and bacon. We continued our debate for a bit longer. I was coming down on the side of Eva while Wall was staunchly in the Leslie camp. This question was not ending anytime soon.

Our coffee arrived and we continued to talk casually. Once the food showed up I masked our presence like before. I didn't tell Wall. He had come to me so I wanted him to open this up. I figured he might be more comfortable if he thought everything was normal. I wanted to know why he had come to me. Maybe the police had something. This could open up my whole investigation.

Once we had our food we ate in silence. I wanted to let him go first and he seemed to be struggling with something. Wall would probably not crack under silence like most people. That trick did not work as well on cops. I might have to start questioning him if only to get the ball rolling. It was possible he was there only to distract me while my room was searched. It had been done before, but I did have mines set against that. He finally looked at his watch and back up at me.

"Trevor, answer me one question. I have a big decision to make and I want you to be honest with me. I think I have a pretty good read on you, but I can't be sure. Were you involved with the murder of Clara Edwards?"

I sat quietly for a moment. His mind was a storm of

activity. I couldn't catch anything in particular without making it known that I was in his mind.

"No. I didn't kill her nor am I aligned with the people who did. I was hired to protect her and I failed. In as much as that I'm responsible. I didn't cause her death but I didn't prevent it either. Now, I am damned determined to solve it. Is that clear enough?"

Wall looked straight into my eyes. Not many people ever do this for a long time. When two people lock eyes, they started to open a link with their minds. It drew close to what I could do. It was part of why staring has always been instinctively seen as creepy. It felt like an intrusion of the mind and it was. Wall had a way about him that seemed to stare into my very soul. He shook his head after a few moments.

"I don't know," he looked down at the table. "Something about you just isn't right. You have a feeling that's different than anything I've ever encountered, but I don't get the feeling you're lying to me. At least not about Clara."

"Good. Glad we cleared that up."

"Shut-up and listen. Galante is certain you're involved but he doesn't have the evidence yet. They do, however, have enough to pick you up for the suspicion of the murder of Annie Shively."

"Who?" That name was new to me.

"Have you never met her? You were seen with her last night."

"Wait? Do you mean the receptionist for the HFC? She's dead?"

"Yes, and they're going to pin it on you," Wall seemed anxious as he spoke. His anxiety seemed to be rising as well. "Once they have you they won't let you out. Can you knock me out with whatever power you have?"

"What?!"

"Look, I was supposed to stall you long enough for them to get their arrest warrant and get to me. I was to keep you in your room or tell them where we went. I sent a short text earlier with this location but also stalling for time. That time will be up soon. They're coming with a team to take you down. That's why my phone buzzed just now. You need to knock me out and run."

"I-"

"Do it!" Wall practically yelled the order.

With no time to prepare I flashed him with the whole of North by Northwest. That might finish making my point about Eva Marie Saint as well. He slumped forward in the booth and I popped up and out the back. I kept the obscuring field around me so that, as I moved away from the table, it fell off Wall. I heard some gasps and a man yelled for an ambulance.

I burst out the back door into the parking lot. I was hoping to stay hidden as I watched the police set up to come in and get me. No such luck, however, as the ability only cloaks casual observation. These guys were looking for me. I heard someone shout "halt!" and felt attention turn toward me. I dropped the whole act and bolted.

Fortunately, I was very tall and I worked to stay in shape. This was going on in the day and the sun was bright. I had nowhere to hide anywhere in sight.

I ran between cars making sure to keep as many as possible between myself and my pursuers. I was trying to get to open space so I could unfurl my legs and get this thing going. I dodged between cars as I moved into the connected parking lot of a YMCA.

I broke free on the large lawn and started running full speed. As I turned around the building there was a large group of young children and their handlers walking toward me. I moved around them as best I could.

I knew they would get more cars involved soon and that would wreck my chances here on the street so I had to get off road. I crossed the street and leapt a fence into someone's back yard. I was still being chased but there was a good distance between us right now.

I kept going and leapt the fence at the back of the yard as well. Hopefully my height made this easier for me. I checked mentally and there were three strong pursuers hot on my tail. Damn there were some really fast guys in their police department.

I doubted that I had the lead to just outrun them in open space. A clear shot might open and someone probably wanted me dead. I leapt another fence into a connecting yard and noticed a tree line to my left. I turned slightly and headed for the fence at the back. Maybe I could pull some shenanigans in the tree to lose them. I leapt the fence at the back and could see my obscuring freedom.

I noticed that the ground took much longer than usual to find me as I fell. I could tell that gravity was still operating normally and that its pull was within standard range for Earth. As I floated there pondering physics and its implication, the ground found me.

It was sloped severely and I started to tumble out of control. I could not see where I was going as I felt trees go by. Branches reached out to slap me. My coat kept me from getting scrapped and scratched, but not from getting banged up.

I rolled and flopped for a bit before I landed on train tracks. I had not realized that I was right by the tracks. That was a painful realization but maybe a fortunate one. Hopefully, they would move slower than I did and give me some time.

I moved back into the trees hoping for cover. I continued to move North with the tracks. There was not a long distance here but there might have been enough for me to break free.

I stopped once I was north and under the cover of trees. I needed to ascertain their location and what I was still dealing with. I could tell that they were still following me but that they had slowed significantly. They obviously didn't take the express route down. My amazing strategy had worked perfectly.

I moved north slowly now that I had a bead on their minds. The trees slowed me as I tried to move silently, but it was a fair trade for the cover provided. I would have to wait and see what they decided to do once they cleared the cover.

Breaking into the open I saw the three of them about fifty yards south of me. They were searching the area. I could tell they were disappointed that I wasn't running down the tracks one way or the other. Sorry guys. Two of them split off and ran in opposite directions down the tracks. Good.

Unfortunately, one of them stayed put and started to search more closely. Why couldn't they be incompetent movie cops and all run in the same direction away from me? Action heroes had it so much easier. I waited in my spot so as to make no sound, but time was not on my side. Eventually he would find something that would lead him to me.

I waited to be sure the others were gone and strengthened my mental connection to the last officer. Minds are naturally drawn to each other because of our social nature. He wouldn't know why but he would feel a draw toward me. I crouched down and waited for him to move closer. He was being very cautious and careful.

This guy was quite smart.

Any other time I would hope to work with an officer like him. Once he got to within ten yards I flashed him with *The Man Who Knew Too Much*. He dropped to the ground. I figured I'd let him dream sweetly of Doris Day for a while.

When he fell his legs were slightly sticking out so I felt sure his compatriots would find him before anything bad happened. I began to work my way up the east side I was on so I could reach street level again. I was checking hard for minds the whole time, but the other officers were too far away now for me to get a good connection with them. No one was at the top either so I walked out calmly on to the street whistling *Que Sera Sera*.

CHAPTER THIRTY-ONE

So, now the police were after me. That cut off many of my options. Going back to the hotel was out of the question. Surely the police would be watching my hotel. I couldn't keep a place to stay in Marksboro. My car was mostly likely also out as an option. I wasn't sure if they had enough to impound it, but they would surely be watching it as long as they knew which car was mine. I had to assume that they did the basic work of running my registration.

Wall might have been able to take some heat off me, but that would take time. Chances were that he would have his own problems since I had knocked him out so I could not count on his help either. He had already helped me enough anyway. After this any suspects I went to talk to could call the police and drive me off. That was going to make it almost impossible for me to really apply any significant pressure. I was not doing well at this whole investigation thing. Of course, if someone was pulling the strings of the police to get rid of me, maybe I was already achieving my goal. I wasn't in prison so that was the brightest side I could find to this entire situation.

As I walked through town I tried to work out my next course of action. I stayed to side streets to reduce the chance of a random police drive by. Though I wanted his help, I tried not to lean on the option of Alan. He was certainly going to be pissed when he found out that I was fucking this all up. I had hoped to go to him when I had real information. Then I could get him back on my side, but I still had only my conjecture. So far, his prediction of events was one hundred percent correct. I also didn't want him to get involved with the police. He had his own safety to think about. I still could see no better action than finishing this thing. I had to find the real killer. It was the only way to clear myself as well.

I had most of the story worked out in a coherent narrative. I didn't know who the actual killer was, but I an idea what that person was like. Important information, certainly. I also had the problem of Annie being murdered now. It was hard to believe that her death was not connected to this whole business, but it was possible. However, the only smart way to proceed, for the time being, was to assume it was all connected. Victor stood to gain the most financially from his mother's death, but he was genuinely distraught by her death. He also didn't have the talent to do it himself. He could have paid someone, but I couldn't run down the money trail with the resources I had at my disposal. All told, I simply didn't like him as the murderer.

It all kept coming back to the Voice. If she wasn't the killer she was in league with the killer. I had to find a way to contact the Voice and get information out of her. I needed to do it on my terms so I could control the connection. That would not be easy. I knew how to push her buttons but I had to keep her from escaping before I could learn anything.

Wait! She never left a mark on my mind because she used intermediaries, but she would have left a mark on those people's minds. The wizard I fought was dead, but, as far as I knew, the person she used at the wedding was still alive. If I could reconnect with that mind I might be able to get the information I needed. I could try to reconnect using the small mark left in my mind from his. Like a psychic redial. I needed a safe place to work and some time. This wasn't a fast and dirty technique.

With my hotel room being compromised I had to find another location to work. The only option I had left was Alan. Great. I couldn't go there right now. Surely someone would be talking to him because of me. I had to wait until a little later to go see him. Of course, I had been meandering around town in the wrong direction, so it was going to take a while to reach him now. I also still needed to avoid main roads to evade capture so this trip would be slower still. I started to head west to get my bearings and head in Alan's general direction. The day was still young so I had time on my side. Of course, if it were dark right now this whole trip would be much easier. I made sure to avoid people and traffic as I began my trek across town to a man who surely didn't want to see me.

As I walked I figured out where I was and began to work out the best route. I made sure it would take a couple hours so I could give the police plenty of time to question him. When I finally arrived at Alan's place I carefully checked the area for minds. People were arriving home from work and greeting their loved ones so I found a shed by the alley behind his house and waited to be sure no one saw me. I kept the scan going for a while. It would be terrible to get caught now when I actually had a plan to end this whole train wreck of a case. I didn't want to walk in if the police had not been to see him yet. How terrible would it have been to be caught through my own stupidity that way?

Alan wasn't home so I decided to wait for him to come home before entering. I figured that the police spoke to him at his office, but chances had not been working out well for me lately. As time wore on I was considering breaking in and finding a place to hide inside. I realized that if someone found me in the shed I had no way to explain my presence. Before I could make that mistake I sensed his approach. He was being very cautious as he drove up and got out of his car. I figured that he felt someone might be following him as well. I gave him time to finish his sweep. The man was extremely methodical and patient.

I decided to give him a little time to relax as well. It probably wouldn't do me well to show up right as he got home. I could sense his anger. I waited another half hour to make sure no one dropped by and to avoid surprising him too much. I moved through the alley to his back door. I did not want to risk the main road so the front door was out. I knocked and then waited.

I felt his apprehension as he approached the door. He was weary. He looked out the glass and saw me standing there. His door opened in a flash and I was swept inside quickly. His door barely clicked shut before he tore into me.

"Just couldn't leave, could you? Had to stay and keep fucking it all up, huh? Why not just leave? What do you have to gain, asshole?"

"Hello to you too."

"Shut your goddamn mouth! Do you even begin to understand how hard you have made things here?"

"I know how hard this has all been for me."

"Do you? I was working to make the HFC go down for this. You kept fucking about which made Galante think you were involved. I had sold him on the idea that you had left since you were just hired help. Then you turn up at the HFC offices and now you look complicit."

I looked down. I had nothing to say. He was right; I had no idea how involved he was in this.

"Then Annie gets killed after you met her in a bar. What the fuck were you doing meeting with my agents?"

"I-"

"No, I'm not done yet. Annie was a wonderful woman and now she's dead. Most likely because she spoke with you. I'm the reason she got involved with them in the first place. Now she's dead. On top of that I look like I've been covering for you and might be involved in this whole thing as well. You couldn't fuck up more if you tried."

"Well-"

"No, still not yet. Then you knock out two cops and lead the force on a chase like some shitty '80s kids' movie. Why not just shoot a cop next time?"

I stayed silent this time.

"How much worse can you make this? The whole department wants your ass. Wall's in for questioning as is Johnson. He's the guy you left by the tracks in case you aren't even taking names anymore. They were both out cold with no visible sign of violence so this whole thing reeks of magic."

"Anymore?"

"I should call the police right now. Your actions have made the HFC look clean as a whistle. Was that your plan? Clear them?"

"I-I don't have a plan. Well, I didn't, but now I do. I have some ideas and some ways to go about it. Are you willing to give me the time to explain? If you do, and you don't like what I've said I will follow your advice for this, however you want me to do it. Deal?"

Alan sighed and walked over to his fridge. He opened

the door and pulled out two bottles of beer and sat down at his kitchen table. He motioned for me to sit and slid one of the bottles my way after popping the top. I sat down and he took a long pull from his bottle.

"Okay, what have you got?"

I took a drink and began to lay out all the information I had. I kept my conclusions out of the discussion as much as possible and tried to lay out only the facts. I included everything about the Voice and the situations he knew nothing about. I told him about my time with the HFC and Annie. Alan sat quietly listening to all of my words. He didn't interrupt me or get impatient as I told the stories that had made him so angry. He sat absorbing all my information with a blank face and posture.

Once I'd finished laying it out as I understood it, I stopped and remained silent. I tried not to prompt him or force his mind. He sat for a moment and then got up and grabbed two more bottles. He slid one to me and sat back down. His eyes got swimmy as he drank in silence. I could tell he had gone to another level of his mind. I had never touched his mind when he was in this state. I was always concerned that I might affect his process if I even touched him. His mind had an amazing ability to process information and I wanted it working at full capacity.

Finally, he looked up and returned to my level of reality.

"Okay, there is definitely something there beyond the HFC at work. I can't speak well to the magical aspects, but I do trust that you've given me the information correctly. So it does stand to reason that someone used the HFC attack as a cover for their own more potent attack. That leads me to believe that the real killer didn't have much faith in the HFC's ability to correctly execute their plan.

"There's also the possibility that the killer didn't actually know the whole plan of the HFC. The killer may not've realized that there was another plot to kill Clara that was unknown to Clara herself. That would make a lot of sense but it creates a big problem. There are now two murder plots for only one victim. The police will never accept this. It's entirely too messy and we have no solid evidence for the magical plot."

"Yeah, especially when I don't know who the other party is beyond a voice in my head."

"I have thoughts on that. The killer would have to gain something from the murder. Victor stands to gain a lot of money from Clara's death. That's the easiest explained answer. Could he be the killer?"

"I don't think so. He simply doesn't have any real talent for magic and all of this requires a great amount of power and ability to pull off."

"He could hire it. He has the money now to pay anyone."

"True, but he was truly distraught about his mother's death."

"Still possible. He could be suffering from buyer's remorse. Just because he had it done doesn't mean he still didn't love her."

"True, but we don't have the ability to run that down... unless you can run down financial records. He stood to inherit her money anyway, and from what I can tell he had a pretty open faucet."

"I can, but it takes a long time to get what I need without police assistance. Okay, we'll table him as a suspect for the time being and explore a few other options. Have you considered Alexander as the Voice?"

"What?"

"Are you blind? He has the power you talked about

being required. He could do this and get his revenge on both Clara and the HFC as a whole. It's also possible that this would cripple the organization if he could work it right. That's a big motive."

"Sure, I had thought about the idea but too much doesn't make sense. Why do it at his house and during his daughter's wedding? That brings the shadow over his people and himself. Why not work it at some HFC event?"

"Good point. At his house he's in complete control. He can setup the events however he likes. Also, there is the presence of the HFC plot that already existed. His opportunity is at the wedding not an HFC event. I can't believe that he's all that excited about the wedding. I can only imagine that he would prefer his daughter marry a wizard instead. Maybe he had hoped to halt the wedding or prevent it from happening entirely. We don't really know if the plot went as planned. Something may have gone wrong and changed the timing."

I leaned back for a moment and thought about that. It was possible. I got up and grabbed another beer. That would explain why he'd gotten so angry when I had talked about investigating him and his family. I had more chance of finding his involvement than the police did. He didn't seem the type to forgive something like a murder attempt against him or his daughter marrying the son of his would-be killer.

I leaned forward in my chair as I spoke, "of course he was willing to fight for Victor as his son. He seemed willing to go to war with me over it. Remember the encounter outside of his place?"

"Of course, I remember. And of course, he was willing to protect him. The wedding is over. The deed is done so he'd have to shift strategy. His best cover now would be to protect Victor and take him as his own. There's emotional power in protecting a son from his mother's killer. He has this set up very well. Alexander has power and could be the one pushing the cops to go after you hard."

"Damn!" I sat silently for a time. Alan was silent as well. His logic was so strong and convincing that I was questioning my own conclusions.

"I still don't like it," I finally broke the silence. "It's hard not to see his possible involvement, but I don't think he's the Voice. That's not the feel that I got from her."

"Fair, but he doesn't have to be the Voice. You have no proof that the Voice is actually the killer. The Voice could work for Alexander. That's not at all hard to believe. He could be the one who figured out how to do it right."

"True, but I still don't like it. It still doesn't feel right. When I spoke with him I didn't get any of that from his mind. I should have seen a few hints."

"I don't have your abilities, but he is powerful. Could he have fooled you? I think he looks pretty solid."

"It is possible that he fooled me, but that possibility is extremely low. I just don't think he could have pulled it off that flawlessly. Not to mention, if he knew the skills the Voice had, I should have had more trouble pushing him around earlier. But, if that is the case, I will know more tonight."

"What now?"

"I have a method that should let me contact the Voice. I need time and a safe place to set up. I was thinking I could use your spare room."

"Of course, you were. Anything else I can offer a violent fugitive from the law?"

"Look, at night she should be asleep. That will give me a bit more of an edge. I could finally get all the information I need including a good identification."

"Information you can never take to the police. What will you do with it to actually help the situation?"

"Let me worry about that later. Once I know who I can better judge what to do with that information. It could stand to be far more useful than you think."

"Sure, fine, I can't stop you anyway. Take the guest room, but try to keep it down. I want to get some sleep. I'm sure I'll be speaking to the police again soon and now I am guilty of aiding and abetting you."

I smiled and Alan got up from the table. He walked upstairs shaking his head the whole way. I had to make this work the first time. He was really going out on a limb for me. For that reason, I wanted to wait until the early morning to increase the chance that she was asleep. She might have defenses but they would be less active and I could take my time in breeching them. I sat down and decided to find a good movie on TV. I got fortunate and *The Night of the Hunter* was playing. I felt a bit like I was facing my own Harry Powell now. There was a charismatic force against me and no one really believed what I was saying. I might be more worried if Robert Mitchum were still alive.

I had to be careful. If Alexander was the force I was against I may not have what it takes to fight him in a long war. Aside from magical power he had the influence to completely bury me. I could fight him hard and possibly win, but only if he were willing to fight in my arena. The police and others he could involve could do incredible damage. No matter what the conclusion turned out to be I had to know who was behind it. If I could be careful enough the Voice wouldn't know that I had figured it out so I would have time to figure out a good path. Alan was on-board now as well, so that increased my chances. I had no other way to proceed so this would have to do.

CHAPTER THIRTY-TWO

I waited until a bit after two in the morning. I hoped that would be late enough to put any minds involved into a weakened state. The source of the Voice may have known enough to put up defenses before sleep, but I had to try and this stood the best chance. I shifted a few things in the room around to set up a good spot for me. I decided to work on the floor so that I had space and no threat of falling off a chair or the bed. That was all proof that I could learn from mistakes in the past. Painful mistakes have been made. I needed to have as little concern for the physical world as possible for this to work.

I lay down on the floor in the space I had created and took a few more moments to prepare myself. I had no concerns about my actual ability to do what was needed; I had the power and knew the technique well enough. I took the moments to lie there and prepare myself for what all might have to be done. I always tried to do as little harm as possible when I did things along these lines, but people could make that difficult or impossible sometimes. If there was a lot of resistance I might have to use more force. That stood to hurt the Voice but it could well destroy the conduits. Seeing as I had no idea who those conduits were, I had to prepare myself for what might have to take place.

Once ready I reached into my mind for the imprint left there by the conduit used at the wedding. A mental imprint was much better than a fingerprint. It was far more like DNA evidence. No one could mask their imprint and it was completely singular to each individual. It consisted of impressions left by a person's thought process and emotions, as well as the general state of that person's very being. The impression did change slightly throughout life, but not drastically and almost none over the short period of time since the wedding. For my purposes it also acted as a point for me to connect to that mind. Here there wasn't a good analog to anything real world. It wasn't an address or a phone number, more a variable that I could plug into an equation that would yield a phone number.

People noticed these imprints all the time as we always left a version on people we connected with. It was one identifier that we couldn't see but used to know people who were closely linked to our lives. That feeling when something about someone was off or when a close friend had a big life change were both reflected in their imprint. All our identifications were made on multiple factors. Most of the time they all lined up fine, but we always noticed when even one was off. If only data security could use such complex factors for security. People were mostly fooled when they overrode their own mind to allow someone through. On every level we were truly terrible at identity security.

I focused my mind and sent it out through the lens of the mental imprint I had. This would enable me cover massive amounts of physical distance with less energy expenditure by only connecting with the person whose imprint I was using. I didn't know how long it took in the physical world. I was not focused on any clock during this process. I didn't feel much time passing and the work seemed fairly easy so I assumed that the conduit was nearby. That was good. I could more carefully control my power and could manage it with a lower risk of harm. I carefully tuned in a solid connection before I tried anything else. Here I wanted a solid anchor.

I achieved this anchor by rooting into his brain. This also allowed me to learn more about the person in the process. Despite people being self-aware they spent very little time actually thinking about who they were. Most tended to think about their situation and circumstances far more. Many considered favorite movies, political ideologies, reading preferences, and the like to be true defining factors of their lives. These bits were almost useless when I dug into his mind; they either changed often or did little to define a person without additional information. I found thoughts of his car and rough paperwork. There were worries about a bank account and a marriage to Sheila. Judging from the length of time involved in the thoughts of the marriage I assumed the conduit was a man and Sheila a woman.

Once I broke through the surface level I began to truly dig in and sift through for information of his mind. I needed to learn what I could so that I could find the imprint I needed to create the next link in the chain. I began to sort through his mind not yet understanding his filing system. People stored memories in very odd ways and recall was very personal. The easiest way for me to get what I needed was to find his recall method. Like hacking, social engineering was the easiest way to get that method, but I didn't have time for that. This would have to be a fast and dirty job. And, most likely, painful.

I began to tug at threads in his mind for information

and almost immediately I could tell it was hurting him. This man was wired to keeping information secret and I was forcing it out. He didn't know how to stop me but hurt himself trying. His name was deeper in than I had expected: Nathan. The next surprise was that Nathan was employed by the HFC. The first conduit was a wizard. So far, I had found no evidence that Nathan had any magical talent. Why use someone from the HFC? Convenience or was this part of the frame job? Did the Voice know that I could trace a mind this way? That would have explained using the conduits.

I kept searching for a specific cluster of memories. Having your own mind used this way created a very specific reaction. It was incredibly violating and most seemed to classify it in their mind similarly to molestation or rape. It was very similar at its core. Someone outside of yourself who was far more powerful barged inside and used you for their own purposes. That feeling and, in turn, the imprint would have been stored together in a memory cluster. I needed to open that and find the imprint. Nathan was about to have a terrible and prolonged nightmare.

More time passed as I searched Nathan's mind for the information I needed. In the end I almost tripped over the memories that I needed. All the time I had been searching his mind for moments of shame. People often categorize memories more by emotion than by time or even the people involved, though there was some very good cross-referencing. I had been thinking that Nathan had simply done few things he considered to be shameful, but the truth was subtly different. Nathan had almost no capacity for shame. I found memories of his horrible mistreatment of service people and hired help. The man was a horror for cab drivers and god help anyone one who had to deal with him on the phone. Amongst all of this I finally found a memory of Nathan dealing with a superior after a job that he felt he had botched. It was the only moment of shame I found and cradled deep inside this one I found something he truly felt terrible about: The Voice taking over his mind for a time.

I accessed that memory and inside I found the imprint I needed. The connection here could mean a few things. It was possible that these both involved the same superior, but my feeling was that it stemmed from them sharing the same sense of powerlessness and vulnerability. Most people, at their very core, hate feeling weak more than anything else. It seems to be a part of the fears of both death and the unknown. I studied the imprint closely and found that it was still fresh and clean. For my purposes that was very good. Its state meant that Nathan had not accessed it much at all. Accessing and exposing memories changed them, but it also eroded them to a degree. People generally made a relived memory better fit the narrative of their life. That was why good therapy helped people so much. They could blunt and dull the sharp edges of painful memories through remembrance. Burying pain was quite rough for the human mind. Those sharp edges began to tear at other memories and twist how people saw their past and themselves.

In this case I was very glad Nathan was the macho kind of guy who buried his pain deeply. I could dig it up and it was still well preserved and ready for my purposes. I could create a great bridge between him and the next link who I hoped was the Voice herself. Of course, doing so would make him relive this memory for the entire duration I had the link open. It would also make this memory stronger and easier for him to relive after I was done. This would also make it harder for him to erode it in the future. Basically, I was going to both make him need therapy and reduce the effectiveness of said therapy. His life was about to get worse.

As I studied the imprint I came to realize that it was also fresh because it was very strong. I realized that there was a very good chance that Nathan was the only conduit involved. With that information I took a moment to be sure I was ready for the next person to be the Voice. Again, I focused the imprint like a lens, but with it being another lens in the chain I would have to pump out more power to be sure that enough could reach the next link. This was the part that could hurt Nathan physically. So much power going through his mind could do significant damage. This was not something I usually like to subject people to, but I had no other option.

Time passed again as I sent my mind out to the next stop. I found it and this time I was prepared to make an anchor quickly. I grabbed on to a few bits of the mind's identity and kept grabbing as I found them. I quickly found out two things: this was the Voice and she was protecting herself quickly. I checked my anchor to be sure I had enough. I had a foothold, but not everything I had hoped for when she woke and tried to eject me. I would have to pour on more power to maintain my position until I could better dig in. I would have to keep working on both my anchor and the conversation. Fortunately, she was a talkative person. I planned to play on her theatrics to buy some time.

"Well well, isn't this a surprise," she seemed genuinely interested. *"How did you find me?"*

"As you had said before, I have my tricks. This one I plan to leave a mystery."

"Fine. I'll work it out later myself. What do you want?"

"Well, aside from the voyeuristic joy of wondering around a

young girl's mind at night, I have a few questions that only you can answer for me. Why did you kill Clara Edwards?"

"Now what would possibly lead you to believe that I killed that poor woman? From what I have been hearing you are responsible for her death. You wouldn't be trying to frame me, would you?"

"Really? You try to kill me, then recruit me, and now you just insult me. We both know you were involved; how do you profit from this?"

"As a wizard isn't the death of any hatemonger like her profit enough? She tried to kill Alexander DesChanes. Why wouldn't I want her dead?"

"So, that's it? Simple revenge? That seems pretty weak. I had you pegged as a higher-minded villain. More of an aspiring Dr. Doom than a mad Harry Osborn."

"What motivates me is the sole domain of myself. You haven't the mind to comprehend my motives or intentions."

"Hmm... Murder, revenge, money, pride. These all seem pretty easy to comprehend. They're motives for characters on simple TV shows after all."

My anchor now was pretty solid. Her identity was still well protected, however. I did get the momentary joy of confirming that the Voice was indeed a female. Got to take victories when they come.

"You only see the short term. My end goal will leave me more powerful than your paltry intellect can even fathom. You had best use the time you have left to hide and hope that I forget your involvement in this affair."

"That's it? That's all you have? Just some stock villain arrogance? Here I had come to think of you as an adversary, not just some little girl who is raging at the slight of not being invited to a school dance. Surely you ended a human life for more than some imagined ultimate power."

"You foolish dick. You have no idea what I do or why I do it.

To think I wasted any time trying to ally myself with you. Laughable."

"Still obsessive over what you cannot have? Now that makes sense. I'm a hard catch to lose and live with."

"You preening cock! You self-centered bastard. Do you think I care about you at all? I had wanted to use you like all the others who work for me whether they know it or not, but Monty was wrong. You mean nothing. To me or the world at large."

"If you believe that I have a bridge to sell you in California."

Something felt wrong. I checked my connection chain and realized that Nathan couldn't handle the power. He was about to pass out. When he fell unconscious, my whole connection would be lost and I had not really learned anything yet. I had to get something fast.

"Fine. Your motives are high and grand. So, convince me. What could possibly motivate you to all of this and justify all that has happened?"

"Now it's my turn to scoff. I'm not going to tell you my whole plan just because you asked. You're not nearly as good as you think you are."

"You don't have one, do you? You're flailing around stalling for time so you can find the right hack motive from the right hack story, aren't you?"

"So pathetic. I can feel you starting to fade. You don't have the time to get what you want."

"You don't even know how she died, do you? You're just a patsy in this like everyone else."

Her reaction to this was twofold. Consciously she laughed as I was fading away creating a great parting image for the villain. Unconsciously she let slip a memory. Not even a full memory just a small part. Not even a full sentence. Twelve words she released twelve words as I was dragged out of her mind. I passed quickly through Nathan's as he blacked out completely.

I snapped back into my mind. I opened my eyes and took in my surroundings slowly. Nothing here had changed so I felt fairly safe. I sat up and took stock of being back in my body. It could be unnerving to come back and worse still to be unexpectedly snapped back. I had no clue as I sat there what state Nathan was in. I had passed through his mind too quickly. I would have to see about following up on that a bit later.

Twelve words.

Yes, I did come out of this whole thing with a victory of sorts. I had information that I think points to many different conclusions, but I would have to think of how best to use it.

Twelve words. Twelve simple words that might contain all I need to know.

"May fate cut the thread of she who stands to unravel ours."

CHAPTER THIRTY-THREE

Sica.

The Voice that had haunted me this whole case belonged to Sica DesChanes. Now I could start to make some of the connections in this whole thing. Those connections quickly made a lot of sense, too. Not only did Victor stand to get the money, but so did his wife. She did have a lot of money from her father, but this would be money she was closer to. Of course, there was the revenge angle, but I still had a feeling that it was at least secondary. She had also claimed some grand power would be hers to claim. That was an end I still could not see.

I stood up and proceeded into Alan's kitchen. I looked through his drawers and found a beat-up notebook and a few pens. I sat down at his table which was vastly more comfortable than his floor. I would have to complain in the morning. The notebook had notes for around his house like measurements of doorways and locations of plugs. This guy was way too organized for my taste. I found a blank page and started to work. I needed to figure out how the poison worked. I was certain now that it was a poison delivered earlier with a trigger set for later. Clara probably had the right time for the delivery of the poison. I had no way to know for sure, but Clara was quite perceptive.

The trigger appeared to be in the vows. Jessica had been very careful in her vows and I now knew why. She had been incredibly devious hiding a trigger in her wedding vows. No one would interrupt her and she could speak in her time and at her cadence. Her ego would make hiding them in plain sight all the better. I had found them to be odd when I first heard them, but the whole day had been odd enough that her vows just seemed to fit. The whole thing fit her dramatic nature so well.

I accessed my memory and started the process by writing down her vows. I had the recording from the wedding so I could play it back exactly.

"Victor James Edwards do you swear to
Stand with me against those who oppose us
Forsake all others before me
Your heart to my heart
Your blood to my blood
Give me of your strength when I need
Together stand forever and a day
Woe to those who stand to make this union fall
May fate cut the thread of she who stands to unravel ours?"

I sat there for a moment and looked over her vows. They had seemed odd then but so much had happened since that I had forgotten to go back and think of them again. Now that I sat and paid attention to them they again felt very odd for wedding vows. I thought about it and realized that she might be going for old world tradition and charm. I took the notebook and went back into Alan's living room. He had a desktop computer. I knew the password so I could get on-line and check a few things out.

I began to look at old traditions and rituals for weddings. I needed to see if Sica had lifted this from some other source. I started by looking at the different lines separately. I checked the lines as a whole as well as segments that seemed ominous. I even made sure to check the more modern traditions. I looked through Wicca and its many off shoots and copies though I did not expect much here. Sica would pull from an older, more authentic source. As I had expected my search came up empty on every front. I even sent messages to contacts I had to see if they knew more or could point me to something. Those might take time but it paid to be thorough.

The more I read and wrote down her words the more certain I was as to their meaning and purpose. Sica had not copied some old mantra or poem to use as a trigger. Sica had performed the whole spell in front of her wedding guests. With this I began to see just how the spell worked. She had pulled energy from Victor as well since doing the spell like that took phenomenal amounts of power at one time. She was powerful, but assistance would be required.

Normally, this kind of poison with a trigger could be prepared fairly easily by most any mage. He could perform enchantments over a potion in the beginning and then slowly feed power into the poison with time even while it was in the body of the victim. With time to replenish and heal great amounts of power could be pumped into it over time to achieve great results. All that would be required was regular proximity to the victim. Here Sica would not have that so she went another way.

She would also enjoy the feeling of showing off. As best as I could figure, Sica had used a magically conductive fluid as the base and then performed the entire enchantment at one time. She pulled from her own immense power as well as the life-force of Victor. Victor's power would have to be given freely so she worked that permission into the whole spell. Even with that help this demonstrated how powerful she was. Very few wizards could have pulled off a spell or poison quite like this one.

Then there was the end effect of dumping so much power at once. Sica would look and feel drained, but here the wedding and Clara's death would stand to cover for Sica's looking tired. Her exhaustion would look like great emotion and serve to sell her distraught reaction. I couldn't help but marvel at both her clever methods and sheer power expenditure. When I thought back Clara had dropped almost immediately after Sica's spell.

I re-watched it play out in my head a few times to get the order of events down correctly. Sica stopped, there was a beat, and then there was the hit in Clara's mind as the poison took effect. I had thought at the time that it was her reacting to her son being married, but it was the poison starting its deadly reaction in her blood. That speed was amazing and could only be achieved with great power. Of course the location made the revenge portion of the whole event even sweeter. There was a bit of a home field advantage at play but more to the point she made Alexander watch the whole thing. She was showing off to her father. I wondered then how much of this he had already figured out. He had to at least suspect some of it.

Of course, he did. That's why he was so upset at the wedding itself. Even if he didn't know the specifics, then recognizing a spell must be second nature to him by now.

There was no way he didn't see it for what it was and recognize the power movement as well. He would have figured out enough at the time to realize she was involved. That could be why he was so quick to close ranks. It also explained why he was so interested in what I thought and how I was doing. I was the lone variable he could not control for certain.

I watched it again in my head and froze. There was one more step in the chain of events before Clara's fate was sealed. The last step changed the tenor of that whole event entirely. It also showed that vengeance was more of the motivation than I had originally thought. With this I knew Sica was the mastermind behind it all. No one else arranged it or ordered it. She was the one. She truly had pulled off a master-plan worthy of Victor von Doom.

The actual order of events was vows, silent beat, "I do," and then the poison hit Clara. Sica had made Victor deliver the trigger. He had been the one to finish the spell and actually speak the words that killed his mother. By marrying Sica Victor had literally killed his mother. That was the act of one truly cold bitch.

CHAPTER THIRTY-FOUR

I continued to think about that whole experience through the night. There was no way I was going to get anymore sleep after that conversation. I spent a lot of my time trying to find a way to make her pay for what she had done. I was under no delusion that I could teach her a lesson, but she had killed a woman and she needed to pay for that. That woman was a client of mine so I figured I should be involved. There was a chance that she was involved in Annie's murder as well. Sica had to be stopped somehow.

I thought about what I knew. I had all the information I needed but no way to give it to the police. My memories would not hold up as evidence. I could appear as a witness, but most of what I knew was hearsay and the direct knowledge could not be corroborated. Of course, it crossed my mind that Sica could be killed, but that was not my business. Who was I to decide that she was to die when the impetus for it was her killing of someone else. That created a whole tree of problems in my mind. I had to find a way to expose her for the murderer that she was, if nothing else, for Victor's sake.

Victor.

He was another factor I had to think about. I realized

during the night that he would be destroyed by the information of his involvement in his mother's death. He had not been aware of his involvement, but that would not change the fact that he had said the words that caused her death. I could see him having a terrible reaction to that information and I was not sure I wanted his blood on my hands as well. With that kind of discovery who could blame him for taking his own life?

That question haunted me for a long time. Could I let Sica go free to keep Victor from learning the truth? Could I live with Victor reacting poorly to make Sica pay for her actions? Then there was the grand plan she had mentioned. She claimed to have a greater purpose than what had already transpired. Could I sit back and allow her to gather still more power?

No. No matter what terrible things happened because of my actions I could not allow Jessica DesChanes to gain more power.

Once I concluded my involvement was necessary, I had another problem on my hands. Sica was sure to want me dead now. She had to know that I would eventually come up with answers and she knew now that I wasn't going to quit anytime soon. Despite her age she was no child in her mind. Sica was a powerful mage with talent and training. Could I survive let alone win a confrontation with her? Fortunately, I had no loved ones for her to use to threaten me. She could go after Alan, but he was very resourceful. I rarely had to worry about him taking care of himself.

No, my concern for my own safety could not be my driving motivation here. This girl was far too dangerous and the stakes here were far too high. I knew what was going on so I would have to get involved. It was apparent that she would kill to achieve her goals, so how hard was it to believe that she would kill again? What if she began to kill victims many at a time? There was no way to be sure what kind of limits she might have. Hell, she may not have any at all. If she could get the power she spoke of, would she become a global threat?

My mind turned in these circles most of the night. There was little forward momentum and no satisfaction. I finally looked up when I realized that something was shining in the window. The sun had started to rise over the horizon. As I sat I heard some rumblings from upstairs and decided to treat my generous host to some breakfast. At his expense, of course.

I searched his fridge and took out a pepper, some mushrooms, and a few eggs. I put some olive oil in a pan to heat up as I chopped the pepper and mushrooms into small cubes. I put some crushed garlic, oregano, and some sesame seeds into the pan and let them brown. I added the peppers and mushrooms to cook as Alan came downstairs. He realized what I was doing and started to make coffee and toast while I whipped up six eggs with milk, salt, and pepper. I added that to the pan. We both moved through the kitchen in silence as we worked.

I mixed up the omelets as they cooked to get a good mix as Alan took care of the toast. Coffee filled the air making me realize how much I wanted a cup. I added shredded cheese to the mix and split it into two equal piles on two plates. I found some bacon in the fridge and put it into the same pan to fry realizing that I should have done the bacon first. Not the first mistake I had made on this trip and probably not the last.

When I had it all done and split onto plates I walked over to the table where Alan had coffee, orange juice, toast, butter, and jam set out for us both. We sat and ate our impromptu breakfast in silence enjoying the first moment that felt like two friends having a nice visit. I would have liked it if the whole week had felt this way.

Alan knew instinctively that I had gotten news overnight and neither of us was quick to open that whole line of inquiry. I assumed he still wished that I had gone away burying this whole thing. Though that would have been much easier, I knew he would be much happier when the real people involved paid for what had happened. None of that paying would do anything about Annie being dead. Alan was going to make sure that I did not forget that one.

How could I forget being involved in destroying both sides of that relationship?

The food was quite good and very filling, but it was nearing its end. As breakfast drew to a close we both knew we'd have to talk. I spent much of the time eating thinking of ways I could improve my omelets. Alan was the one who finally decided that we had been quiet long enough. He knew there was a real problem and that it needed to be resolved soon. Possibly, he wanted me to leave and knew I would not until this was over. Either way, he spoke first.

"So… eventful night?"

"Yes. I didn't get everything I wanted but I got enough to move this all forward a lot."

"Well now, calm down there, pal. My floors can't handle your acrobatics."

"I didn't get good news."

"Oh! Was there good news to be had? Was it possible that Clara or possibly Annie were still alive?"

"Fine, dick, I get it. No, there was never going to be any good news here, but that doesn't make me happy when I realize how bad the news is."

"So, are you glad that you stayed? Maybe you

should've gone home. That would've lead to one better possibility."

I knew he wasn't going to let up.

I sighed, "You know I had to figure it out. I can't just let the wrong people pay for a crime even if they're bad people."

"Fuck you. That is not why you kept going. Your pride was hurt because you failed. You may have gotten some info, but that doesn't change your motive. Your pride got me wrapped up in this and got Annie Shively killed. Kudos to you for doing the *right thing*. I'll put you down for an award."

"You're right. I was mad, okay. But now I know that there is more going on. I should've listened to you... but only to a point. You were willing to let the killer off to prosecute the wrong people. How is that any better."

Alan paused before speaking.

"True. Okay, we were both assholes. Let's move forward and finish this before anyone else ends up dead. Especially me."

"Thanks. You're all heart."

Alan gave me a big shit-eating grin. I sat for a moment and finished my orange juice. I got up to get another cup of coffee taking his cup as well. He was going to need more once he heard what I had to say. When I got back in my seat I took a drink and then started to lay out what I had learned during the night. As always, I gave him all the details, including the prep so he would realize that I'd been thorough in my preparations. I gave him the info I had on Nathan and told him how I found the imprint that lead me to Sica. I recounted our conversation and how I got booted out when Nathan passed out. All I left off was my thoughts after that. I always wanted to hear his thoughts from the information alone. He didn't need to be colored by my thoughts yet. His were probably better anyway.

After a few moments of quiet he spoke up.

"Okay, that's one fucked up story."

"I know, right? She's a seriously cold bitch."

"Yeah, she is. So, how do you handle all of this? As far as I can see she's covered her tracks very well in any real-world way. You know but what can you do? The police will never buy any of this."

"True. I will just have to be the one to finish this… somehow. I just need to find a way to do that."

"Alexander will protect her from you."

"Not if he knows the full extent of what she did." I took a sip of coffee. "I need to find a way to make him see the full story."

"He won't believe you."

"True, that's why I can't tell him. I'll have to make him see."

"So, show him your memories."

"He won't buy that. It's too easy to believe that I would make changes in what I show him. He'll assume I'm manipulating it to be what I want. Whatever I show him has to be iron clad."

"So, you need her to confess to him."

"Yeah, but she'll never confess with what I have if Alexander is around. She's not stupid or easily intimidated."

"Make a link between his and your mind."

"Maybe, but he might still think I'd change that. Most wizards don't understand mental abilities well. I can't move forward with any plan that might be less than entirely convincing."

I sat and thought about it for a bit. How could I get Alexander to see Jessica confess? How could I get her to confess? No, one problem at a time. If I could get him to see it, I could probably get her angry enough to say something incriminating.

"Could Alexander put some kind of magical bug on you?" Alan asked as he finished his second cup of coffee. "Something he made that he would trust?"

"Hmm… that's an idea. Wait. No, Sica would surely check me for any enchantments when I spoke to her. She's got to be fairly paranoid at this point."

"She might be arrogant."

"True, but do I want to bank on that possibility?"

We sat there quietly for a bit longer. We were both sitting there hoping that the caffeine would wake our brains enough to kick start an idea. I was so close to finishing this; I only needed one last piece.

It hit me.

It hit me hard.

"I have it," I almost shouted as I began furiously scribbling in the notebook. I tore the page out and shoved it into Alan's hands. "I need you to get these things for me as soon as possible."

He looked at the paper quizzically.

"And what might you be planning while I shop for you?"

"I need to see a man about a confession."

CHAPTER THIRTY-FIVE

I knew I had a lot to do and a shrinking amount of time in which to do it. The newlyweds would go off on an amazing honeymoon soon, probably in another country or two. The funeral had postponed their leaving, but Sica was too bright to stick around through the worst part of the investigation. Were they in another country the police would eventually get weighed down with the rest of their work. I didn't know when they'd be leaving, but that was my hard deadline to meet.

I thought out my plans as I walked to the diner where I had left my car. I hoped that it would still be parked there. I had no clue whether they could come up with a reason to impound it or not. I had also forgotten to ask Alan if he knew. The list of things I had forgotten or had done wrong on this one was growing to be a story of its own. I needed wheels if I wanted to get everything done in the little time I had. With a vehicle, a little luck, and freedom to… well stay out of jail I could finish this.

The details of my plan began to coalesce as I walked. My first, and most important necessity was Alexander. He was the keystone to actually achieving anything with this plan. I had to get him to see what I was going to get from Sica and believe me. I'd have to talk to him first. If I failed on that part there was no point in continuing with my plan.

Once I could secure Alexander's involvement, then I could move forward with the confrontation itself. Anytime there was going to be a situation that could goes sideways I preferred to have home field advantage. Marksboro was in no means my home field and it was, in fact, my opponent's. So, the next option was to simply rig the game to give me an advantage. Sica was an exceedingly powerful mage and I hate fighting powerful mages. She also had no qualms killing an innocent by-stander, so she might actually enjoy killing someone who had caused her so much trouble, i.e. me. If possible, I would try for a nonviolent confrontation, but that could be impossible.

Since a fight was lodged firmly in the land of probable, I would have to be sure to prepare for that. I had no intention of underestimating Jessica's abilities so I would prepare lethal force. This would also require finding a location where I could control the variables to protect both myself and any innocent people in range. I would also want a place that would grant me more advantages than her or at least no more either way.

She had to at least guess that I was on to her scent. Even if she really did believe I was too stupid to harm her, she would be careful at minimum. I was being sure to take extra caution to shield my mind from any outside incursion. I didn't need her breaking in with her voice or getting any information out. I was sure I could keep her at bay in this arena.

I would also like to get Victor to see what transpired along with Alexander. While I was certain that it would hurt him to know his involvement, I could not protect him if he remained unaware of what his wife had done. My hope was that Alexander genuinely cared for the boy and might help him after they both heard this terrible news. At some point Victor would have to learn what really happened and his involvement in it all. He would have to own up to his part even if he had been blinded by love and ignorance.

Those two often went hand in hand.

I heard that so often as if it were a shield against wrong doing. Acting in the name of love or guided by love doesn't absolve a person from responsibility any more than being drunk did. Maybe some people can't handle their love. Maybe it weakens them too much. They could have a predisposition to love addiction. Far too many people tried to use it to excuse actions and, surprisingly, too many people allowed them to.

This society seemed so willing to accept terrible things done in the name of love. Love excused sins old and new alike. When did this one emotion become all good? Isn't love jealous? Isn't love selfish? Were these good things? How willing were most people to share all their love with all the people they met? Love had never lead to only good actions any more than joy, anger, sadness, or wonderment. When people allowed emotions to rule life the result was a truly harsh world.

My diatribe continued in my head as I neared the diner. I slowed down and approached more cautiously. This was the moment of truth for my car. I peered around a corner to the lot my car had been parked in.

It was still there.

Good. Then I looked around to see who was around. After a moment I spotted the two guys sitting in a car facing my car trying to look casual.

Shit.

They were focused and alert. Their shift had probably

recently begun. I assumed they were hoping to catch me coming for my car. It was a good plan. I would need it even if I left town. That probably wasn't an option now. This would require a careful touch. I pulled back around the corner and worked to prepare my mind. I calmed myself and split off a section to control this setup. I worked to zero in on their minds and get a solid connection. I then carefully latched the split section of my mind to theirs creating an open transmission pathway. Then I fed them a scenario.

The two officers jumped when they saw me walk casually around a corner and head for my car. I got in and pulled off slowly down the street. They pulled a quick U-turn and followed my car as it drove east out of town. I led them out of town and into the country for about twenty minutes before I allowed my illusion to fade. The concentration was taxing and I had bought myself enough time. They would see my car wink out of existence. That should cause some major confusion.

After they had driven off I walked to my car and drove off. I looked to see if there were any secondary viewers, but I doubted it. This was a small town with a small police force. I would still have to work very quickly and then hide my car. They would be back for sure. I hoped that Alan would allow me to use his garage to hide it. I was putting a lot of strain on his generosity. First, before I could work on that, I had to go see Alexander.

CHAPTER THIRTY-SIX

I drove out to see Alexander once again. The route was well known to me at that point so I took a bit of time to enjoy the scenery. The houses here were large and gorgeous with amazingly well manicured lawns. Many had ponds and small wooded areas as well. When people accrue enough wealth, they tend to either bring nature back into their lives under their control or destroy it entirely in large buildings surrounded by concrete. People were probably still a little resentful over that whole predator thing.

Once again, when I pulled into his drive, Alexander did not welcome me to his house. We spoke out on the lawn but he was more hospitable this time. I didn't know exactly what caused this, but he did seem more agreeable. I carefully laid out my plan leaving out key details. I didn't want him to know who the mark was to be or what I might have to do to her if things went awry. I held back a few details so he wouldn't figure it out. I simply labeled the target as a rogue wizard who was trying to create chaos and gain power.

After our very tightly worded conversation, I asked him for a legal favor. I didn't think he wholly understood why I asked, but he was willing to acquiesce to my request as long as I agreed to his terms as well. Maybe he thought he was getting the better part of the deal. I was glad to see that I still had some of Alexander's trust though my plan could finish that all off and create a new and powerful enemy. I didn't feel that I had enough of those yet.

After our conversation and agreement, I left to finish getting my details all arranged. There were things I needed to have setup before anything could go awry. Some of the details I had left to Alan to arrange. He had connections that I didn't. Now I had to rely on his ability to do what was needed fast enough.

I had faith.

The next big item on my agenda was to find a location to stage the whole confrontation. That was quite a huge part for me to do. I needed to find a location away from people where I could control the environment. Many cerebro-mines would need to be set to swing things in my favor. Anyone who entered a fair fight deserved to lose. I wanted to gain all the advantage I possibly could. That was one side of the coin. I also wanted to see to it that Jessica could not gain any more advantages; she already had many that I would have to contend with. In a town this size I was having some trouble finding that location.

I spent some time cruising town. Fortunately, the locations I wanted were not near heavily populated or commercial areas. I had less to worry about with patrolling police cruising by. Parks had the space needed but they were too public. I could never be sure that innocent people might not walk through at any time. Parking lots ran too much risk of mines going off early. People did use them and I didn't know the area well enough. If I tried to pick a spot out of town I ran a huge risk that she would smell a trap and enter too prepared.

This was paramount and my search was proceeding much too slowly.

I drove around for hours. The risk of getting caught kept escalating and my results were non-existent. I was contemplating picking a place outside of town and losing the element of surprise when I turned a corner and found my location. It was as close to perfect as I was going to find. As it was the remnant of a factory or warehouse there were still some walls up and the entire lot was fenced off. The walls would help contain the fight and judging by the weed growth people tended to leave it alone. The sun was going down, but I had found my home field.

I drove back to Alan's from there. I took my time but the location was a bit over a mile from his house. I would park and hide my car and continue the rest of the work on foot. Walking was the safest mode of transport since I could neither fly or teleport. With the sun going down I could do a lot of work after dark as well. I would hate to get picked up now when I was so close to my goal.

Alan was home when I returned. I hoped this was a good sign. So much could go wrong and I didn't have time to troubleshoot much. I was shocked when he met me outside and gestured for me to drive into the garage. He already had it empty and ready for me. I pulled in and he closed the door from the inside.

"I figured your car would be safer in here," He spoke as he turned on a light and walked toward my car.

"Wish I had thought of that."

"Shut up. I knew you were going to ask so I got it all ready. I got everything you asked for but I had to pay a premium on almost everything."

"I figured. Time is more important than money right now."

"Maybe to you."

"Bill me later. I have another favor to ask."

"Sure, why not? How many miles until I rest?"

"Shut up, smart ass. I need you to go see Alexander and set things up there. I had expected to have time but it's running short. I'll contact him and let him know to watch for you. He knows the plan but not the target. Don't let anything slip."

"You suggesting I'd rat you out?"

"No, just letting you know what he knows. I'd go, but I need to prepare the location."

"Did you find a place? Can you set it up how you wanted? This bitch is dangerous. From what you've told me you need to prepare for a real knock down drag out this time."

"Yes, mother, I found a place."

"You better not be meeting that Hansen boy. You two just cause mischief whenever you get together. I don't know what his parents think he is doing."

"Jesus, lay off. I'll call Alexander. You go ahead. I don't know how long it will take, but I'll let him know that time is important and that it must be now. I'm going to wait until it is completely dark to go do my setup. The fewer people who see me the better. I still have a ton of shit to do before I'll consider myself ready."

"Will do, boss," he spoke sharply as he brought both of his rubber heels together in a barely audible click. His right arm shot out in a very inappropriate salute. I shook my head and walked inside to call Alexander.

CHAPTER THIRTY-SEVEN

Having called Alexander and let him know that Alan was with me and that he would be doing the setup, I waited for the sun to finish setting. Once it was dark I made my way back to the location I had picked. My basic Internet research informed me that I had chosen an abandoned chemical plant. There was a big debate over who would pay for all the clean-up leading to it being left to lie empty for years. The EPA costs were high and as of yet no one thought the land was valuable enough to undertake the cost. I would probably change all that when everything went down. Destruction changes many opinions.

Though the land was near the center of town it was a large lot and people left the area alone. That would make for privacy during our encounter. Some collateral damage was inevitable but maybe I could justify that by calling it land development. It had enough structure to give me cover if I needed it, but it also had space for me to move. With no better spot around, it would do well. Marksboro didn't have an arena for us to square off in.

As I had done before I went to work creating traps and laying mines around the area. This time I created more powerful mines. I needed the advantage and she would be able to slough off my weaker versions. I assumed she had shields that could take a lot of damage. I didn't want to kill her, but that did not seem to be the real problem here. With her power and skill, I had to concern myself more with her trying to kill me. I would have to resist my inclination to pull punches; I wanted her alive. She would turn that into an immediate advantage and destroy me. This was going to take most of the night.

Trap setting was very delicate work. When I set them up I had to infuse them with some power. This was like a battery powered ignition switch so that a trigger could cause it to draw more power from me at the time of execution. I also had to setup the actual trigger mechanism. It could be hard choosing what would set them off. I needed to set something that I, and most people, would not engage, but something that my target definitely would. Malicious intent toward myself was usually a good starting point, but I wanted to avoid them all going off at once when she arrived. That meant setting the range for the trigger along with the inciting act or thought. I also had to set the range and power of the effect at creation. These were not a "fill in the blank later" kind of thing.

With so many different functions chosen at the beginning was it any surprise that I had to fraction my mind to keep all of them controlled? With my mind powering them all, I had to dedicate a section of my mental capacity to each mine and its function. This usually limited me to five at any one time, though I rarely used that many. I did have some standard traps I tended to leave where I am staying that require much less attention. Those I can keep straight with very little mind use and no fractioning, but these would be different. Usually, with most opponents, one or two is more than sufficient.

Six.

To combat Jessica, I decided to go with six. I wanted to leave little to chance or poor timing. She was sure to be that tough. Aside from taxing my power with each there was another possible problem: after the fight, if any were left, I had to disarm them. With my connection as it was I couldn't simply disconnect them from my mind. I set my traps so that my being rendered unconscious did not make them dissipate, but triggered them instead. I learned that this could be a great motivator in a battle of words.

The final decision was how much power to give each. I didn't want to kill her, I really didn't, but I assumed that she could shield herself from physical damage quite well. A mental trap might work better, but she had shown quite a bit of proficiency in that realm as well. No, I would have to hit her with some serious power. In this regard I chose to use potentially powerful mines but not throw my full weight behind them. This would allow me to add on the fly if absolutely necessary. Adding like that was far less efficient so it would cost me more energy than the output received, but I didn't want to go to max power to start.

I smiled as I worked, "Great name, Max."

The first I set was an electrical mine. There were large power lines nearby that had powered the plant with a large transformer station as well. I could draw power from the grid to give some serious punch with less danger to the city's power. This kind of trap worked better if a portion of the environment was conductive. Since it was not I would need serious power to make it work. I couldn't create electricity with my power, but I could channel it with enough will.

I searched the area and found some copper in one of

the walls. Great. This would make the mine so much more useful. With a better physical path found I could begin adding my power to the trap. My abilities meant that I could over clock the line to carry far more power than it originally could have carried. If I had magic I could create a conduit for the power flow with magic that would bolster the copper. In the magical case the copper would act more as a magical symbol or focus than an actual power line. I couldn't really say exactly how it works with my power. There were no scholars studying my powers and how they worked. Maybe I could create an endowment at some university to study my abilities. I have never been good at studying so the mystery remains. I just know it works.

Since the line ran through the wall already, I used my mind and some physical muscle to rip some of it out of the wall. I laid that out of the ground and lightly buried it. This would make the connection. I then set a trigger that would go off when an aggressive mind was in close physical vicinity to that line. When that condition was met a circuit would open pouring as much electricity through that line as it could hold. I left room for me to increase the conduit size as well. With that set I moved on to the rest of the mines I had planned. All told that one had taken over an hour.

Considering what all had to be done I was not at all surprised when the sun rose as I finished my final trap. I stood up dirty and exhausted both physically and mentally to watch the sky lighten. It always seems to re-energize me when I felt the sun hit my flesh. I felt the hope and possibility of a new day raise my spirits. Maybe I had been born on a dying world and sent here by my father. That would have made this easier.

Feeling the rush of morning helped me get moving

again. I still had work to do before I was ready for the actual confrontation. With the traps set, however, I had another timer set. I didn't like leaving mines out in the open for long. I had no way to be sure someone wouldn't set something off somehow. With the power I put into these there was no way an accident wouldn't kill that person. I had a mental dam on them for the time being, but that also used my power. All of this was very taxing.

By that point Alan should have completed the work at Alexander's home. I had faith in Alan's ability, but not in Alexander's trust in me. He had seemed accepting of my plan, but he could have a change of heart. There was a real possibility that he could figure out my target as well. The man was brilliant and devious. Any actions I took to obfuscate the truth may well be apparent to him. I also felt certain he already knew who had killed Clara. There may have been evidence given to shift him from the true answer, but I couldn't be sure without asking and that carried too much risk. I needed to talk to Alan, prepare my last bits, and get some rest. Finally, I needed to be rested for all of this to go smoothly. Sad that that one was the last on my list.

If this all went correctly tomorrow morning would be my confrontation with Sica. I would use her pride and arrogance to draw her into my web. Her youth would make those strong points for manipulation. If I could pull this off Victor and I would be free, Alexander would be alerted to Sica's plan and end her power grab. Then everybody would come together and jump up for a freeze frame high five. If this thing went tits up, well, I die. With the conclusions laid out in front of me, I was pretty sure which side I was on.

I walked back to Alan's thinking about all of this. For some reason I kept focusing on the part about my death. I had to keep reminding myself to stay off main roads. I was entirely too exhausted to run from the police at that point. As I walked the whole of the last week began to weigh down on me more. I thought about Clara and Annie and lost all that energy from the rising sun. Clara's death had been so vicious and gratuitous. Why kill her so horribly? Then I thought of Annie. Why did she have to die? She had already talked to me, and apparently Alan as well. Was her death just to get me arrested? That put her life solely on my hands. Both deaths were so different. It was still possible different people were the cause of each. I might have more work after I took care of Sica.

I walked through the alley to the back of Alan's house. He was waiting on the back deck when I walked up. I braced myself as I walked up to him.

"So?"

"He is not keen on the plan?"

"Which part?"

"All of it? He doesn't like the link with you. He's not sure he trusts it. He doesn't like the setup either. Oh, and he doesn't like you going after his daughter. He made that abundantly clear."

I sighed, "Wow. So, he figured that out. Any good news?"

"The Cubs look good this year."

"Well, fuck, Hell has frozen over. Will he do it?"

"He said he'll wear them. Quote: 'he had better produce.'"

"Fuck."

"You bet. Did you get it all set up?"

"Yeah. I need some rest."

"True. Also, I never spoke to Victor."

"What? That's key. I need him almost as much as I need Alexander. It'll help him stay safe and clear."

"He refused to talk to me and Alexander stood by Victor's decision."

"Fuck me. I guess I could talk to him this afternoon after I wake up."

"Also-"

"Really?"

"Yes, now shut up. Alexander also said it had to be tonight at the latest. He would wait no longer for you to do whatever you had planned."

"Shit! I guess sleep will have to wait. I need to speak with Victor now." I realized that sleep might be a dream I never realized.

"Are you sure you have to go this way?"

"I know what happened, Alan. I know the whole course of events now. I just need to prove it to the people who matter. I can't walk away this close to the end."

"Okay, I just had to ask one last time. Is there anything else I can do?"

"No, the rest is up to me. Thank you for what you have done already. Please remain available. I don't have a great feeling about all of this."

"I had already planned that."

I went inside with Alan and called from the kitchen. Alan went upstairs for a shower and to give me a little space. I called Victor's home number. I didn't want this to be a cell call. It rang for a moment and then a member of the household help answered.

"Hello, Edwards residence. May I inquire as to who is calling?"

"I want to speak with Victor Edwards."

"Of course, you do. Who may I say is calling?"

"An employee of his late mother."

"Sir, may I have a name?"

"You have all you're getting."

"Fine." He set the phone down and headed off. It was obvious he didn't like my answer, but knew he would get no more. I was sure he assumed that Victor would put me in my place.

After a few minutes I heard the phone picked up.

"Hello, Trevor."

"Hello, Victor. No need to ask my identity?"

"Who else would leave a message like that? What do you want?"

"I need to talk to you. In person."

"Fine. One last time. I will meet you at Alexander's in the back garden. I cannot stand the idea of you on my mother's property. Twenty minutes, just you and me. This will be the last time that I see you or talk to you. That's the deal. Take it or leave it."

He was flexing what little muscle he had left. I saw no reason to fight him on this. I was also very tired and running out of time. I would lay out my case and if he wanted to remain ignorant after that I could not be held responsible for what happened in his life. I felt that I owed Clara the attempt to save him from himself.

"Deal. I'll see you there," I said and hung up. Maybe, if this went quickly, I could salvage some rest before I had to move the plan to its conclusion. I would have to risk using my car again. I hated tempting fate so much, but if I needed Alan to move I didn't want to saddle him with my car as his only means of transportation. I'd have to take another big risk to get this all done.

CHAPTER THIRTY-EIGHT

I didn't have much time to fit this all in. Alexander had pushed my schedule to its very shortest and Victor added yet another thing to do. I had to hurry, but there was no need to be stupid about it. It was possible I would be required to go straight from seeing Victor to drawing Sica to the confrontation so I gathered the items I had asked Alan to get for me. He said all had gone well with Alexander so I trusted that it included the favor I had asked of Alexander. I hoped this wouldn't take so long, but things had not been going my way here lately. My mind was quite fractured with all the mines I had set. I couldn't keep up this level of focus for long.

I drove to Alexander's estate taking the fastest route I could. I grew more annoyed as I drove. Time was running low and here I was running off to coddle some little *prick* so that *he* could see that it was all in *his* best interest to know the truth about *his* new wife. Maybe I was getting more than a little worked up. I realized that I was screaming in my car as I drove to Alexander's. Had to stop that. Cool tough guys don't yell to themselves in their car.

I pulled into my usual spot in the long driveway and contemplated how odd it was that I had a usual spot. I took a bit of time to calm down. I may need to yell at this kid, but I needed to be in control here. He was not accustomed to life and death situations. It really wasn't his fault that his life was more calm, stable, and boring than mine. Lots of people lead boring lives. Hell, they liked it that way. They craved the banality of all the trappings in their stable lives. I really needed him to stay by Alexander and do what he did. That would get us all through to the end.

I got out and walked to the back garden. My pace was brisk as I was trying to think of the correct wording to get Victor in line quickly. This had to go as smoothly as possible. I figured that if I could think of the right words to say he'd get in line and go along with the plan. Maybe then I could pull a bit of rest before things got crazy. I needed this kid to get in line.

I turned the corner into the back and saw Victor sitting on a bench with his head down. He was shaking slightly, which made me stop. I took a moment to look at him. In all my running around and deciding what was best I had lost sight of how much this must truly be affecting him. I had been thinking of him as a part of my plan. Sitting there he looked so small. He was really a little, lost boy in a scary world without his only protector. He was confused and scared and here comes the big bad wolf to take whatever he had left away from him.

"Hello, Victor," I spoke quietly.

He turned his head toward me and looked blank for a moment. His eyes were shiny. I doubted that he had many tears left at this point. After a moment he recognized me and shot to his feet. Quickly, he cleared his throat and stood to his full stature. He never managed to regain the same aplomb he had before his mother died.

"Good morning," his voice trembled a bit. "What do

you so badly need to talk to me about?"

"Look," I took a seat as I spoke. I wanted to put him at ease and my size tends not to do that. "This must be hard on you. Your mother was an amazing and powerful presence in your life until the other day when she disappeared quickly. Now I come along and talk badly about the one good thing that has happened to you this week. I truly am the world's largest asshole. I get that."

"I'm glad you realize that. Did you come to say that you are leaving us alone?"

"No. There are things that you must know. You don't want to, but it's important. I wish I wasn't the one to have to tell you, but that's how this is going to work. You know that you want the truth-"

"Truth? What do you know about truth? You're just a bottom feeder. You're scum. You con people with stories and promises to get their money. I want nothing more to do with you. This conversation is over."

"Kid, leave the tough stuff to tough people. You're scared but don't be stupid. There's a lot of shit going on here and you can't bury your head in the sand on this one. You have to know what's going on. After that you can do whatever you want. Don't like me? Fine. Don't trust me? Good. All you have to do is listen.

"I talked to Alexander. He's going along as far as that with my plan. If I turn out to be wrong you can be assured that I'll have to answer to him and he will not be happy with me. All you really need to do is stick with him and keep an open mind. Please."

"If he is truly going along with you, I will comply as far as he does. No matter how this ends I want you out of our lives. That is the price of my compliance."

"You and me both, kid. You do that much and I assure you I will be out of your life."

I stood up. He had never sat with me. He made no move to shake my hand and I did not press that issue. He was trying to be strong in a stronger world. I thought I could let him have this gesture. He was way out of his league and he knew it. Victor had to ally himself with more powerful people simply to survive. I walked away feeling pity for the boy. It must be hard to have others control the outcome of your whole life. As I neared the front of the house a familiar voice touched both my mind and my ears.

"Trevor."

Turning I realized instantly the mistake I had made. When I had arrived, I had never scanned the area for minds and this time it had cost me. Anger came instantly to my mind but the target was myself. How could I get so careless now? This mistake was going to cost me dearly. I slowly turned to face Jessica DesChanes.

"Of all the houses in all the towns in the world, you walk into yours."

CHAPTER THIRTY-NINE

Not good.

That's what kept blazing in my mind for any interested parties to see. I was not ready. This was the worst possible place and fairly close to the worst possible time. I had to think. Could I come up with a way to both get out of here and draw her to the location of my choosing? Quickly.

Damnit.

"I take it you were not looking forward to seeing me today. Pity."

"Well, I prefer to prepare for my dates with recently married women. I don't even have a hotel room yet. Do you prefer queen or king size beds?"

"Funny. You really are a funny guy."

"Yeah? I'd been thinking about starting a new career. Can I put your review on my advertisement?"

I quickly checked the state of the traps I had set. The were holding steady and my links were strong.

"Well, I wanted to see you. In fact, I was just thinking of you. We can see who gets what she wants here."

"Wow. Would you say that I'd been haunting your dreams? That kind of quote sounds great on dating site profiles."

I checked the grounds for the locations of any other people. Due diligence a bit too late. I really didn't want to keep this here. Nothing was coming to me, however. I was too exhausted.

"I've been watching you a lot. I've noticed a few patterns. Quite interesting patterns, really."

"Yeah? What kind of patterns?"

"Well, I have noticed that you make more jokes when you're nervous or scared. When you're deep in thought and working hard your mouth runs… a lot. Now, what at this moment could possibly have you nervous or scared?"

"You got me. I get nervous when I talk to beautiful women. Especially, beautiful women with magical talent who tell me that I haunt their dreams. That is what you said, right?"

I located the other people on the grounds. There were eight nearby aside from myself and Sica. Not good again. Most of those people had no involvement in this situation at all. One of them was Victor. All eight needed to stay safe.

"I doubt that. Trevor, I don't think that any woman has ever made you nervous. I don't know that any could, not in that way. No, you have something planned. You're running that mind of yours trying to accomplish something."

"Well, I do need to go shopping and decide what to have for dinner tonight. I think I feel like chicken tonight."

"Stop. Just stop this. Right now," the playful tone in her voice dropped out entirely. Her mind shut down hard. She wanted to have this out here and now. I thought quickly and sent out a general mental command and another very special request.

"Okay, you're right. I'll be quiet and get out of your

hair."

"Oh, you're not going anywhere. I know what you have planned and I have no intention of being lead to your cute little playground. I've taken steps to take care of that. No, we're going to handle this right here and now."

"Fine. I guess if this has to go down, it might as well be here. Your dad will love that."

I pulled out my sunglasses and put them on. I checked again on the mines I had set. I would have to start disarming them carefully. That would reconnect the fractured parts of my mind and make that area safer. I couldn't let them go off in the process. I was currently at a major disadvantage. I had very little to match her magic normally, and right now I was too fractured to bring any of that to bear. I could do little if this turned into a fight.

I could still have been able to end this with a war of words. I needed to get her to speak either way. Maybe, with Alexander and Victor here I could find a way to use them to end his without violence. A new plan started to form.

"Now you seem angry. Why? Why can't this go smoothly? Can't we talk like a couple of adults?"

"What do you think is happening here? Aren't you planning to stop me or kill me? Isn't that what arrogant types like yourself think?" Sica almost seemed to be enjoying all of this.

"So, are you labeling me the hero in this story we have going? Are you saying that, for the good of mankind, I need to stop you?"

"That's what you think, isn't it? You see yourself as some costumed hero fighting crime for the good of all mankind, right? I read stories like that when I was a child."

"Okay, you're still a kid and I think you're exaggerating it just a bit. This isn't a hero/villain situation, really. I just want to find out what happened to Clara and I'm pretty sure you're involved." I wanted to make her angry. I had to keeping tugging at her short temper.

Sica tilted her head to one side as she spoke, "That's your big deduction? That big brain of yours went to work and figured that all out, huh? You know, I'd heard about you. Not a lot of people know you but I had heard some things. I guess I'd expected far more from you. Kind of disappointing, really."

"Okay. Yeah. I've figured out a few things. You had a group working for you. You had that group kill Clara with a nasty magical poison so that you could take her son and her money as revenge. Of course, you have plenty of money, but you're greedy so that's to be expected. Nothing so amazing really."

She laughed. She genuinely laughed like a super-villain. I almost laughed with her. It was so unexpected and most laugher was contagious. Wouldn't do to laugh with the villain. Looks bad.

"You're a moron, you know that? You have no clue what is going on here. No idea at all."

"And you do? Did one of your lackeys fill you in? We both know that your father is the real mind behind this whole business."

Sica kept laughing. It was a clear laugh and would sound charming had I not known what she had done. I was taken aback by how genuine her amusement really was. I could see small flares come from around her shield as her mind experienced real pleasure. I felt sick at the perversion of joy in front of me.

"You really thought you could play out that that old

trope with me? Thank you, Trevor. That's the funniest thing I've heard in a very long time."

"Well, I guess I'm glad to entertain you a bit today. I'm just a big clown turning cartwheels for your entertainment."

I was still trying to disarm the cerebro-mines I had lain. I drew closer to closing out the first one. Once I could close it this would get a bit easier. Each one would bring back a bit of my mental capacity making the job less stressful on the whole of me. I had to be careful with the triggers as I went. Of course, I had made them strong. Too strong to set off and be done with. This must be what it felt like to be on a bomb squad.

"Even now you're trying to get in my way. You don't even know what you are trying to stop, but you're so sure you need to stop it. You never give up, do you?"

"I gave up tic-tack-toe once but doing that almost lead to Thermo-Nuclear Global Warfare so I learned my lesson about quitting."

"Jesus! How old do I need to be to understand all the bullshit you say? You're so damned ridiculous. However, you're becoming a bit of a bore now and I've wasted enough time with this. Since you wouldn't leave on your own, I'll have to make you leave myself."

"Oh! You'll make me? Who do you think you are?" I couldn't see or manipulate her mind through her shield. Words were all I had at my disposal. "That's a laugh. Why not just tell me what I want to know so this doesn't get ugly?"

"Maybe you're right."

"Really?" I felt a *click* in my mind and knew what had happened.

She took a step and began walking toward me as she spoke. She stopped when we were standing apart from each other like an old western movie.

"Yes, I did it. I engineered Clara's receiving the poison. I made sure to make use of the HFC plans and my own to make both sides of this whole thing look suspicious. They would both blame each other and go to war. My father would lose either way. His people would see him as weak for allowing it to happen at his home or he would be the aggressor in a war that would turn many regular people against him. The HFC could not stand long against his wrath if he truly meant war so others would get involved. Once things were bad enough I could slip in and offer a better solution. Everyone would gladly give me the power and let me take over.

"I even get Clara's money should I lose my connection to my mine for a time. My father most likely won't find out my involvement until too late, but if possible, I still need to be able to operate. The best part, are you ready? The best part is that you think you are the random element that will put a stop to my plans. The actual spell that did the deed was in Victor's vows. He said the words that killed his mother. He cast the magic that did it. His mother's group will blame him for it all when that comes out and disown him. My father's side will kill him for the treachery he performed. Your meddling is what kept them looking long enough to see that it was more than a simple poison. You were a part of it all.

"Try as you might you can't stop me. I knew about your mental link with my father. I also noticed the enchantment he put on your sunglasses. I broke both easily. The only hope you had to clear this up was if they heard me lay it out. My father is the only power anyone could bring against me and you lost it. Now they will move forward suspicious of each other. It's perfect. All your stalling to get me to talk? I've let you think you were in control. No one else will hear this. I've told only you what you wanted to hear. That's my gift to you. You get that? Is it clear? I won. I've completely overpowered you and cut you off at every turn. I won! The day is mine."

She had thought of everything. She covered my every plan. I'd known she was smart, but there's only so much anyone could do to combat a truly resourceful and intelligent person. I could think of no other course of action. My shoulders dropped. I lowered my head and took off my sunglasses.

I looked down at them for a moment. The idea had been brilliant. Her talents were as well. I sighed and looked back up at her.

"Good idea, though. You gotta give me that," I tossed the sunglasses to her. She caught them and chuckled a little. She looked them over and put them on for a moment. She looked squarely at me. They were too big for her.

"How do I look?" she asked me. "Maybe I'll keep them as a souvenir of my victory-"

"Good morning, Mrs. Edwards," she heard her father's voice from the ear piece.

"What?!" Sica's eyes doubled in size as she ripped the glasses from her face like they were on fire. She stared at me in disbelief.

"You outsmarted yourself, Sica. I knew you'd look for any link or enchantment that I could place. Your father refused to trust those anyway. He thought I could easily manipulate them. The one thing he would trust was the one thing you'd never think to check for: a simple camera and microphone. A plain low-tech camera and microphone hidden in a pair of sunglasses. He's been watching the whole feed live from a secure location. You lose, Sica. Everyone will know. Recordings are being made as we speak. No one will give you power now. No war, no money. Nothing. It's over. And. You. Lose."

"You... no. You can't... It can't be over."

"Sorry, there's no way out. There's no need to change or stop. Nothing you can manipulate. It's been seen from your very face in your voice. Consequences are starting as we speak. Can't you feel it? I'm sure that your father has already begun to act. I have no idea what he'll do, but you and I both know what he's capable of. Why not stop? He may be lenient if you go to him now and talk things out. The police probably won't be, but your father might."

"No. This can't be over. It just can't be." Sica was getting frantic. I had managed to disarm two traps. My mind was clearing but I still had four to go. I was working on the third when I felt minds nearing my location. Children's minds. Lots of them. I would have to move quickly, but I needed to finish this first.

"I refuse. I won't let this happen. Not to me."

"Sica, it's over-"

"Don't say that!" she waved her hand toward me and I felt a blast of force hit me in the chest. I was off my feet and flying through the air in an instant. Flying, that is, until I met the side of the house. Ouch.

"You did this," Sica looked straight at me with fire and madness in her eyes. "You did this to me!"

This wasn't going to be pretty.

CHAPTER FORTY

"You son of a bitch!" Sica screamed. Her voice was amplified by her magic. At this point she was enhancing everything with her magical power. Power radiated off her so that anyone could see it like heat waves on a hot day.

Her level of magical affinity was insane. Most magic users never reach her level of either power or intricate use. Those who reached that level of use tended to have age and training restraining them. Those with the sheer power rarely got the training needed to be so dangerous. She had both to such a degree that she was subconsciously enhancing her actions with her latent magic. Yippee.

"Look-"

"Fuck you!" she screamed. She threw her arms wide and another burst of force shot out and finished pushing me through the outside wall of Alexander's house. I landed in the room and tumbled a bit. My natural strength kept me from breaking, but going through an outside wall is a painful event no matter who was doing it. I took a moment to send a message to Alan.

"Got to (I sent a picture of the mined location). *Kids. Do not let-"*

"No messages! No help," I heard from outside. I

needed to keep moving.

I got up and out of the rubble in the house. Sprinting for the front door, I could feel that the people in the house were exiting out the back and running away.

Good.

I ran for the front to aim the magical cannon away from them. I needed a plan. Distance was my enemy and her friend right now. It gave her room to cast and keep hitting me with projectiles. I had no way to counter her power right now.

I couldn't flash her mind in her current state. She had closed off her mind fairly well and I was still too fractured trying to disarm my mines. I couldn't muster the force to break through her shield. I'd have to weather the storm for a time and hope she tired or gave me an opening.

I burst out the front door and broke to my right. I didn't want her to start throwing magic in any direction. I'd already endangered too many innocent people. There had to be a way to break her concentration. It was taking too long to disarm my traps to rely on that, but I couldn't stop now.

A wooden arch flew about six inches in front of my face. I rolled down and barely missed it.

I'd broken to the side of the house Sica was on and she stood with her legs wide like a power lifter going for a record. She was gathering power to herself; she was building up to something big.

My attention went briefly to the trap location. The children's minds were getting closer. I still didn't have the third trap disarmed.

Shit.

I had to stay focused, but on which spot? I was spinning my wheels trying to do too many things at once.

The power around Jessica surged and I let my mind

control me for a moment. As she thrust her arms forward I telekinetically pushed one of her arms up. Her aim went wide enough for me to duck underneath and find safety.

A blast of fire flew just over head and lit two trees on fire behind where I was lying. The heat off the wave when it passed was intense enough to cause burns on its own.

I heard her roar incoherently. She was completely lost in rage now and my continued existence was to blame. I got no respect. I realized that weathering the storm may not work out. I may not have enough time. Before she destroyed everything around us. She seemed to be increasing her destructive capabilities the longer I lived.

I got back to my feet and stood facing her. Taking a moment, I focused much of my mind on the third trap and finished disarming it. I felt that fractured part of my mind return and began to feel some of the cloud lift.

Three to go.

I could do this.

Took too long.

The coldest blast I'd ever felt hit me full on. The icy wind of a bitter winter storm washing over me except it felt more like an all-encompassing wave of icy water, but not even that covers the pure lack of heat. It washed over me quickly, but took with it all the heat in me. I felt heavy, cold, and slow. Frozen.

I took a moment and looked down to see if I was encased in ice like a video game. I wasn't, but the water in the air around was frosted over me and the ground everywhere the wave hit. Plants were dead and frozen. I looked back at Sica to see her smiling at me. Her eyes glowed with power.

I tried to move as quickly as possible, backwards, toward the burning trees. They were still on fire so the cold must not have reached them. That or the two magics canceled each other out. I hoped that heat might help me out.

Another blast of force caught me squarely. The frozen ground allowed little friction so I slid backwards. As I neared the trees I did begin to feel better. That one had not felt as powerful. She must have been baking something large and holding power for that; she had way more power drawn than she was using currently. I was at her mercy if I stayed on the defensive.

My coat thawed out enough to be flexible again along with my pants. I had lost my hat a while back. Back on the move I was straying wide of the frozen lane; I needed to stay moving. I couldn't afford to be a target for too long.

Maybe she would slow down if she had to spend more time thinking and less time throwing. Back at the warehouse the children's minds were searching around the perimeter.

Shit.

They must be at the fence looking for a way in. Three to go and I was out of time. My message to Alan must not have arrived.

Alone, no cavalry, and a superior foe.

This was the exact situation I never wanted to face. Sica had stayed ahead of me in almost every way and the one way in which I had won was about to get me killed. I could never seem to get one up on her. I had to find a way to level the field before she leveled me.

I might have to consider shooting her dead. Maybe alive wasn't possible.

The power around her surged again as she began to cast again. I stopped dead and gave her a target. She took her aim and I waited until the very last minute. I gave her a small telekinetic blast to the backs of her knees. Her legs went out from under her and she finished firing up into the air.

On its way up, the blast connected with a flock of passing birds. They completely disintegrated on contact leaving no trace of birds at all. She was moving on to the big guns. I knew I could not wait for her to get exhausted. That one would've hurt.

Something touched my mind from my intended battle site. Alan had arrived and was rounding up the kids. I wasn't sure the specifics of how, but the young minds were moving away. Authority worked well sometimes. With his physical presence there I could focus more here and finish the disarming later. I needed to finish this fight.

Sica was getting up.

I got an idea. I knew how to finish this fight without killing either of us, but it could be fairly rough. I gave her arms a mental push so she fell again and ran forward. I needed to close the distance.

She got to her knees and saw me running.

"You fucker! This ends now!" She thrust her arms forward almost like she was delivering a ki blast. I felt a sickening feeling run through me and slowed for a moment. I had to hold down my stomach to keep going. She rose to her feet with a surprised look on her face as I closed.

Sica raised her arms again to throw something else at me but the look of sick shock never left her face. That is until I got close enough. With no time to hesitate I put all my weight behind it and hit her with a hard right hook to her jaw. I felt the sickening crunch as my fist connected; I think her jaw broke on contact.

She dropped like one hundred-ten pounds of dead fish.

For a moment, as I looked down, I thought she might be dead, but then I found her mind. She was unconscious. She probably had a concussion on top of the broken jaw. That was a very close call. Fortunately, I was much bigger and more accustomed to physical violence than she was. I had never been so glad to have hit a girl.

I took off my shirt and tore strands of it off. I used the sections to tie her wrists and ankles. I also tied her mouth down so she could get it to the hospital for repair. I sent an image of what I saw to her father with the location so he could get here to take care of her. I relaxed a bit and began to feel some of the wounds from the fight. This one would hurt for days.

Her last blast must have been a rushed form of something else. That's the only reason it had so little effect. I had no idea what it was supposed to do, but it had hit me squarely. I sat down there by Sica for a moment and took the time to focus more on my traps. It was much easier now to finish the job and I got the last three disarmed. I then let Alan know everything was safe.

I surveyed the area and looked at all the damage. Alexander was not going to be happy. His home was busted up, his lawn was both frozen and burning, and his daughter was unconscious and broken. This looked really bad. I had to see it through to the end, though. I looked down at Sica and saw that her eyes were open.

She stared at me with rage and shock in her eyes. She didn't move or struggle, only stared. I received a message in my head.

This isn't over. I know about you now. I know what you are.

I looked at her for a moment and was about to question her when she glowed with blinding light and disappeared. Her ties and all her clothes were left there on the ground in her outline, but she was gone. I checked, but her mind was completely gone. She must have triggered a quick teleport spell. Great. Now I had to explain to Alexander why his daughter was gone but her clothes were still here. Damnit.

CHAPTER FORTY-ONE

I sat on the grass by Sica's empty clothes and waited for the interested parties to arrive. I waited for about half an hour before I saw Alexander's car drive up. The fires had gone out and the ice had thawed. Unfortunately, his home had not been repaired in that time. The scene must have been horrific. I, however, had stopped caring about how this scene appeared. This whole business had gone on for too long and had gotten too crazy. With my cerebro-mines disarmed I felt my mind become whole again and felt extremely tired. I was ready now to leave this town, but that was not to be… yet.

I stood up as I saw them approach. I looked around again for a moment and realized that this had truly become a cluster-fuck and it was on my shoulders to explain it all. Great. Victor went quickly to Jessica's clothes and began to inspect them. Alexander stopped a few feet in front of me and looked clearly up into my eyes. We stood locked eye to eye as Victor stormed around us with frantic energy.

"What happened?" tears were in his eyes. "Did you kill my wife? You weren't happy simply killing my mother so you went after the only woman I have left. You fucking bastard! You'll pay for this. I will be sure that you pay-"

"Victor," Alexander spoke with a steady clear tone that made Victor stop still in his tracks. It was as if Alexander had slapped Victor in the face. "Jessica is not dead."

"She's not?"

"No," Alexander kept his eyes locked on mine. It was clear who he was really giving this information to. "She has used an old teleportation spell I had helped her develop in her youth. It was unpolished and flawed. At the time she found it funny to show up at her new location naked, so she never corrected the flaws. You must have truly hurt her if she resorted to that old spell. I am not entirely sure how you did it."

"I doubt that you want the details," I measured my tone carefully. This was not a time to have Alexander mistake me for making a joke.

"Correct. I assume now that this is finished. Your involvement here is done."

Neither statement could be mistaken for a question. Alexander was telling me what was going to happen now.

"I have one thing left to do here and you'll be rid of me." I turned toward Victor and caught his gaze. "Have you seen the exchange?"

"No," Victor was knelt by Sica's clothes. He stood and had her shirt in his hands. "Alexander picked me up on his way here and told me about it. I believe that he told me what he saw truthfully."

"Your mother wanted you to see what happened. She knew something terrible was going to happen. Your protection, even in her death, was the most important priority. She didn't want you to marry Jessica. She didn't want you involved in all this business she was in. At this point, how it started has nothing to do with where we are now. Is there any chance that you have heard her and will capitulate to her wishes? There is still time. I am sure that the marriage could be annulled with no legal repercussions for yourself. That is the special favor I said I would ask of you before."

I looked at Alexander as I said this last bit.

"I can help you get out of your vows cleanly. I offer that now and only now. After this I will no longer help you hurt my daughter. I will guarantee no reprisal from myself or any of my people."

Victor stood still clutching Jessica's shirt. He looked down at it and clutched it tightly. He looked so deflated standing there. After a few moments he looked up at both of us with tears in his eyes.

"You're both trying to help me, but people have always made decisions for me. My mother's dead. I have no one else. I cannot believe that Sica's involved like you say. There must be another explanation. I don't know what happened, but I'm certain that you were involved. I'm making this decision for myself. I will not leave my wife. I never want to see you again. Is that clear? No, I need to go find my wife."

Victor picked up her clothes slowly and carefully. After he arranged them he looked at both of us again and nodded at Alexander before he slowly walked back toward the house. He looked small and broken like a little boy in an adult's world. I turned back to look at Alexander who had never stopped looking directly at me.

"The boy wants what he wants. Now, are you satisfied?"

"No, but I know when it's over and time for me to leave. Thank you for telling Victor what you saw. What are you going to do?"

"I will fix my house, help my new son find my daughter, and hope to never see you again per our agreement. You have done well here, but I never want to cross paths with you again. You do not want that either. Now, leave my home and never return, Trevor Harrison."

"Goodbye, Alexander. For what it's worth, I am sorry."

"It is not worth much. Goodbye."

I realized there was nothing left here to do. I turned and walked toward my car felling a great sense of loss. I had survived the fight, but nothing had truly been resolved here. I needed to go see Alan to finish up the last of this. The police were still looking for me and that needed to be fixed. Alan would have to help me clear that business up. Once again, I'd have to rely on him for so much. Too much, really. Hopefully, that would go better from here out.

I fired up my beast and drove through some country rods outside of town to enter closer to Alan's house. I was almost too tired to evade capture. Maybe things would have worked out better if the police had just caught me. Alan could possibly agree with that sentiment at this point.

CHAPTER FORTY-TWO

Alan wasn't at home when I arrived at his place. I hid my car again in the garage and picked his home lock with my mind. I was entirely too tired to wait outside. I did not last more than five minutes in his house before I passed out on his couch. My mind and body were done. I simply couldn't hold on for any longer.

I woke up the next morning when the sun rose. I'd been asleep for hours. I walked into the kitchen and brewed some coffee, I felt much better after a long night of sleep. I was stiff and still a bit tired, but better than I would have expected after that battle. I filled a mug and sat in silence drinking coffee. It felt good to drink and not have to prepare for some huge undertaking. As time went on I began to think of the last week and my mood sank.

"Good morning," a voice came from the living room. "Anything else you want to break before this is over?" Alan walked to the pot and filled a mug with coffee as well. He sat down across from me.

"I didn't do it on purpose, you know. I didn't want all of this to happen."

"But it did, and it often does. There is a storm that follows you through your life. That is one of the reasons I don't refer many cases to you." Alan was quiet for a moment, taking a drink before he spoke again, "well, are you going to tell me what all went down yesterday and why I had to chase a bunch of kids away from an old factory to save their lives?"

"Yeah, let me fill this up and I'll go through it all. Thanks, by the way. I would not have been able to handle the kids and what I was doing."

"You got lucky that I was eating nearby. It would have taken too long to get there from much further away. I stayed ready, but that was still fortunate."

I sat down and looked in the eyes. "Truly, thank you."

"Okay, so what the fuck happened?"

I told him about the setup and confrontation with Sica. I tried my best to give him the details of the battle. I had no real idea how long it lasted. One surprising thing about fights was that they were usually shorter than you thought. Part of the reason fighting sports had rules was to slow the fight down. The story seemed long and I was getting tired again simply telling it. I told it all through to my passing out on his couch.

"I figured that much when I found you there. You were out like a light. So, after it all Victor is going to stay with her?"

"Victor can't leave Sica. He's like a puppy. He needs someone to be loyal to and who takes care of him."

"His mother was very strong and domineering."

"Maybe. Maybe she realized that she had to be that way to keep him in line. Maybe Victor was lucky to have Clara as a mother."

"Maybe. Who wouldn't want a hateful woman willing to plot the murder of an ideological rival for a mother?"

"True, but who doesn't have flaws?"

"Just wanted to be sure we weren't ready to apply for sainthood just yet. I know she's dead, but she had some serious flaws."

"Yeah, I guess it can be really easy to forget that. I've spent so long trying to figure this out that I've lost sight of things a bit. Enough time in anyone's mind and you start to see things from their perspective. Well, either way, Victor feels a lot like a lost puppy. I may have to check on him occasionally."

"Yeah? I don't think he'd like that. Just remember, puppies have a way of doing pretty well. I think he'll do alright with Jessica DesChanes as an owner. I think she'll take care of her puppy."

"Possibly," I took a sip of coffee and sighed big. "So, what about Annie?"

"I wondered if you remembered her. I know she wasn't Clara Edwards, but she was a person."

"I deserve that… and a lot more. What can I do here? I don't know where to start with her death."

"No. No no. Stay clear. I'll take care of this one. No one else needs to die here. I have some leads and I will take care of their justice. Just, step back and relax."

I put my hands over my head. "Sorry, I'll just leave this to a professional."

"Exactly. You've done enough," Alan took another sip and put his cup down. "Now, my turn. Thank you for going after the real killer. I would've taken part in framing the HFC and, while they deserve it, I would've been wrong. I'm not good with magic."

"I know that was hard for you. I assure you that I'll only remind you of it when it suits me in arguments and at random when I deem it necessary."

"Ass."

We both laughed. It felt good. For the most part we were releasing the last of our tension about the whole case, but that laugh felt really good. It felt a lot better than worrying about Sica who'd be very angry with me and incredibly dangerous. Laughing was easier than realizing that I'd burnt my bridge with Alexander DesChanes, one of the most powerful wizards in the world. Laughing was a vast improvement.

"So," I spoke after I got my laugh under control. "Should we take the recordings to the police?"

"Why?" Alan replied simply.

"So, they can go after Sica and close the whole case."

"Oh, no. They'll never believe it. That video could've been doctored."

"Alexander saw it live."

"Oh yeah? And he'll verify it and help get his daughter convicted."

"What about them looking for me?"

"I'll take care of that. I've been working to clear Wall and Johnson already. I'll use this info to get them cleared and get you off the hook but it'll never convict. Alexander will see to it that he fights. His lawyers would crucify all this evidence. Accept what is."

"So that's it? I figured it all out and nothing changed?"

"Yup. Welcome to the detective business."

"I knew I didn't want to be a detective."

"Good. You're no good at it."

"So, I should just pack up and leave?"

"Yes, and soon really. You can't keep taking chances. It'll take me time to work this all out. Don't come back until I tell you it is all clear."

"Seriously? You're still running me out of town?"

"Yeah. I already packed everything in your car except what you're wearing now. In all seriousness, you need to leave."

I finished my cup and stood up. "Well, I guess this is goodbye."

Alan stood as well, "Yeah. See you later. Wish I could say it had been a good visit."

"Me too," I shook his hand and walked out the back door. I was more than a little upset that it was all shaking out this way. I got into my car and saw that what I had left was packed into the back. I could think of nothing left to say or do so I just pulled out and drove west out of Marksboro. There was nothing left for me to do but see what else I could find out there. I left the city with people dead and their memories in my head. This would be a long drive.

Clear from town in the flat rolling plains of Illinois I saw a truck gaining quickly behind me. At first, I assumed it was some kid opening up his new truck to play around on the country roads, but then I saw the flashing red and blue. Shit. I kept going hoping that there was a call that would see the car fly on by. No such luck as I watched him slow his approach and pull in behind me at the same pace. I considered running. My car could tear up these open roads and I could probably get away. However, a long chase across multiple states did not sound like a great time, so I pulled off to the side. I had one thing left to take care of.

I readied my mind as I waited. It wasn't an official vehicle. A red pick-up truck with a portable light on top slid in behind me. I saw a tall man in the driver's seat with messy hair. I took a chance and got out of my car. Once again, we met between our vehicles on a lonely country road. I had no idea where this might take us. I felt no malice but official duty tends to carry no malice. We stood for a moment looking at each other. Wall moved forward. I was prepared for a fight but not for an outstretched hand.

I stood blankly for a moment as I had not fully grasped what was happening. His look changed and that broke me out of my disbelief. I took his hand and a smile grew on his face.

"Thank you, Trevor."

"For what? I fucked everything up." I released his hand and took a half step back.

"I could never've gotten the people responsible for Clara's death. I had a feeling you were the right man for that job."

"But I couldn't save her or even prosecute them. I failed totally."

"No more or less than I did. Clara was never the type to rely on someone else for her own well-being. I figured she brought you in because she thought her death was inevitable. Killing her could not have been an easy task. She knew she needed help after that. She was mostly worried about her boy."

"You know there was a plan to fake her death, right?"

"No, I didn't know that. Was that an HFC plot?"

"Yeah. She was involved. Her compatriots at the HFC had a counter plan to kill her anyway. Alan has all the details."

"I was going after them at one point. I never liked them or what they stood for, but they were smart enough to have me talk to Clara. She never convinced me they were good, but she calmed me on the whole situation. She convinced me that she was turning them into a political lobbying group. I thought it would be best if I let her work."

"Your sister thinks differently."

"You talked to her? Of course, you did. Lori hates the HFC because they're trying to run her out of her bar."

"They're the ones? She said a big developer wanted

her out."

"Yeah. They make a lot of money through land development around here. They own a bunch of property around her bar and want it all. If not for that she might have joined them. Maybe not, she hates most everyone, really. I'm not sure she sees any differences in people. She just hates people."

"Hell of an attitude for someone in the service industry."

"Easier when they are giving you money."

"So, I gotta ask, did you and Clara have some kind of a relationship?"

"We were friends. She was never interested in me beyond that."

"Your name wasn't Annie."

"You know about her, too? You seem to have gotten most of the information on Clara."

"Yeah. I spoke to her and figured it out."

"Now she's dead too."

"Talking to me isn't good for anyone's health."

"Seems that way," he looked me up and down as he spoke. We shared another secret now.

"I knew her secret but I never told anyone. Helped her if she needed a quick date with a guy for show. She was still certain that the truth would harm her future."

"With the HFC? I can believe it. I can't imagine that their hate ends at magic users. You're a good man, Detective Wall."

"Yeah, maybe. I secretly hoped it was just a phase after her husband died. My sister was right on that regard. I did love Clara. Probably always will"

"So did Annie, and she may have died for it."

We stood quiet for a time. There was really nothing to say to that. He seemed like he didn't really have a plan doing this.

"Did you come out here to bring me in?"

"You are still wanted… but no. This is my personal time. No one knows that I came. We're a ways out so no one should drive by. I felt that I had to thank you. I don't want details. It's too soon for that."

"Thank you for having faith in me back in the diner."

"I knew I couldn't get it done. I wanted results and you seemed like the only man to get them. You better get out of here. Plenty of people are still looking for you."

"Thanks. Seems everyone I like in this town keeps running me out of town. Goodbye, Wall." I turned and walked back to my car. A few steps away he stopped me.

"Oh! Hey. You're clear for that house fire."

I turned back toward him, "yeah? Thanks."

"No questions?"

"Only good news I've heard. I'm not looking in that damn horse's mouth."

"Funny thing. No one can connect it to anyone yet. The HFC weren't involved and they have found no proof of arson."

"Alan will explain some of it. I set traps and one of them went off. I just can't figure out where the body went. I assumed someone's buddy dragged him off."

"Yeah, that's the funny thing. There was one witness, a kid who was out past curfew. He didn't come forward because he didn't want to get his girlfriend mad. He was with another girl. She ran off when a guy approached the house, so the kid thought about getting tough until he got a look at him. Said he was a big guy who looked really scary. He decided against getting tough."

"Sounds made up."

"Maybe. He only gave us one solid detail aside from his size. Said the guy had a patch over one eye."

I froze.

"A patch, huh? Still sounds pretty fake."

"Yeah, probably. Kid was pretty shaken up. Said the door blew the guy back into the yard. Knocked him flat."

"Yeah, my trap would have had a punch. So, where's the body?"

"Said the guy laid there for a moment and then sat bolt upright and got up."

"That sounds like a movie."

"Yeah. Then he said the guy walked into the house. After another moment he heard another boom and it all caught fire big time. Said he thought he saw the guy walk out from around the back."

"Pretty thin."

"Sure, but I thought I'd let you know. I have a feeling it might not be as thin as all that. Take care of yourself, Trevor."

"You too, Wall. Thanks again."

He got into his truck and drove on by me. I slid into my car and sat for a moment. One more thing for me to think about on the drive out of here. Great. This was just a wonderful visit to Marksboro. I simply must do it again soon. Just as soon as my life became too easy again.

Glad you've enjoyed your time with Trevor Harrison.

Please rate and review this book on Amazon to help other people find and enjoy it.

If you'd like to hear about additional releases and find the next books to release about Trevor please visit my website and join my mailing list.

Mattoon Underground

If you want to read another book in the same world but with a different character please check out

The Hunter Overture

Trevor Harrison Returns in the next book in the Mind Over Magic series.

Organized Magic

Made in the USA
Lexington, KY
09 December 2018